Polishing Jade

Polishing Jade

A Novel

By Tekoa Manning

ISBN-13: 978-0615923710 (It's All About Him, Inc.)
ISBN-10: 0615923712

Second Edition

Picture on Cover from ©iStock.com/KCline Photography

Dedication

This book is dedicated to my sons: William, Robert and Samuel and all the other brave stones that have been through intense heat or the rock tumbler to become precious jewels; and to my mother who loved diamonds for reasons unknown.

Acknowledgements

"Every good and perfect gift descends from above, from The Father of lights with whom there is no change nor a shadow of variation." James 1:17.

I would like to thank Jo Zausch my English Professor, who first told me that I could write. I would like to thank my best friend Debra Testa, who has read and reread all the stories in my heart. I would also like to thank my dearest friend Charlie Manning, who helped breathe new life into Ellen Cotton and other characters. My brother Norman Green, who read the first chapter of this story in 1999 and never forgot it. I want to thank my sister for always supporting me and for naming her daughter 'Jade' from whom the main character gets her name. I want to thank my parents for raising me in a home where God the Father, was the main Character. I would like to thank my sons for sticking with me through the worst of times and the best of times. Last, I want to thank Jeff Manning, for polishing me and holding me through all the intense heat!

Prologue

Sometimes at night when I lay my head down and the waxing crescent moon suspends above my window, I can still see us sitting under the porch light. Daddy plucking his banjo and Johnny taking Mama by the hand and dancing her around the porch making her eyes sparkle like the stars, and then there was me, Jade. It seems I was named after this precious jewel by my mother, from whom I acquired my blue-green eyes. The Jade stone was thought to be the stone of love in times past. It was said to bring joy and luck, but all of these things seemed to be hidden from me. I was just a young girl underneath that porch light, talking to the man in the moon about my fate. I wasn't aware that translucent Jade gemstones were born from intense, high-pressure heat within the earth's crust. Nor was I aware that I would have to go through that same intense heat in this life to become Polished Jade.

Chapter 1

In 1965, I was a junior at Braxton Bernard High School. I was young and filled with distrust, fear, and worries. My classmates thought I was a nerd and only interested in schoolwork, but it was just an act to keep them from seeing the real me. Dime store novels were my escape, and they could take me as far away from Braxton as their pages could carry me. The closer I came to the last page, the more my stomach seemed to draw up into knots, dreading the ending. I found myself reading more and more slowly, putting off facing my own present reality for as long as possible. I would close each book with a long haggard sigh and wonder what it would be like to be one of the main characters. Their stories were over; mine seemed to hesitate. Like a tightrope walker, I felt suspended, wobbling, teetering and struggling to find balance. The characters in the stories I read seemed to extinguish all their pain, but here I sat, empty and scared, waiting to turn a page. If only I could start a new chapter.

During class, my fingers would fidget with my long auburn hair and twirl it nervously. I was painfully shy and would have rather chewed my pencil down with my teeth than to walk to the front of the class and sharpen it. I walked with my head down and seldom looked directly into anyone's eyes, instead inspecting the texture of linoleum, the pebbly concrete, my worn shoelaces or the indentations left in the grass. Yes, others may have missed the frosty morning dew, where the sun tilted and caused the autumn leaves to bleed into the earth, but I noticed. It was amazing the amount of people whose names I didn't know, but I could pick them out of a line-up by their shoes.

My mama swore that I walked on my tiptoes until fifth grade when I was stung by a bumble bee on my left big toe and was forced to move the arch of my foot towards the earth. Among the other peculiarities and unappealing habits that plagued me, I was a chewer. I gnawed my fingernails down to tiny cube shapes and then when they were mostly invisible, I chewed the skin around them or the skin inside my bottom lip. Mama threatened to put turpentine on my fingernails and that would stop me she warned. Of course, she never did follow through with much.

I had few friends and was living close to the edge of "not enough of anything". Lack was a word I knew, it seemed to greet me at the door and drag me in. There was more than enough lack in my life to share with others. I lacked love and yet I knew somewhere underneath it all, it was there in the hollow places. It came through smiles the shade of cumbersome yellow and sighs that were weighted down tired like an old stump. Mama said that perfect love made fear flee. I wondered what perfect love tasted like. I wanted to gulp it in like chocolate milk and leave a moist coating of it above my lip. Fear was something like lack that seemed to engulf me, like the puddles that filled my shoes and left them soggy and my feet a pruned mess of wrinkles. The fear had crept into my pores, like the silt of rain.

My family and I lived in Mississippi near a pocket-sized town called Braxton. In fact, Braxton was so minuscule in size that after the sign depicting the number of the population had been hit by a truck, no one bothered to fix it. The bent up, leaning rectangle left the township with a rusty caption that said "32?" Maps admitted its existence with a shy tuck of their head. It was a small farming community with the families making up most of the town, but the town wasn't the only thing small in Braxton; folk's minds seemed even smaller.

All twelve grades were in one school. The school was a two-story brick building. Air conditioning was achieved by opening the large windows to let the breeze blow upon our sweaty necks. In the wintertime, the heat came from the steam produced by a mysterious contraption that resided in the basement. The janitor banged around on it from time to time to keep it going. The lower grades had around fifteen to twenty kids in each class, but by the eighth grade many students had dropped out to help out on the farm or had transferred to the better school in Cleveport. That school was twelve miles away and more advanced in academics. Only the poorest children like my brother and I would graduate in Braxton. Our senior class was never over eight and sometimes as few as four.

There were no factories, grocery stores, or businesses to speak of in Braxton. We had Taylor's General Store; it had some gas pumps out in the front. There was a display case filled with sweet tooth items that Miss Rita Taylor baked, and they sold an assortment of other necessities. For most other things, folks drove to Cleveport.

My daddy, Albert Gentry, worked at the saw mill in Cleveport. The scent of fresh cut hickory, birch, and oak seemed to linger on him. The wood shavings clung to his clothes, hair, and skin, giving off their pleasant aroma. He was a strong man, with broad shoulders, large hands and black wavy hair that draped along his neckline. His skin was bronzed from working out in the elements and when he was sober, he had a presence about him that drew people to him. His eyes reminded me of a wolf's. They were large smoky rings, layered by tiny specks of blue that seemed to whirl in a circular motion pulling you into them. His eyes, along with his words, had the ability to grasp me like the suction of a tornado, then leave me empty and destroyed.

When I was but a little thing, Daddy used to rock me in the big wooden rocker, which he had constructed out of scraps from the mill. We would sit out on the front porch many nights listening to the crickets sing or the owls hooting calls. I would lay my head on his chest and inhale the woodsy scents, wishing to stay forever in the safety of my daddy's arms. These nights were peaceful and left me feeling safe and protected. Occasionally, he sang a hymn or a Bluegrass ballad, and I'd drift off to sleep with the sounds of angel's wings brushing my ears.

Of course, in time I began to see there was another side to my daddy, and he wasn't really my daddy at all, but some dark monstrous creature. This grotesque being seemed to take over my daddy's body making him ill-tempered, and hard. All those feelings of protection were swept away and replaced with a feeling of trepidation that no little girl should ever know. My mama said it was the good ole' Kentucky Bourbon that entered his body, and unlike the fragrant wood, this was a smell I came to detest. The strong arms that rocked me to sleep, the large calloused hands that patted my head, and the voice that sang *Amazing Grace* --- they all became something different when he drank. I think this was the hardest thing, for I never knew which daddy would appear. At those times, when a mean spirit had entered into him and his calm wolf eyes were replaced with daggers that was when I sought a means of escape.

My brother, Johnny, and I, we'd run off into the woods traveling as far as Cottonwood Farm, where a fence row of pallid honeysuckles called our names. We'd pluck each one and savor every drop of the sweet nectar. I picked clovers or daisies to pass the time, pressing my fingers down deep into the rich soil. I'd make sure each stem was long enough to braid or tie into knots, and then I would create beautiful necklaces or head bands. Sometimes I'd just lie back in the grass and stare up at the clouds that took the shapes of people and animals, and me peering with great intent for an angel's wing.

"I wish we could escape, Sissy, but where is there to go?"

"Could we make it to Uncle Ed's?" I rose up and propped my head up on my elbow.

"No, Sissy, Uncle Ed lives way out in Kansas, and I don't have a car or any money to get us there. All the guys at school have already labeled me the son of the town drunk. I can't stand this anymore! I gotta save up for a car. I need a job real bad, but how can I get to Cleveport to even look without transportation?"

Johnny ran his fingers through his coal black hair, then cracked his knuckles, a nervous habit he'd acquired of late. It was as if we were merely buying time until we could escape, and yet we both hated to think about what would happen to Mama without us there to protect her.

“Do you think we can go home now, Johnny?” The grass had left indentations in my legs and the earth seemed to be hardening beneath my body.

“Naw, Sissy, I don’t think it’s been long enough. Dad probably still got that whiskey on his breath. Just a little longer Sis.” Johnny’s pale blue eyes held a sadness that seemed to envelop both of us.

“Maybe we can walk down to the creek bed and try to catch salamanders after while,” I said. Johnny sat with his head down, arms crossed and resting on his bent knees in a posture of defeat.

His furrowed brow and aging soul progressed almost daily, forcing me to watch as my brother lost his childhood. Johnny was seventeen, going on forty. He always called me Sissy, just about everyone else called me Jade. My real name is Clara Marie. Mama said I had eyes the color of the gemstone, dark pools of green, and she began calling me Jade when I was a toddler. Anyhow, the name stuck and I spent countless hours in front of the mirror trying to see what Mama saw.

I raised up out of the grass and brushed myself off. "You ready Johnny, let's go!"

Johnny and I walked into the deep woods where the sweet gum trees stood. We braved the water moccasins and cottonmouths to get a taste of gum sap for chewing. The creek ran cheerfully past us, a small cool stream that was unaware of our troubles and the tall pines enveloped us, hiding us from the outside world for just a little while.

"Johnny, I'm getting real hungry, my tummy's growlin'. Can we go back now? Mama is making country fried steak and biscuits." I had my lips pouted and looked up at him with my sea green eyes, and I knew that he secretly wished to save us. After turning over several rocks and tossing a few smooth stones into the water, Johnny said, "Alright, alright, but don't go makin' a big racket. Maybe we can sneak some leftovers outta the kitchen. If we're lucky, Dad has passed out for the night."

We made our way over the hills and passed Cottonwood farm. I spied the Cotton's house. A warm glow of light spilled through the windows and I wished I could just knock on Ellen's door and step into that warmth.

The grass felt cool and damp under my bare feet. Johnny was my hero and my strength, protecting me from the night creatures that came out to spook a child's soul, and the dark monstrous creature that lay ahead, with his stale breath and bloodshot eyes.

Mama never let on like anything was wrong when we came through the side door. She was sitting at the kitchen table with the swelling of a fresh bruise on her cheek. Her tanned freckled skin made the welt less noticeable. A frozen smile showed as if painted on. Her large doe eyes reminded me of a deer frozen in a bright beam of light, only they revealed the truth. Mama pressed her lips together firmly, taking long draws off her cigarette, inhaling deeply into her lungs. She pushed the smoke down further and further, like her pain. Her lips had etched lines and deep creases that seemed to expand when she exhaled. Her hands were shaking, and she had a look of regret that only an abused women can.

"Johnny, help me get your Pa to bed now, son." My daddy roused himself where he was lying on the sofa and slurred, "I don't sneeeed any shelp, Virginia!"

Johnny grabbed his legs and my mama took hold under his arms, and they shuffled their way down the hall towards the bedroom plopping him atop the mattress. Where they left him to sleep off the demon that had entered him.

Me? Well, I sat at the table and began to reminisce about the honeysuckles Johnny and I had tasted earlier. My spirit felt like those fragrant flowers that had been spent. We had sucked out their sweet sap and daddy had sucked out our joy.

Chapter 2

No one knew why Miss Ellen Cotton planted corn in front of her living room window. She claimed it just made it easier for her to pick a couple of ears before dinner. The ears stood encased in their husks as the silk-like tassels spilled out and adorned the porch. Large sunflower stalks bent their heads under the adjacent window, nodding and smiling at me; they seemed to beckon callers with their vivid colors of golden wheat and buttery yellows.

Miss Ellen was a sturdy little woman, plump and ample-bosomed, with high cheekbones and pursed full lips. Her hair was charcoal streaked ashes, highlighted by silver strands done up on top of her head. She was a hard worker, keeping her house, yard and garden immaculately cared for with the energy of a woman half her age. There was almost always some cookies, a cake, a cobbler, something I could sink my teeth into real easy, and paired with that treat was good, cold milk, fresh from her cow named Bessie.

Miss Ellen also owned three Boston terriers, her "house dogs" as she called them. "The Girls" were named Bitty, Peggy, and Cookie. What a bunch of fun they were! They chased squirrels, birds, and the occasional cat that had the misfortune to slip into their space. They never caught much except rabbits, and between the three of them a rabbit didn't stand a chance. Miss Ellen said there was something wrong with a dog that couldn't catch a rabbit. After a morning of squirrel chasing and almost constant barking, they jumped onto the back porch tired out and ready to come inside. These little dogs were world class nappers. Sometimes, after I'd had my milk and snack, Miss Ellen would shoo me off to the couch with The Girls to sit awhile. They would huddle around me or on top of me, and soon enough we would all four be snoring away, rocked to sleep by the sound of Miss Ellen humming as she worked in the kitchen.

Miss Ellen surmised more of what went on at my house than she ever let on. She never pried or asked probing questions, but she was always there for me. I can't remember what age I was the first time I wandered far enough to make it to the top of the hill where I discovered her little house and found her tending her garden. It seems to me now like we were always friends. Spending time with Miss Ellen was sometimes the most attention I got all day. Her kindnesses kept me from falling into a greater despair over all the things that were wrong in my home.

Miss Ellen was a bit peculiar and had a plethora of superstitions I never knew existed. She advised me to only cut my hair on a full moon and to place a lock beneath my pillow that same night for good measure. "Jade, this is something my mother taught me, never take a broom with you when you move! Throw it out and leave the dirt behind. Always start off with a clean sweep." In an odd way, this made perfect sense to me, but when I shared it with Mama she said, "Leave it alone – all her beliefs and strange superstitions ain't nothing but hogwash. Jade, honey, no black cats crossing your path can harm you and umbrellas opening indoors don't stop the rain of blessing over a house."

"Well, what does stop them?" I asked, looking at the jagged crack that ran from the ceiling down the wall and thinking about the dark tension that held the walls together in our own home.

"People do, they stop the blessings with their tongues," Mama said, with her eyebrows raised and that sharp look in her eye. "They speak death. The good book says, 'Life and death are in the power of the tongue!"

I wanted to stick my tongue out at her for some reason but instead spilled my true feelings out for her to see. "What about all the words Daddy speaks when he's drunk, is that what's stopping our blessings?" I said it abruptly and then caught Mama's eye and lowered my head quickly. I was shocked that such bold words had sprung from my lips. We never mentioned the dark secret of my father's alcoholism. My daddy's words were soaked inside the plastered walls of our home. My eye's peeped up under my copper-colored bangs to see Mama's reaction to the taboo topic.

"Jade, we both know your daddy isn't himself when he's drinking. He's under the influence of a force that's greater than himself." Mama looked saddened by my comment, and I could see it had hurt her deeply. "Jade, I wish I could change things." She looked up at me with those large deep set eyes of hers that spoke with more emotion than her words and wrung her hands, then pushed the invisible wrinkles out of her paisley dress. Her fingers were long and slender and olive vein lines popped up on the tops of her hands that had known much hard work. She tucked a strand of hair behind her ear and reached for her vice, a cigarette, and I immediately regretted saying anything about my daddy.

"I'm sorry." I said it half-heartedly and pushed my toes hard into my shoes.

"Well, honey, it is true that your daddy's hurtful words cut each of our hearts and they affect us all." She inhaled deeply and blew a perfect line of smoke into the air.

"I know," I said softly, feeling ashamed that I had spoken about our shadowy secret and yet oddly relieved. I had caused Mama to realize she could pretend it didn't exist, but no matter how hard she tried to keep things together for us, she couldn't make the monster go away.

"Jade, you stay away from Mrs. Cotton and her craziness. Why, who ever heard of planting corn in your front window?" She tapped the ash tray and shook her head with a smirk. Her long slender face and green hollow eyes peered back at me, and for a second I wanted to shake her, shake the fear out of her and the sleepiness. It was just like Mama to change the subject and move the conversation in another direction. I dismissed Mama's warnings about Miss Ellen. I was sixteen and past ready to break free.

"Yes Mama," I uttered tiredly, but it seemed there was always a reason to venture off our property and on to the Cotton's.

It wasn't an hour after Mama's warning that my brother Johnny and I walked up to see if Mr. Cotton's new Beagle had birthed her puppies. He had ol' Butch for several years, and he was a good bird dog. Mr. Cotton bought the little female from a man in Cleveport for a small price because she was over six months old and had not sold yet. She came home with him and nature took care of the rest. We walked on past the house and found Mr. Cotton in the barn milking, Bessie. The litter of puppies lay in a stall where he had placed fresh straw for whelping.

"Awe, Johnny look how cute they are! I want one!" I sulked. Their eyes were not even open yet, and they were not much bigger than a rat.

Johnny picked one up, inspecting it. "This here is the runt Jade. These small puppies aren't big enough to fend for themselves. They miss too many meals and don't gain weight like the rest. After a few weeks of that, most of the time they just die. Seems the bigger, larger pups just pushed them out of the way at feeding time."

"Die?" I mouthed, my eyes saddened by this news. Johnny nodded his head and looked away. "I want to take the runt home and save her Johnny. Please, please, we could feed it milk with an eyedropper or get a baby bottle!"

He shook his head and said, "Jade even if our folks said we could have her and Mr. Cotton would let her go for free, it wouldn't be good, not with Daddy and his temper." I guessed Johnny was right because I could see Daddy giving it a good swift kick after he'd drank one too many. "Men like our Dad, well Jade, they always pick on whoever or whatever is weaker."

I nodded and looked down at the squealing runt, and I pondered how my mama was like that runt. My daddy was bigger and physically stronger than my mama, and she was the target of his anger almost all the time, until lately when I seemed to be the one he had on his radar.

Johnny spoke up and said, "Thanks, Mr. Cotton for letting us look at your pups!"

"No problem kids, you come back anytime." He smiled and waved from his milk stool. His hair was a thick mass of silver and he wore bib overalls most the time. Before we'd walked a few feet, he raised up and said, "Johnny, it will be hunting season before you know it, we'll have to take one of them out and shoot us a quail or a turkey or two."

Johnny smiled and said, "Yes sir, by all means!" We left the barn and went on up the hill.

"I've got homework to do Sissy, and I need to help Mama, you coming home?"

"No, Johnny, I think I need some fresh air." My mind was still visualizing that runt probing for some milk and Daddy was home by now. I walked up the path that led to the blackberry bramble that grew on the fence line of Miss Ellen's yard. I squatted down, hiding beneath the vines, and I began to pick the plump berries. I ate until my fingers were stained a dark crimson and juice was dripping down my chin. Sometimes dinner in a bramble bush was better than eating at home.

It was peaceful at Cottonwood, it seemed as soon as my feet hit our land I was filled with dread, and I knew why I walked on my tiptoes until I was five. I raised my head and I soaked in the sun that only caused more freckles when suddenly I heard him. Before the voice ever reached me, I could feel his presence. It seemed to stomp the ground in anger, and no matter how hard I tried to hide on that farm adjacent to our place, it wasn't far enough. I felt like the wild goats that had traveled to the tops of the crags in the mountains, only to be hunted by the larger creatures lurking below.

"Jade! choo out heresss?" Daddy's voice lurched in the distance. Then I saw his steel toed boots coming up the path, stumbling. "Shade Gentry, I'mmm gonna tan shhour hide! Shhou hear me?" I sunk down deeper into the vines that were now scratching my arms, trying my best to avoid being discovered.

"Albert, what are you doing?" My mama had come looking for him, and she was trying her best to convince him to go back to the house. Poor Mama had come to save me.

"Done choo 'Albert' me, I'm cuummins soo see Jade." He slurred every other word and reared up with anger. Daddy had reached the point where he was past hurting me or Mama. Now he was what Johnny called "sloppy drunk."

"Come on Albert, Jade is fine. Leave that young'un' alone. Don't you remember what it was like to be a teenager?" Her face seemed to stretch and sag from grief. Mama took hold of his arm and they began to shuffle back down the path, leaving me alone with my thoughts and the ache in my heart that never left. I sat still listening to Mama and Daddy's voices fade away as she steered him down the hill toward home.

Even though I was sixteen, I still had nightmares of my father beating my mother in front of me. I still remember certain scenes, a blimp of his fist hitting her belly, her face, or any place she couldn't cover fast enough. I remember her lying on the floor in the fetal position, a pool of blood and a baby that would never carry the name "Gentry" because of a blunt blow to the abdomen. I plucked one more berry and sighed long and hard, the sun was growing dimmer and I felt stuck.

It wasn't a minute later that I heard a screen door bang and the unmistakable humming of Miss Ellen Cotton. The sound was a sweet moan, and I could see her shoes from my hiding place as she began to pick berries. Her shoes were not made of steel, but softly worn leather. She was wearing an apron that depicted roosters crowing, and her hair was a mess of bobby pins holding a braided bun-like twist in place. Her pale blue eyes held a gray film that made it hard to tell what color they actually were, but when she smiled they ignited my soul. I guess you could say, Miss Ellen had an elegance that you wouldn't expect her to possess. She came closer to where I was and peeked through at me, pretending to gasp with surprise. "Why look at you, girl, out here giving me a fright! Come outta there now!"

I raised up displaying my fingers that were as stained as my lips and smiled for the first time in a while. "Okay, Miss Ellen, I guess I've eaten 'bout half your ripe berries by now anyhow."

She laughed that bubbly kind of laughter that people with real joy have. It's a happy sounding laugh that came from a deep place I hadn't found yet. I slipped carefully away from under the berry bushes and stood up, hiding behind a layer of embarrassment. Miss Ellen enveloped me in a loving hold that I returned awkwardly. I guessed she had heard Daddy's slurring and saw Mama take him off down the hill.

"Come on girl, let's go on to the house and sit awhile. You can entertain me and the dogs for a bit." We went into the house and she poured two glasses of lemonade and handed me a plate of sugar cookies that helped wash the blackberries down. She placed her apron on the chair next to us and then went to work at removing the hairpins holding the bun. A long charcoal braid fell down her back, and soft wispy pieces fell about her face. At times, she reminded me of an old Indian woman that should have been living in Wyoming wearing leather and beads. "Tell me how your school work is going, Jade. You keeping your grades up?"

"Oh, yes, ma'am, I am doing my best, I think, and I'm glad we are getting closer to summer." I looked down at the scratches on my legs from the bushes and wiped at an imaginary spot of dirt.

"Jade, when I went to school, we had a one-room school house like yours and all grades first through eighth were in that one room. There was no second floor and we had an outhouse. If we misbehaved Miss Crane would take us right outside behind that outhouse and put a switch to us. Often times she would send a note home about our behavior and then we'd get another switching when we got home. If I took a notion to throw the note away or destroy it, I also took a chance of Ms. Crane asking my parents if they read it at church on Sunday." Miss Ellen raised up and washed the crumbs off the side of the table into her palm. "Right smart walk to the schoolhouse as well, three or four miles I surmise, but may be off a bit."

"Wow, things were tough back then," I said, "I would never have guessed such a long walk to school and Ms. Crane sounds meaner than my principal!" I wondered what Miss Ellen might have looked like as a small girl and if that braid down her back had ever been cut much. "Did you like school, I asked?"

"Yes, Jade, very much so, but my sister Kathy became sick with the Typhoid fever and so did my mama shortly after. I had to stay home and take care of my brothers. By the time, things settled down and I could go back, it just never happened. Before I knew it I was marrying Mr. Cotton and having babies!" She smiled and poured me more lemonade.

I felt normal around Miss Ellen, like what I thought other kids in a regular home might feel. I didn't yet know that everybody has troubles in life. I thought my family was the only one with a secret and I always felt ashamed. I was humiliated that Albert Gentry was my daddy, but for some reason unbeknownst to me, Miss Ellen had a way of making me feel like the most ordinary person in the town. She also had a way of making me feel like an adult instead of a child.

"It won't be long until dark, Jade, so I 'spect we should finish up our lemonade and get you goin' on down the hill."

"Yes, ma'am, Miss Ellen. Thank you for the lemonade and for being my friend." I smiled at her and looked down at the kitchen floor. I noticed the checkered pattern and the way my shoes fit into the blocks just right. My bottom felt glued to her chair at the mention of 'get goin down the hill." I desperately wanted to walk down her hallway to her guest room and sleep one night without fear.

She clapped her hands together, waking me out of my daydream and gave me another big hug, squeezing me real good. It felt so nice to be wrapped in those loving arms. Really nice. I stepped down the porch steps and gazed in the direction of my house. My heart felt like the sun, sinking in the background. A flushed haze covered the sky-line and the lightning bugs brought a hint of light. I still had a picture of my mama's bruised face in my mind, so I listened intently for any commotion as I stepped into the yard. All seemed quiet at the Gentry house. I held my breath as my feet slid across the hardwood and gently turned the doorknob to my room. The screech of the door challenged the silence, and I stood still and waited to see if the silence would speak. My heart chimed with the clock in the living room as I quietly released the door knob and clicked the lock. I hesitated, but no one stirred, perhaps the demons had grown sleepy. I had learned to be painfully quiet in order to not rouse them from their slumber. Rousing them could be most fearful.

Chapter 3

My mother used to be pretty, her auburn hair long and parted down the middle. Her huge emerald eyes, like mine, were captivating. It was the worrying, abuse, and the constant smoking to calm her nerves that stole her beauty. She'd light one right after another, but she never smoked in front of company, and no one at the church was even aware that she smoked. She was very ashamed of her addiction, and I think she compared it to my daddy's craving for alcohol.

Once Johnny and I tried to smoke a cigarette we'd stolen out of my mama's pack. We walked plumb across Cottonwood farm and hid behind a large sycamore tree. I didn't think Johnny would ever get the thing lit, between the strapping winds and the constant fear of getting caught. "Did you get it?" My hands were shaking and I knew that even though my mama was full of love and forgiveness, she'd take a strap to my hind end for this.

"No, it's too windy and the matches keep going out!"

I put my hands in front of Johnny's and tried to block the gusts that were blowing up around us. He puffed and puffed his lips and finally I saw a cloud of smoke arise. Johnny's eyes were large and round and his lips puckered as he blew the white smoke into my face. "You got it, Johnny!"

He smiled and handed it to me. I looked in all directions making sure no one had found us out, then placed the cigarette between my lips and swallowed a big mouthful of smoke.

"That's not how you do it, Sissy, you have to inhale it down into your lungs." Then he proceeded to display the correct form of smoking. I don't think he had enough practice because he began to choke and cough and his eyes were watering.

"I don't like it Johnny; it makes my mouth taste funny and my head is spinning." My mama smoked enough for all of us and she swore constantly that each pack would be her last.

Johnny continued to puff as if he had to suck down the whole blame cigarette at once, blowing smoke like a choo choo train. He passed it back to me, but I just refused. I only saw my brother turn that shade of green once before and that was when he caught the stomach flu at school and hurled for a solid week.

"You don't look so good Johnny."

"I don't feel so good Sis." He stumbled and then sat down on the ground. "My head feels like a merry-go-round." He stared at me kind of funny like and then stood up, hunched over and began to spew a steady stream of vomit out of his mouth, gagging and making moaning sounds.

"Whew wee Johnny! You okay?"

Before he could answer, here came Mama! "And just what do you kids think you are doing out here smoking?" She had a thin switch from a tree in her hand and was shaking her head back and forth. "I see you got sick Johnny Gentry! Well, it serves you right smoking one of my nasty cigarettes, and with your sister, of all things!" Mama took that switch and she just swatted by our feet and across our legs one time. She wasn't going to hurt us with it, we knew that. Mama couldn't stand to give us a whooping. We had to be acting mighty bad for her to even think about it.

The lump on Mama's back created a false impression from the rear. Even though her shoulders stooped inward, her spine curving like a crooked road, she was actually quite young. She said it was scoliosis and it had been with her since childhood. I wondered if it was because of Daddy, if perhaps before they met she was unbending. My daddy towered over her like a tree; his strong branches surrounding her until they suffocated her very soul. She tried to escape; yet with every step he'd reel her back in, like a spool of yarn he kept her wound to him, enveloping her in fear. His voice was sharp and controlling, shattering her self-worth, her dreams, her very being, with a volume that could rattle the dishes in the cabinets. My mama would flinch and try to retreat back into her shell, the hard calloused shell that safely protected her. Every once in a while my daddy would gently coax her out and lift her spirits again. Her curved back with the crooked spine would begin to straighten. She'd start to bloom again; the scared doe eyes would appear calm. Yet, it seemed he was kinder to the scared doe. It seemed the stronger and straighter my mama became, the shorter the leash he gave her. Like a controlling tyrant, his boisterous words kept her wings clipped.

I know there is good and evil in all people. The evil beast just stays hidden behind a dark curtain. This black forest of darkness is unveiled when the drape is drawn open and brought to the light for everyone to see. We all try to keep the evil hidden safely behind that curtain; we try to keep wickedness hidden in that deep dark space. Daddy never could let his problems surface; he kept them safely tucked behind the screen. My mama couldn't get him to open up to her about a place called Pork Chop Hill and a war he never wanted to fight.

My daddy, PFC Albert Gentry, was shipped off to Korea in 1950. When he returned, he had a son who was two and a half years old and a daughter who was conceived during a Christmas leave. Of course, neither seemed to recognize him; his wife felt just about the same way. My mama said it was as if she had a new husband. He was not the good hearted carefree man she had kissed goodbye at the bus station just two years before.

Daddy had nightmares, night sweats, and a halo of darkness that came over him periodically. My mama just thought in time that he would heal and the man he was when they first met would be restored. My mama was a dreamer of sorts and lived in that fairy tale world for a long time. This imaginary place was her way of coping. She held on to the past and the man she fell in love with. I loved to hear her reminisce about the early years with my daddy and especially about the evening they first met. That was my way of understanding my mama.

She was just out of high school. It was late August and her best friend Maryann had accompanied her to the county fair. Evening shadows were growing long, as the sky turned to dusk and the sun dipped low on the horizon, a fiery, glowing ember. Mama said Daddy had been trying to get her attention all evening. "Now wait up, pretty lady, I'd like to buy you and your friend here a cotton candy?"

Mama twirled around, tilted her face out of the sun, raised her eyebrows up curiously and said, "And who are you?"

Daddy shifted and looked a little nervous. Mama's hair was deep rust, her cheeks were healthy and radiant, and she had those emerald green eyes with thick dark lashes. The only thing that marred her beauty was the fact that she was a little on the plump side. "I am Albert Gentry, and you are…?"

"Virginia Tillman. Nice to make your acquaintance, and we'd love some cotton candy!"

They walked down to the concession stand and Albert purchased the sugary treats. He had an unlit Camel tucked behind his right ear, and an eyetooth that bent to the side just enough to give him character. "See that big Ferris Wheel?" My mama turned and gazed up at the ride while Maryann giggled. "I've had a hankering all evening to get on it." He slid his hands down deep into his crisp new Wranglers. "I've walked clear around this whole midway looking for the prettiest girl to ride it with me."

He smiled, his eye tooth just catching his full mouth. Virginia blushed, her cheeks as red as the bright sailor dress she was wearing. Maryann urged my mama, "Go on Virginia, go now, I'll wait."

The Ferris Wheel cost a whole twenty-five cents. Daddy tipped his Stetson hat and walked up to the ticket booth. Mama said the night was perfect and the Ferris Wheel was filled with soft multi-colored lights that cast a glow on the crowd below. They took their seats and teetered all the way around until every last passenger was boarded and buckled in safely. My mama said she was so frightened of the height of the ride that she placed her hands on the iron security bar and gripped it for dear life. My daddy said, "Virginia, just sit back and relax now; take in all the beautiful scenery, I know I am." He smiled, never taking his eyes off her, and then reaching over, he unwrapped her fingers from the bar and slipped her hand gently into his. Mama said his words seemed to swim around her, floating like a symphony of colorful magic that illuminated the darkness. He was stirringly handsome and he was sure of himself. I wished I had known my daddy back then, back before he became someone else.

The other side of my daddy never reared itself during this time; my mama wasn't even aware that he existed then. The demon of the forest stayed behind the dark curtain. There were flowers and dances to attend. Daddy had a fine paying job for a country boy and the promise of a fulfilling life. My mama's heart was soft like fresh baked bread, then came the war.

When Daddy came home he never talked about the war, at least not to Mama. She told me he only said, "No person should have to go through war, especially women and children." It became a topic as taboo as the drinking. So, he hung out with guys he knew from town or his work, they all had been in the war, too. Mama told me that at first it seemed the late nights with his buddies helped my daddy begin to heal; he seemed happier for a while. Then gradually, the nights grew later and he became worse. The more he drank the more the leftover anger came out. He wasn't getting better anymore; he was getting worse.

The abuse began with language. Cursing and saying Mama was good for nothing, she was stupid and that other wives managed to live on what their husbands brought home. Then later he began to hit her, mostly slaps to her face. Over time, he escalated to bruising her arms in his gorilla grip fashion, and a few times he even hit her with his fists. She never let on like she needed any medical help, but she did begin to retreat further into herself. Daddy also found time for Johnny, to smack him around for this reason or that. I mostly got away by hiding, but over time I was the recipient of his wrath now again, too. He strapped my legs with his belt a few times. Those colors were stained and embedded in my memory. There were blue and purple welts that took days to fade away. I never would look at the meadow rue or the purple sweet pea petals the same again. My dresses didn't seem to cover them. Mama saw, but she wasn't sure what to do, but I did overhear her tell Daddy she'd pack up and leave if he did it again. I believe that was her best attempt at standing up for me. I just stayed home from school and went to Miss Ellen's. I knew she saw my legs and knew the truth; I felt bad, but she never let on. She fed me and let me rest on the couch with her dogs. I don't know what I would have done without Miss Ellen and her compassion.

Chapter 4

Mama opened the can of salmon and dumped it into a glass bowl. She began to take a fork and dig out all the bones and brown pieces and toss them back into the can. The can had a picture of a large fish smiling up at me. "Girl, go get me an egg out of the refrigerator. Go on now." She pushed her shirt sleeve back up to her elbow.

I scooted down off the stool and dragged my feet all the way to the ice box. My feet were still a tad too big for my body, and I hadn't quite grown into them yet. I knew when Mama made the smelly fish cakes, she and Daddy would be fighting. Having fish always meant we weren't eating real meat for a while because Daddy had drunk the grocery money.

"Go get me a can of peas, Jade, and don't shuffle." I knew that meant pick up my feet and quit dragging them. I focused on picking them up all the way to the cupboard which was painted white but chipping away to reveal a much prettier yellow color underneath. "Get two cans, Jade."

"But Mama, we don't got two cans."

"We don't *have* two cans," she repeated, correcting me as she chopped an onion on the cutting board. "What about corn, Jade?"

I reached up to the second shelf where the corn sat and grabbed a can. "When is Daddy coming home?" I was trying to mentally prepare.

"Soon, Jade."

"How long though?" Mama ignored the dread in my voice and continued to order out chores so that there would be less for him to find fault with. "Jade, you run along now and sweep the porch and have Johnny bring in some wood."

Mama crushed saltine crackers in her hands and tossed them into the bowl. I could tell she was worried. I tried to think of how to help her, but nothing much came to mind. And being a teenager, I had enough problems. This school year my body seemed to change overnight, right about when I began to get my monthly visitor, as Mama called it. I found myself wanting a little more privacy than what I was accustomed to getting, and I was closing the door to my room all the time now. All I was doing was homework, but shutting my door just made me feel better.

I watched Mama stir the can of corn and add a dash of salt to the cast iron skillet. Her hair had come loose and was all sweaty from bending over the stove. No matter how hard she tried to put it up in a bun, it came out, and strands fell all around her neck and earlobes. She never wore jewelry anymore except her plain gold wedding band.

Lately, she had become very thin. It was as if one day the weight suddenly slipped down her thighs and fell through the cracks of the wooden boards of our kitchen floor. I thought she had grown pale too, but the changes in her appearance hadn't seemed to weaken her. I still got plumb tired just watching her work.

I walked outside and grabbed the broom and began to sweep the dust and leaves, wondering which daddy would come home tonight. If he had been drinking or had a bad day at work, we knew. All we had to do was look in his eyes. They told us whether it was a night sighing from relief or if it was a night of not speaking and barely even breathing.

I watched the dust kick up from a row of gravel as his truck pulled up at the side of the barn. I saw his gait and focused on his eyes as he drew closer and felt the color drain out of my face.

"I swear, Jade, you get uglier every day." He reached his hand under my chin and smiled down at me, and an evil chortle escaped his mouth, coming from the dark place deep inside him. I lowered my head and waited for the screen door to bang shut before I allowed the silent tear to slip across my cheek and released the breath that I had been holding.

“Johnny, Daddy’s home, Mama wants you to bring in a pile of wood.”

“I know, Jade, but I have to burn the trash first.” Johnny was dumping the trash into an old barrel, and the smoke was rising, filling the air with a putrid smell. His pale skin was rosy from the heat, and his cheeks were smudged with soot.

“Gosh, that stinks!”

"What did he look like?" Johnny asked. His sad blue eyes weary of the evening that might lie ahead of us.

"He said I get uglier every day." I lowered my head and thought about how Mama was right about his words and how words did have power over us.

"Jade, he gets uglier every time he drinks, and you are far from ugly!"

I wanted to believe him, but when I looked in the mirror I secretly wished to be a blonde with a flawless complexion. My hair was red like Mama's, only not as dark and it had just a hint of golden highlights. I guessed I was what folks called strawberry blond. Like most redheads, I loathed my freckled cursed skin. My eyes were sea green, and I knew they were intriguing enough to make up for what I lacked, but Daddy's words still cut like a knife.

About that time we both heard a commotion. "I swear if he lays a hand on Mama tonight, I'm gonna knock his head off!"

"Johnny, what if he wins? What if he hurts you real bad?"

"I'm not scared of him, Sissy. He has already hurt this family enough!" Johnny walked in the house with a stack of wood in his arms. I followed behind him as he laid it on the hearth.

Mama was on the floor in the corner of the room. Daddy had the Hoover vacuum cleaner hose in his hand, hitting her with it over and over again. She didn't make a sound. She was covering her face and head with her hands the best she could. Whimpering.

"You damn lazy woman! Didn't I tell you to have all this done before I get here? Didn't I? Answer me! Makin' fish cakes, and I should be eatin' steak as hard as I work for this family." His face was red and he was swearing at Mama, using words that flew through the air and stabbed us all in the heart. He stopped swinging for a couple of seconds as if to catch his breath and then started hitting her again.

"Albert, don't! Aaaaalberttt!! Please don't. Oh God, please stop you're hurting me!" Her words were blubbered and distorted; snot and tears were running down her face and hanging off her chin. It was like a horror movie. I didn't want to watch, but I couldn't move from the spot or even shut my eyes. I was frozen right there, breathless, waiting for it to end.

Daddy raised his arm up again with that hose, but Johnny grabbed it in mid-swing. "You leave my mama alone!" Johnny's pale blue eyes had grown hard and cold. His voice was trembling but at the same time, quite strong.

That was the first time I ever witnessed my daddy in a predicament in which he didn't know how to react. At first, he just stood there and stared. Johnny repeated, "Leave my mama alone!"

This frightened me even more; I didn't know whether to run and hide or just wait. Daddy snapped out of his trance and wrenched his arm out of Johnny's grasp. His eyes were watery and very bloodshot. "Oh, yeah, and what are you going to do about it?"

Johnny took one step forward, and in a flash wrapped his arm around our daddy's neck and put him in a headlock. "If you just even once touch her again, I'll kill you." His nostrils were flared and the veins in his temples were throbbing, keeping tempo with my heart beat. "If you so much as harm a hair on her head, I will kill you! Do you understand?" His words were trembling. Johnny let go and stood staring my daddy in the eye. For seventeen, Johnny was built. He was just as tall as Daddy now and even more muscular.

"Oh, you want to be the big man of the house, do you? Don't eat my food anymore, and don't use my water either. You want to rule the roost, go ahead, you can pay the bills! Dag burn kids think they know it all!" Daddy kicked the lamp table and staggered off a few paces.

Johnny stood his ground as he wound up the vacuum cord while standing between Mama and Daddy, watching to see if he made one wrong move. The vein line in the center of his forehead was throbbing and for just a few minutes I felt safe. Safer than I'd ever felt. The air in the room felt cleaner and somehow easier to breathe. It was as if a different sort of vacuum had sucked out all the fear.

Mama pushed up from the floor and began brushing herself off. She hid behind the hair that had fallen around her face and began to set the table, trying to pretend that the scene we had just witnessed had never happened. She took a handkerchief out of her apron and dabbed at her eyes and wiped her nose. Daddy picked up the keys to his truck off of the counter and tore up gravel as he left. We three sat around the table eating the salmon cakes in silence. I thought about the fish adorning the label, its eyes and big gaping mouth smiling up at me hauntingly.

After supper, Johnny told Mama to take a nice hot bath and we would clean up the dishes. She went on and stayed in there soaking for a long time. She reappeared in her cotton housecoat and joined Johnny and me in front of the fire. We sat quietly, watching the firelight dance across our faces and listening to the crackling embers. Finally, Mama spoke. "Johnny that was a very brave thing you did tonight. I want to thank you for stickin' up for me. It took a lot of courage to stand up to your daddy like that, but I don't want you to ever do that again because he might hurt you real bad."

Johnny shook his head in an exasperated motion, "The next time he comes home in a rage we need to call Uncle Ed to come and get us."

Mama looked sad and fiddled with her housecoat for what seemed to be a very long time. It was tangerine orange with a ruffle around the hem and a belt that had seen better days. She looked up somberly, and her forehead drew up in a crease. She lit another cigarette and inhaled deeply, before releasing the smoke towards the fireplace. "But I love your daddy and I always will Johnny, no matter what. Sometimes God puts people into our lives for His purpose. I heard a preacher say people were like gemstones in the rock tumbler. Some are very ugly or dirty, others have sharp edges, but when they are tumbled around together the rough edges are smoothed, and the grime and filth are worn away to reveal a beautiful polished stone. Abrasives and water are used to buff out the surface and create a silky smooth finish. Johnny, can't you see all of us need each other. We have to keep praying for your daddy and keep tumbling around until we become polished." She pulled a tissue out of her pocket, dabbed her eyes and wiped her nose. Then she looked up at Johnny and me and said, "I hate this, I never wanted it to be this way. Your daddy was different before he went off to war. Do you believe me?"

We both nodded and softly said, "Yes, ma'am," in one voice.

"I love your daddy and I know he has pain inside that makes him like a wild ox at times." She rose slowly from her chair and looked Johnny in the eye, then looked at me and said, "You two get yourselves to bed now before he gets back here. If you hear him come in, do not get out of bed. I mean that you hear?"

We both mumbled, "Yes, ma'am," and went on toward our rooms. Johnny took my hand and squeezed. I reached around his neck, and he hugged me good and tight. Mama turned the lights off and went into her bedroom somberly. I never heard Daddy come in, but he was sitting at the table the next morning looking humble and beaten down. The demonic monster was gone from his eyes, and now they just appeared weary. He was talking quietly with Mama when I came into the kitchen.

"Good morning," I said softly. I hid behind my copper bangs, while getting a cereal bowl out of the cupboard. They said in unison, "Good morning, Jade." Mama smiled and when I looked at Daddy, he smiled, too. Their smiles were comparable to a picture placed in a photo album to be cherished. The only thing was, their smiles were as empty as the smile on that fish adorning the can of salmon and their hollowness grieved my young heart.

I thought about our family dynamics. Mama wanted to protect Johnny and me from Daddy. Johnny wanted to protect Mama and me from Daddy. Unfortunately, no one could protect Daddy from himself.

Chapter 5

My mama started an ironing business the year I turned sixteen. While my daddy was at the mill, she went to work making her own money. By this time, quite a few women in Braxton were working jobs in Cleveport. There were secretarial positions, clerking in stores, and some even found jobs in a couple of new factories that had moved into the area. There was a factory that made house shoes, another made women's purses, and still another made candy corn. The downside of this, for those women, was washing and ironing and housework to do on the weekends.

Mama heard them at church talking about work and keeping house, too. The wheels started turning for Mama.

She knew she couldn't take in washing because the water use and soap would be a financial burden. Also, her wringer washing machine and the clothes line outside for drying would be too much work beyond what she did for her own family; but she could iron. Mama told a couple of women at church her plan to take in ironing and that got the ball rolling. The women brought their clothes in bags on Sunday night and picked up the finished products the next Friday afternoon. I helped Mama label the bags so we knew whose garments they belonged to. When the ladies came on Friday, I would help her with the money and getting the clothes into their cars.

She didn't make much, but it was an extra few dollars and gave her some sense of independence. At times, it bought a few staple grocery items we desperately needed. Of course, Daddy took her money, when he remembered she had it. Or, if someone arrived to pick up and pay after he got home, he took all of it. But Mama stuck some of it back and kept that hidden from him. That was the only lie I ever knew my mama to tell. He would look into the shoebox under their bed, and she would swear a few dollars was all she had. Mama had to become very clever in hiding her earnings. She had so many stashes. I don't know how she remembered them all! She removed the back from a picture frame and put some behind the picture. Her coat pockets at the back of the closet usually contained some of the cash, as did her Bible.

Johnny and I also helped her all we could with the cleaning chores around the house. We had to have everything finished before my daddy arrived home from the mill. If Mama's job interfered with his supper being on the table at six o'clock or if the housework wasn't done, it could cause a night of heartache for all of us. Fortunately, Friday was the night Daddy usually arrived home very late and pretty drunk. When the clothes went home on Friday, Mama rewarded Johnny and me with a dollar each. Then on Saturday, we would walk to town to buy a soda pop and a candy stick of our choice from Taylor's General Store.

I loved to watch Mama ironing the white collared shirts and nice-looking dresses of the town folks. The steam floated off the iron, vaporizing, and then trickling down her neck, leaving a damp spot on her chest. My mama's dark auburn hair curled up as the moisture filled the air. Sometimes she'd sing songs along with the radio and tap her toes to the beat. She seemed to take pride in her work, making sure each shirt was smoothly pressed to perfection. This ironing business seemed to give her a renewed purpose and hope.

Her mood began to change the closer the clock reached my daddy's quitting time at the mill. We quickly got rid of the ironing board so Daddy wouldn't get angry that Mama was not in the kitchen at the stove. Each finished piece of ironing was hung in my closet so Daddy would never see it. Johnny and I started supper, and with the evidence of ironing whisked away, she would take over. We all seemed to hold our breath until he arrived, and we got a good look into those wolf eyes. Would they be calm and sober or swirling with evil?

If it was a good night we'd all sit outside after supper on the front porch. The night sky would light up the stars that danced. The sliver of the moon would make me think of the man who supposedly lived there. I could picture him seated in the arm of its bowl-shaped edge. His arms crossed behind his head staring down at the earth and our small porch. He'd wink and drink in the music coming from our farm house. Daddy played the banjo, and Johnny tried to learn how by watching each skillful move of his fingers. My daddy didn't own a capo clamp, so he used a short pencil and held it by rubber bands to slide back and forth.

"Now, this is a G chord and this is a C," he'd say, handing the banjo to Johnny, patiently instructing him. This was the daddy I wished I could kidnap. The father I wished would never leave. Sometimes he did stay in this calm manner for weeks, teasing us and getting our hearts to trust him.

Johnny would take the banjo and strum it like a guitar, swinging his hips to the beat. My mama tried to hold in her reaction but laughed all the same. "Oh, Johnny, really! You are something else, boy!" He was a cut up when he was happy enough to be one. Johnny was definitely outside the box. He reminded me of Elvis with his smooth pale skin, powder blue eyes, and hair as black as coal. He'd gotten all the best features from each side of the family. When I was a little girl, I often wished he wasn't my brother, so I could fall madly in love with him and marry him one day. He was certainly my hero.

Daddy would take the banjo back from Johnny's clowning and begin to pick it and sing with that great big ole' voice of his:

"The blue velvet moon fell from the sky last night-

The stars all lost their glow-

And the sun froze becoming total ice -

Which slowly melted my blue, blue, soul..."

The daddy that sat outside with us laughing and singing would indeed leave us all blue. It was just a matter of time and we all secretly knew it. He tried many times to stop the drinking. He'd look my mama square in the eye, those wolf eyes spinning, twirling, and drawing her into him helplessly. "Virginia Marie, honey, you know I don't want this family torn apart. You, believe me, don't you?" He would furrow his brow, then look intently into my mama's eyes with such pureness. "I can't believe how I have treated you. I am so sorry." He'd hold the word sorry out in a long vowel sound that went like this, "soooooorrrrry."

He'd run his hand smoothly along her cheek, the one he had struck just the night before. "You are so gorgeous and so loving. I could spend my nights holding you and loving you instead of arguing and fighting, but I guess I'm just a fool." He'd begin to pace the floor from one end of the kitchen to the other. It was very dramatic, and yet he seemed so sincere about changing his ways.

"I must be out of my mind to do the things I do. I hurt you, Virginia. I raised my hand to you." He pulled his hands away and stared at them like they belonged to a monster. "You know I don't even realize it is happening. I would never deliberately hurt you, not with words or these hands that belong to a coward. I'm a coward Virginia Marie, a weakling! How could I be so stupid? I'm never drinking again. I'm pouring the last of it down the drain." He would stand by the sink shaking his head. "Why, a grown man like me oughta be ashamed of himself, cussin' and rantin' and carryin' on. I've got children, and Virginia you know I want to be here for them. That there is Satan; that's all it is." He would glance at the bottle of whiskey, "Peeeyewww, I can't even stand the stench of it. It doesn't even taste good to me. I just drink to forget, Virginia. You know I saw a lot over there in Korea? This liquor is just some temptation sent to destroy my family. Well, I ain't having it! My family is my life. Virginia Marie, look at me." And of course, she would, those wolf eyes spinning like a top. My daddy would choke up, and tears would well up in his eyes. His voice would become humble. "I love you; always have, since the first day I laid eyes on you at the fair. Remember that night Virginia?" And of course, she would. "I'm getting back into the word of God, and I'm going to prevail this time. You'll see." Of course, my daddy would fool us time and time again, going weeks without drinking a drop. Then one day he'd show up with that awful breath.

"Cold turkey's hard to do, Virginia," he would say. "You can't expect me to quit overnight. Why, as much as you smoke and as much money as I dish out each week on tobacco, I just know you understand. You do understand vices, don't you, Virginia Marie?" Of course, she did. The thing was, smoking didn't make my mama mean. The only person she hurt was herself. "Now I'm going to stop. It just might take a little longer than I thought. God, don't care if I have a drink or two. You, believe me, right?"

My mama did believe in Daddy or maybe in the fact that deep down he wanted to quit. Those two eyes of his had distorted the truth once again. I often wondered why Mama kept holding on, believing in him after he let her down time after time. I, too, used to believe in his words, the empty words that held no truth. The words seemed to float off his lips, traveling to a far off place. Sometimes when he spoke I would say, "Yes, Daddy," or nod my head in agreement, not knowing what he said. At other times, I'd catch myself getting hypnotized just like my mama. Then I'd have to pinch myself quickly and look away from the eyes that sucked me into them; making me believe in something that never could be.

Mama took us to church on Sunday mornings. Daddy would come when he was sober and trying to win our trust back. Still, other times I believe in his heart he went to better himself. My mama seemed to glow on these rare occasions. She would talk of her faith in the good Lord and her posture would begin to straighten. Her scared doe eyes seemed to gleam and shine, lighting up the sanctuary. I loved getting dressed up for the service. My mama went to great lengths making my dresses. She had a variety of McCall's patterns to choose from and Mrs. Cotton was forever giving her leftover material. The skirts were usually flared and narrow in the waist. Mama trimmed a sage green one with cream lace and added a satin bow. I'd twirl in front of the mirror and inspect my appearance. These dresses usually came after a dark episode of daddy's drinking. They were "I'm sorry Jade" dresses.

The church we attended was small and befitting a poor town like Braxton. The pews were pine benches, unpadded and hard. They were sanded smooth and stained dark walnut. There were slots on the back of each pew that held the hymnal books and envelopes for tithing. Since there was no air conditioning, there were fans that the ladies waved nervously. The hymnals were well worn, a faded burgundy color. The only expensive thing about this modest little church was a stained glass window behind the pulpit depicting Jesus on the cross. There was no baptistery. A couple of times during the summer, folks who were needing to be baptized were properly dunked in the Hudson creek. Johnny and I both took our turn in the chilly waters of grace the summer of 1962.

Brother Caldwell preached on seeds most every week or at least that's the sermon that stuck with me. He was also a carpenter and worked to supplement the meager salary the congregation came up with weekly.

"Now, church, if you have the faith of a mustard seed, you can tell a mountain to move! Jesus said, command it to move and go into the sea! What does your mountain look like? I want everyone here to picture their mountain right now!"

I wondered if Mama pictured a bottle of bourbon. I thought for sure we all did, but what was Daddy's mountain? Only he and God knew the answer to that one.

Brother Caldwell raised his voice and slapped the pulpit, "What does your mountain look like? Jesus said if we spoke to a mulberry tree and told it to be plucked up by the roots and cast into the sea, it would have to obey. People, too many of us keep looking at the tree and making friends with it when we need to pluck it up and cast it out!"

I scooted down in the pew and pondered it all. I had never even thought of commanding a tree to move, let alone a mountain. So, I made a request to Johnny after service, but he just shook his head. I told him I believed if we had faith it could work. "Do you have faith, Johnny?"

"I don't know, Jade." He shrugged his shoulders and looked off in the distance.

"Johnny, we ain't got nuthin' else to do today. Why not give it a shot, and see Mr. Cotton. Maybe he's got some work you can do."

We ran to the tiptop of Cottonwood farm and standing in the highest point overlooking the vast hills, we began to stretch out our hands. I pointed a finger at the biggest hill in sight. I began screaming in my most faith-filled voice, "Move Mountain, cast yourself down in the name of Jesus Christ of

Nazareth!" Johnny stood and watched me; his face studying me with a quizzical look. Maybe he was yearning for my child-like faith. Then we waited in silence. Our feet were planted firmly in the red clay.

"Johnny, I don't hear a thing." There were no tremors, no shaking of the earth, and to our disappointment, nothing happened. That's when I realized it wasn't easy to obtain faith, even the size of a mustard seed.

"Maybe it's not talking about actual mountains, Jade."

"What do you mean?"

"Maybe, your mountain is more of a *big* problem? Maybe it's a situation that's in your life. So you ask God to remove the problem or help you deal with it. Like praying, 'Remove me from this place to a place where I can fly.' Does that make sense?"

I nodded, trying to understand how speaking something could cause it to happen, and how I could fly away from Braxton and the mountains that seemed too big for me to conquer.

Chapter 6

October turned into November, and Daddy was laid off from the mill shortly after Thanksgiving. Winter was sneaking up on us, and a chill blew all around us. Construction is always slowed by the winter's rainy weather. Not much call for lumber meant less work at the mill.

I had begun to notice Daddy couldn't hurt Mama anymore because Mama couldn't feel anything. She was as numb as a paraplegic. Only it wasn't on the outside; it was the inside that had lost all sensation. It seemed that last burst of hope the night she told the story about polishing the gemstones was gone now, completely. It almost seemed that not only could my mama feel no pain, but she couldn't feel anything else either, not even love. She became hollow like a tree that termites had eaten away. The empty shell walked around portraying a bent trunk and crooked limbs. Daily chores were done only to benefit Johnny and me and to keep the peace with Daddy. Her eyes became lifeless, staring into space at nothing in particular.

My daddy started making rocking chairs to sell that winter. He'd finish three or four and haul them in the bed of his old pickup truck to Taylor's General Store. Most the time they didn't sell but were used by the farmers to take a load off or play a quick game of checkers. The men folk would sit in their bib overalls conversing on the weather and the best time for planting. They'd discuss the economy and political issues. Sometimes they'd eat pickled eggs, gnaw on beef jerky, or chew tobacco.

Mr. Thomas Taylor had owned the store for as long as I could remember. He lived in a small apartment above the store with his wife Miss Rita, who never was able to bare children. Miss Rita made quilts and homemade jams to sell in the store. These items sold just about as well as Daddy's chairs. She was a talker if you know what I mean. And if she hadn't heard any gossip for the day, she'd create her own stories to tell.

Miss Rita was a pear shaped woman with a tiny waist that blossomed into a large bottom. This vast behind was attached to thunder thighs that made it hard for her to navigate the crowded aisles of the store. Mr. Thomas was a slow talker who never got to finish a sentence if Miss Rita was around.

"They had to shoot one of them Coyotes up on Pioneers Ridge last…"

"Now, Taylor, you know good and well it was two Coyotes, and we ain't seen the last of them." Miss Rita had her hand on her tiny waist and her hip stuck out as she talked. "Taylor, never mind the fact that Lois lost a calf last week to them coyotes."

As soon as Taylor threw back his hand to disagree, she started on something else.

I had always loved going to the store when I was younger because Miss Rita would just dote over me. "Well, if it isn't Lil Miss Jade! Look at those sea green eyes! Open your hands up and let your ole' Aunt Rita give you treats!" Then she would fill my pudgy hands with her homemade fudge. I think she was good hearted, just empty from never having her own children to love.

Now that I was sixteen, boys were taking a notice, and going to the store had become an adventure. I first met Dillon on a Saturday morning when Mama had run out of flour for biscuits. He worked there at the store on weekends, stocking shelves, sweeping, and cleaning aisles. One thing Dillon never could be found doing was running the register or handling the money. Reasons behind that I guess, was his skin. He was what Mama called colored. Daddy, on the other hand, said, "nigger." Mama had taught me that this was an ugly word, and I should not say it because it hurt the colored people's feelings. I hated when my own daddy used the word. I couldn't understand why he did. I loathed that word that seemed to be filled with hatred and intense ignorance. When I looked at Dillon, I just saw Dillon.

I felt some anger over Mr. Thomas and Miss Rita's decision to keep him from the handling of their precious money and stereotyping him because of his skin color. I guess the Taylors felt they were doing him a favor just by giving him a job. The majority of folks in town seemed to think their status as "white" made them above Dillon and his family. He was a soft brown, not near as dark as most. There had been some talk in the town of an affair between his mother and Judge Barrels. Some folks said that this explained the lightness of Dillon's skin and the reason behind his job at Taylor's Store.

I didn't care about any of the town gossip but had secretly taken a liking to seeing him at any opportunity. Dillon had eyes the color of caramel. When I looked into them, I could see clear down to his soul. He had a warm smile that showed teeth so white and so straight they looked almost false. I'd lay in bed at night thinking about his hand in mine; the warm chocolate hand and the pale cream colored hand entwined. I thought about his full lips brushing my thin mouth. I thought and I thought, but knew deep down Daddy and everyone else in town would never stand for it with their small minds. I felt like there were too many mountains to cast down. I had run to the top and spoken with all the faith I could muster. Now I would just have to wait.

Chapter 7

Winter soon turned its ugly head towards us and blew a chilly wind. The clouds opened up and a cold, steady drizzle would pour out on us for days at a time. Then the temperature would drop, turning the flooded roads into sheets of ice, closing the school and trapping us all inside for days. Our stove was filled with wood, and the house smelled like my daddy. I resorted to painting pictures in my bedroom. The art teacher had given me some paints that were nearly empty because she noticed how much I enjoyed painting. The first one I did was of Miss Ellen Cotton's dried up corn stalks behind a grey-blue sky. The second one was of horses galloping through an open field. Their manes were purple and their coats were a pale yellow. I liked the overall effect, but it was still missing something. I decided to paint tennis shoes on their feet, hot pink, red and orange, with shoe laces and bows. The outcome was very bizarre, and I wasn't sure the world was ready for my artistic vision. Yet, somehow dipping the colors into the brush and creating something from nothing made me feel alive.

Winter was the hardest time of the year for my family. Work at the mill was slow. Although Daddy had been called back, he wasn't getting the hours he was accustomed to. This meant more time off for the bottle and less money to make ends meet.

My mama acquired a cough that December that turned into a deep low sound that seemed to echo through her chest. Of course, this didn't stop her from smoking. She was already thin and listless, but as the cold settled in, she lost more weight and got very pale almost overnight. We all just suspected bronchitis or whooping cough, but then her condition seemed to worsen. She'd heat Vapor Rub and inhale the icy blue scent or stand at the stove with a towel over her head, a pot of boiling steam engulfing her lungs, trying to open the air passages that had tightened. Her eyes were sunken and lifeless, and her energy level dwindled to almost nothing. She was forced to stop her ironing business because she was just too sick. She had a terrible peace about her, which I know now was resignation.

I was seventeen now, and my birthday had passed without anyone noticing. It's odd how things change when a family member gets sick. Mama was in bed a lot, so I had taken over the cooking. I seemed to feel hungry all the time. If it weren't for sneaking away to get fed by Miss Ellen, I don't know what I would have done. Johnny had started working for a family we knew well from the church. He began helping with their livestock. He kept the cows fed and assisted with calving when spring came along. He worked every day after school and ate supper with that family. We both found a way to get through the dreary days and cold nights.

After my mama missed four services in a row, Brother Caldwell stopped by to check on us. I could tell he was shocked when he saw Mama as white as the sheet she was lying on. She smiled a thin smile and thanked him for coming. He looked at my daddy and just shook his head. Of course, he prayed for my mama, asking the Lord for mercy and healing, but I could feel the urgency in his voice when he spoke to Daddy, sitting in the kitchen.

"Albert, she don't sound good, don't sound good at all. I am shocked at how she has changed in a couple of months. I think you better get her to a doctor."

My daddy agreed and seemed to be blindsided by how sick Mama had become. I guess sometimes when you are around a person, day in and day out, you don't notice the severity of their condition, or maybe you just try hard not to see it.

By the time Daddy took her to the hospital in Cleveport, the cancer had spread into every nook and cranny. The cancer was far too advanced for any treatment. The doctors said it was out of their control, and all we could do now was wait. For now, we should just try to keep her comfortable.

Johnny hardly ever went to school, so he could care for Mama at home. I think it bothered Johnny, giving Mama the morphine shots and trying so hard to take good care of her, but at the same time it made him feel like a man. He grew up almost instantly. He was eighteen years old and nursing his dying mama.

A woman from Braxton who worked as a nurse in Cleveport came by a couple of times a week to make sure everything that was needed was being done. She bathed Mama and monitored her medication. She never took a dime for this care. People in the church gave us money to help with expenses. Miss Ellen came with a cake or a hot apple pie. At other times it was more substantial food like a casserole with rice and chicken or a small bag of grocery supplies for each day.

We were so grateful for all the help, but not surprised. It was just the small town way. As gossipy and judgmental as they might be, in a crisis they took care of their own. But even Johnny wasn't prepared for what happened next. Our daddy quit the bottle.

He became a real father; a daddy I never had before, and I actually hated him for it. All those years and now that Mama was at death's door, it seemed he was trying to redeem himself for all the neglect and abuse and cruelty he inflicted on her.

He was now someone who held my mama, wiped her brow with cold compresses, cooked homemade soups, and gave her sponge baths. When he made chicken noodle soup, I'd help him roll out the dough cutting it into strips. He swore there was healing in the rich broth. He purchased books on healing and natural herbs. He even went and talked to an old Chickasaw medicine man and had him come with a bundle of sage to burn in Mama's room. That man prayed to the Lord in a way that made Brother Caldwell seem like an amateur. Johnny told me that after the smudging of the sage smoke and praying in Mama's room, he and Daddy sat with the old man and his son in the kitchen over coffee. The old man told them that he had seen in a vision Mama rising up from her bed still in a prone position, and then, suddenly she went upright and stood several feet above the bed. She looked up and like a rocket went straight up into the clouds as the ceiling and roof of the house dissolved to reveal the sky. He told my daddy to give her peace and faith along with the pain medication. His parting words were, "Keep her mind on The Great Spirit as much as you can." Then he and his son shook hands with Daddy and Johnny and walked silently out the door.

After this, Daddy and Johnny took turns sitting next to Mama when she was awake. They read the Bible to her, going over her favorite verses. Each night Daddy had Johnny and me gather around her bedside and pray for her healing. Sometimes we sang the hymns that she loved. I secretly wished my daddy would have done these things when my mama was well because then maybe the evil cancer would have never been strong enough to defeat her. Oh, why did the mountain move too late?

Cancer slowly overtook her body, leaving her brittle and weak. Even her hair was dry and lifeless. I watched my mama age that winter. She reminded me of the trees with their branches bare. All the flourishing green leaves had fallen to the ground waiting to decay into the soil.

I wondered if my daddy thought that if he changed his ways at this point, God would forgive him for all the evil he'd committed or perhaps have pity on his soul by healing my mama. Maybe he thought that God would send him to purgatory, instead of the lake of fire the preacher talked about on Sundays. I still wasn't sure a loving God could cause people to burn in flames forever. I wanted to get to know the Creator, but that side of Him that men preached about, pounding their fist on pulpits and wiping their sweaty brows, did not make me anxious to begin. They all said it was due to Him giving us free will, but I wasn't sure about that yet either.

It sickened me that my daddy had the power to change all along. I guess that was his free will! I believed he could have done this anytime if he had really wanted to. He wasn't motivated until Mama was on her deathbed – literally.

Brother Caldwell came by often, always smiling and bearing treats that his wife had baked. But, the rhubarb pies and broccoli casseroles were only a temporary comfort. Our hearts were heavy as we waited for the Lord to take my mama away from the never ending pain and suffering with which this awful disease tormented her.

I wanted to ask Brother Caldwell about that mustard seed of faith and why none of us had enough to heal my mama or enough conviction to ask properly of the Maker of heaven and earth to move this mountain of sickness. I wanted Him to uproot this cancerous tree and cast it into the sea. I decided it was best just to keep quiet. I felt sick at my stomach when he mentioned the miraculous healing of my daddy from alcohol. Why couldn't he see people make choices in life? My daddy had made a choice to stop drinking, a choice made about twenty years too late. I had so much anger inside of me, so much heartache, and my mind was working overtime.

My mama was the person that held our family together. She was the light, the warm glow and now she was leaving us. I decided my mama was too holy to tarry here on earth and that if there were a God, he must have a greater mission for her. At any rate, she seemed completely content with leaving this world and told us all we'd do just fine without her. She had finally given up the fight.

One evening when Mama had done fairly well that day, she told Daddy she needed to talk to me alone. I wondered what her words would hold. I entered her bedroom; the humming sound from the humidifier gave a soothing effect, but the smell of death was all around her. Her lavender quilt was tucked tightly around her and her auburn hair lay mussed around her head on the pastel sheets. Her doe eyes full of wisdom from a life of pain held me still. I could hardly breathe. My mama took my hand and tried to prepare me for the future.

"My beautiful Jade," she said in a voice so weak it was almost a whisper. "You are becoming a strong young lady. Daddy and Johnny are going to need you now more than ever. I want to tell you I was wrong about so many things. I want to tell you how sorry I am for staying here, but I did the best I knew how. I was raised that divorce is wrong and that God hates divorce. I think God hates for a person to be treated the way Albert treated you kids and me. He should have given up the bottle. Our lives could have been much more comfortable financially and certainly more peaceful. I just held on thinking things would change and I guess now they finally have."

She began to sputter and cough up into her tissues, and the sound of her struggling for breath was one I will never forget. "Now, Jade, promise me you'll never marry a man that drinks?" Her eyes were saying so many things. It was hard to keep up with their urgent warnings. I nodded vertically, as to say yes.

"Never let a man lay his hands on you; always remember your self-worth. Don't be so meek and gentle like I was. It would be better of you to be hard than to have just anybody take advantage of you that way. Be strong and wise and take good care of Jade." Her hand gripped mine with what little strength she had left, and the tears began to well up inside of me. I wanted to mourn for the woman who lived such a life filled with grief. I wanted to cry for the young woman who lit up the Ferris wheel that night so long ago. I wanted to scream for the passion, joy, and dreams, my daddy had stolen from her. I wanted to hold her until she felt safe and loved and whole.

"I promise Mama," I said through lips that quivered. "I promise!"

She rose up and reached under the mattress, "It's not much, but it might be enough to get you help if you need it." She held in her hands a roll of money tied with two rubber bands. "Here, Jade, take it and don't tell a soul. It was meant for you all along. I need to rest now. Remember what I said, and if your daddy starts drinking again, take this money and go stay with your Uncle Ed."

I had met my mama's brother, Ed, just once. He had come to visit us one summer when I was around six or seven years old. I remembered the long, olive green, station wagon, with paneled siding, and his big round belly that eased out of the seat. Uncle Ed smiled all the time; seemed as if he didn't have a care in the world.

His wife, Julie, was severely obese and weighed close to three hundred pounds. She had long dark hair, with choppy bangs. Her square-shaped teeth were a grayish color, and her nose was plugged, creating a dull nasal tone when she spoke. She was an exquisite guitar player and could strum with her eyes closed. She sang folk music mostly, but on occasion she'd sing a ballad or country tune. I held her microphone proudly and wished to sing as lovely as she did. For some reason, the plugged pitch left her when she sang.

My mama was worried about Julie sitting on our furniture and breaking it due to her large size. I remember her getting Daddy to move her side chair with its dainty legs to the barn, just in case Julie decided to sit there. Mama even took time deciding what bed would be best to put her in. This didn't seem to matter because the box springs fell anyhow, and Julie didn't seem the least bit embarrassed about her weight. She just commented on how furniture was not being made very hardy these days.

Ed took Johnny and me out for ice cream at the Dairy Delight in town on Saturday. We had hot fudge sundaes with peanuts and whipped cream. This was a special treat and Ed gave us each a dollar on the ride back home. Nevertheless, when we returned, Julie had their bags packed and was sitting on the front porch looking rather anxious. Within minutes, Ed became just one of many to witness my daddy intoxicated. It was always an embarrassing sight for me. His slurred speech and the fierce glare out of his bloodshot eyes was awkward. His words resonated with evil. They seemed to fly through the air and slap our cheeks. His thick tongue was filled with ignorance even a child of my age could detect and the tip of it could cut you to pieces. I cringed at the sight of him. Ed had heard about Albert's drinking, but hearing and seeing were two different things. The truth was, that was his baby sister, his only sister, and Uncle Ed couldn't stand the abuse and refused to watch. That day he took one look at my mama's swollen lip and begged her to take us kids and leave with them in their station wagon. My mama just put her head down avoiding Ed's gaze.

"You don't understand, Ed. I love Albert, and he loves me. He doesn't mean to act this way, and he is so sorry for what he's done afterward. He was in that war and something terrible must have happened. I know God can take the cravings away. I just have to be patient. God is slow sometimes. The Israelites wandered through the desert forty years. God's just slow, but we have to put our trust in Him no matter what. Why, Ed, what kind of a wife would I be running off leaving like that? These children need their daddy."

I remember holding my breath and waiting to see if Ed could convince her. I prayed under my breath. I prayed with all the intensity an abused child could muster. I wanted to grab her legs and wail at her feet. I secretly was screaming, "Please take Johnny and me and run like the wind from this wolf-eyed monster!"

"PLEASE!" But my heart sank with each word she spoke. It was one of those times that I hated her almost as much as I hated Daddy.

Ed just shook his head and said, "Virginia, our Daddy would turn over in his grave if he knew how Albert treats you." I guess Ed couldn't stand to see Mama like that. It must have made him want to shake her like my daddy had so many times. Ed grabbed Julie and her suitcase and opened the door of the ugly green station wagon. Julie's eyes were wide as she forced a smile and blew a kiss towards me. I was smiling but inside my mind was screaming, "Please, Ed, try harder, please, ask to take me with you, please, please, please!" But to no avail. They drove off ever so slowly, and I ran down to the creek and sat on a rock in the sunlight. I was wishing I could empty my stomach of the sickly sweet ice cream that seemed to be curdling there now. Ed stayed away and prayed his sister would find the strength inside herself to leave. But it seemed no one I knew had even a tiny grain of mustard seed, nor the faith it would take to move my mama.

Sitting there beside what was left of my slowly dying mama, I held the money in my hands and reflected on the severity of the situation. My mama was leaving and I couldn't go with her. My life was going to be forever different. I felt as if I had jumped off a cliff and was falling but had no idea of how or where I would land. My mama was the strong person in my life, the one who answered my questions and encouraged me when I was down. How was I supposed to live without her? I felt like a little child. I couldn't even muster up teenage bravado.

I was grieving over my mama's suffering. Cancer is a dreadful way to expire. At the same time, I was worried sick about how I was going to live my life without her. I kissed her cheek, whispered, "I love you, Mama," and retreated to my bedroom, where I tucked the money into a safe hiding place. That night I lay in my bed and stared out my window, wondering what the future held for all of us, especially me.

"Dear God, it's me, Jade...Where can I purchase some mustard seeds?"

Chapter 8

It was the 27th day of April. I walked the path past the pecan groves and the wild crab apple trees that Mama used for making pies and jelly. I walked briskly. I was coming home from school, and the trees were full of leaves and buds of fruit declaring springtime. It was almost three miles from school to my home, but more peaceful than the school bus on many a day. This particular day I wasn't in the mood to be cooped up with classmates.

I made my way to the opening that held gravel roads and sunlight, along with roads named after the farm families that owned the land. I kicked stones all the way down Elm Street. Elm turned into Hadley and Hadley to Cottonwood. Now the town had slowly disappeared, with the wisteria vines held by wire trellises adorning walkways. It had all turned into farmland and pastures populated by cattle and hay bales. I slowed my gait. I had a knowing before I reached the house that Mama was gone. I had felt her spirit leave hours before. It was as if emptiness flooded me and I was missing some sacred piece of my soul.

Mr. Earl and Miss Ellen Cotton were sitting at the kitchen table when I arrived home. Miss Ellen's hair was a silver mass, piled high atop her head, and lowlighted with streaks of charcoal that hadn't faded yet. Her eyes were soft and almost the same shade of faded gray. She grasped my hand and rubbed my shoulder.

"Your mama passed away about noontime, Jade. Brother Caldwell has taken your daddy to Cleveport to make the funeral arrangements. Her last words were about you. She said, "'Please take care of my Jade, I love her so.' "

I stood motionless, wishing I could get her hand off my shoulder and that I could run away from all this. She drew me into a tender hug and said, "There is a pot of beef stew on the stove, and Jade, I am here if you need to talk."

"I know," I said softly and deep down I was glad she was there.

She had a look of confusion, a jumbling of awkwardness, mixed with sorrow. She removed her hand from mine and sat back down. Johnny sat in Daddy's easy chair; his eyes saw nothing as he stared through their glaze. I walked over to Johnny and laid my head on his.

"Oh, Johnny, what will become of us?"

"Sissy," he said ever so softly, just "Sissy," and he patted my head.

The house had a strange feeling of loneliness and the lingering smell of death. Part of me felt a sense of peace because the suffering was over and we all could somehow move on with our lives. I knew a shifting was coming, but I had no idea what lay ahead.

Brother Caldwell, of course, preached my mama's funeral. Most all the congregation was there for the viewing. There were crock pots filled with pinto beans and potatoes, a sugar cured ham, roast beef, and sweet potatoes. There were more food and desserts than I had ever seen the likes of before. I didn't have an appetite, though. I only felt numb. The whole two days from Mama's death to her burial seemed to suffocate me and I feared the future for us all.

My mama was buried in a dark blue dress with a white corsage pinned to her lapel. The large doe eyes were closed forever. I would never again see the green eyes that were just like mine. Her mouth appeared to be drawn upward in a peaceful smile. I patted her hand and deftly slipped off her wedding band and placed it slyly in my pocket. I wanted to take away the symbol of abuse. I was secretly thankful, knowing my daddy couldn't harm her anymore. "You're safe now, Mama. Perhaps, you're already up in Heaven with your Jesus."

I stood and looked at the lifeless body that didn't resemble my mama much at all. Her face had sunk in and her arms were thin, pale sticks. There was no spirit left, but just a body that was empty, cold, and worn out.

I think Johnny took it harder than we all expected. His tears flowed freely with no shame. He had tried to protect her and be the man my daddy never could be until it was too late. My nose was filled with the strong aroma of carnations and the mixture of perfumes the ladies wore. My ears were buzzing with the activity of friends and family member's conversations. As I stood there, I didn't feel myself drifting. But I must have, because the next thing I knew, I was on the sofa in the prayer room surrounded by church ladies, the pastor, Miss Ellen, and Johnny. The ladies determined that I had not eaten for several days and brought me a turkey sandwich and a cup of coffee. I sat up, ate the sandwich, and sipped the coffee. Slowly, my strength came back to me. I wasn't even embarrassed. At this point, I didn't care what anybody thought of me. Johnny sat there with me after the pastor and women had left us alone. Both of us were crying for Mama, as much for her life, as for her death. I felt strength in the two of us. We were the only ones who witnessed exactly what Mama went through during her life with Daddy.

My Uncle Ed showed up for the viewing without Julie. He never once spoke to my daddy. However, I overheard him telling others,

"It wasn't the cancer that got her. He killed her and that's all there is to it!" I thought he might be right about that, but I couldn't be certain. He gave Johnny an envelope with some money in it and told him to call if we needed anything. He talked to him about work and finishing school. He kissed me goodbye and left.

The next day, the funeral went on without a problem, except the weather had turned cool and it was pouring rain. They lowered Mama into the ground as lightning and thunder rang from the heavens in a fury. My umbrella blew straight forward, and it was all Pastor Caldwell could do to get through the prayer. We laid our roses on top of her casket and bowed our heads. I stared at my daddy's face looking at his posture which now ironically had become like my mama's. He was like a broken, bent tree. We all went home and waited for something. Yet, we didn't know what that something was.

Those last few days of school were a daze. I came straight home and stayed up in my room most the time. Daddy was working and he and Johnny tried to fix meals. I guess the three of us were shut up in our own private grief.

I walked by the General Store one day, hoping to see Dillon. The colored kids had their own school. All the other businesses in town were segregated. Since he worked at the store, it was the only place that I might run into him.

Miss Rita Taylor hugged me so tight I had to gasp for air. "Jade, honey, come here and let me get a look at you." She was wearing a knee length black dress that made her hips look smaller. "You poor child, I am so sorry about your mama, Jade. How are you doing sweetheart?" She peered into my eyes with deep compassion, and I knew she was one who really cared.

"Thank you, Miss Rita! I am well, I think. I miss my mama something awful, though."

"Awe, Honey. You come by this store anytime. I'm working on a new quilt pattern that I just know you would adore. I can teach you if you would like to learn. I've sold plum out of my strawberry jam so maybe you can help me make another batch? Sometimes, I tend to get bored with all these men folk around." She winked, looking sympathetic but a little bit anxious to find words that would soothe me.

"That sounds real nice, Miss Rita, real nice."

"Jade, you'll be fine. You are such a strong, brave young lady, and I just know you are going to make your family very proud."

I thanked her again and got a stick of licorice candy. I didn't see Dillon, so I headed for the door and told her I'd be back soon to help her. I wondered how Dillon was, with his caramel eyes, and his warm bronze skin. Wondered if he knew my mama had died.

Chapter 9

Johnny managed to graduate, even though he had missed so much school when Mama was sick. Next year, would be my senior year. I wondered if things at home would be bearable enough for me to make it through. I doubted I would get clothes for the new school year. Mama had always made my clothes and collected hand-me-downs from church folks. I had grown a little that year, so I thought probably by fall I would need bigger dresses. Mama's medical and funeral expenses had to be paid, too.

I stayed up in my room most the time. The house had a hauntingly empty feeling to it now. There was no singing, no cussing, or ranting, and no Mama to cover me with her love. Under my bed was a velvet jewelry box that contained the fragments of my mama's life. There was an old diary she had written years before when my daddy was at war. She filled each page with memories of Johnny and it read almost like a baby book. Of course, there were words of missing the man she had fallen in love with on that hot August day at the county fair. Her Bible was in that box as well, with its worn pages and curled up cover from much use. There were three prayer cards with pictures of Jesus on the cross and one of His mother Mary. The box also contained her marriage certificate, and the wedding band I had slipped from her hand. I had added her death certificate that had broken the cycle of my daddy's abuse. The last item was the money Mama had given me, rolled and wrapped with a rubber band.

I put the box back under my bed and lay down. I wrapped my arms around myself giving myself a hug. I drew my knees up and curled in the fetal position. I felt the weight of a tear sliding down my cheek, racing to escape the hole of emptiness. "Dear God, It's me, Jade. Is my mama with you or is she just lying in a pine box? And God, can I please get me some seeds?"

Time went along into summer. Sometimes I became so angry at my daddy I wanted to explode. I wanted to scream at him, "Drink, go on drink your bourbon, throw things, cuss. Why don't you put holes in the walls!" I hated him with a passionate hatred that filled my bones. I despised him for sobering up now that my mama was gone. I abhorred his presence and the food that sustained him. I loathed his words and the oxygen that kept him breathing. I knew the seeds I had asked God for weren't coming. I had gotten seeds from the evil one, bitter, nasty seeds. This evil kernel had grown and planted roots inside me, turning my heart to stone.

Daddy started attending AA meetings in Cleveport right after Mama died. That's where he met Verdi, short for Veronica. All I knew was Verdi made me nervous. She chewed gum constantly, making a popping sound over and over again. Her lipstick, always a hot pink, stayed smeared across her two front teeth. When she smiled, there was excess gum space; it was like watching a horse nay. Her hair was bleached blonde with dark roots that led to a high forehead. She had a pointy chin and eyes of blue that held no knowledge.

Daddy moved Veronica into our home shortly after they met. My mama hadn't even been gone two months. Verdi worked as a secretary in Cleveport and was always bragging about her ability to type sixty words per minute. She'd tap a long fingernail in my direction and tell me how she could teach me to apply the false fingernail tips. "I got 'em down at the Five and Dime, Jade, do you want to try it sometime?"

I had no desire to go anywhere with her and secretly wished Daddy had never seen the likes of Veronica Peyton! Daddy started drinking again just about the time Verdi unpacked her belongings. She went swiftly to work changing the décor of our home, stripping away any traces of my mama that were left. She took Mama's doilies and the afghan throws she had crocheted and packed them all up into boxes. All the while she was telling me that my Daddy needed to move on and just get on with life. She even applied a fresh coat of paint throughout the house and hung black velvet matador paintings above the couch. `There were ceramic bullfighters with blood red capes and ceramic statues of gypsy women with black hair and silver hoop earrings. She played Elvis and Eddie Arnold albums at a volume that could wake the dead while she danced around the living room in her miniskirts, the latest craze.

Veronica's legs were her best feature; traveling the length of them sometimes distracted me from her annoying presence. There were rare times when she tried to befriend me by taking me shopping for clothes or getting me things for the new school year. She would inquire about my schooling and if I had a boyfriend or the likes. Other times, Veronica looked at me as if I were a pile of cow dung she'd accidentally stepped in. Or perhaps I was a pesky nuisance that had made my way into her new home. Nevertheless, I was put out by the whole situation and longed for escape more than ever.

Johnny stuck around for most of the summer. He didn't care for Verdi either. He had looked for work, found a couple of temporary jobs, but it seemed there was no steady work to be had, even at the mill. Finally, he called Ed, who arrived the following week to take him to Kansas.

I heard they have golden wheat fields and sunflowers as big as your head there. He promised to write me and said he wished there was a way to take me with him, but I needed to be strong and finish up my schooling. I stood in the driveway and watched Ed's olive station wagon until it was out of sight. Then I walked to Cottonwood Farm and reminisced about me and Johnny's special time spent together there. My heart felt like tiny holes had been drilled into it and sorrow was oozing out like a watering can. My life would be forever changed.

Daddy didn't seem surprised to see Johnny go and acted as if he'd done nothing wrong. If he missed Mama, it was never brought up in a conversation. He never asked me how I was doing with my grieving. He seemed thankful for Verdi and almost grateful she had buried my mama's belongings, along with her memory. Daddy even complimented her on how she had fixed up the place. The only time Daddy spoke of Mama was when he was drunk, and sometimes he accidently called me by her name. This frightened me, and I hoped he would not mistakenly abuse me like he did her.

On the weekends, my daddy and Verdi entertained her friends. They would play poker or spades 'til the wee hours of the morning. There were six of them total, Jed King and his wife Tilly, Conner Duncan, his better half Frieda, and, of course, Daddy and Veronica.

Jed was a large man with a beer gut the size of a watermelon. His white T-shirt was always stained with perspiration and it never quite covered his belly. He had hair growing out of his nose, ears, and neckline, but none on top of his head. His wife, Tilly, was straight and narrow with a large nose that took over her face and made it hard to notice her pretty blue eyes.

Conner Duncan was all mouth, cracking jokes left and right. He'd finish one joke, yell "Hell-fire!" and then start in on another one. He kept an unlit cigar in his mouth, which he chewed on 'til it was frayed at the end. Conner was the charmer of the bunch, who had a witty or sarcastic remark for each comment his wife Frieda made. He had a cleft chin and dimples even Shirley Temple would have envied. Frieda was a hoot, ketchup red curly hair, which kinked up against her head, and enough freckles for a small child to play dot to dot with until eternity. Her eyes were brown golden flecks. Every time her husband, Connor, made some funny remark and joked, she would squint her eyes and shoo him with her hand. Frieda taught fourth grade at Gillman Elementary School in Cleveport. She was by far the more educated one of the group, and she had a nine-year-old son by her previous husband.

Jed always brought a twelve pack of beer, and Daddy would perspire as much as Jed each time he'd open a can and it made a sizzling pop. Jed would guzzle half the ice cold brew, set the can down and belch loudly. Daddy tried to quit drinking but as a dog returns to his vomit, so did he. Veronica, well she never really had a drinking problem. The AA meetings were just a place for her to meet men who needed help. The men never even saw it coming. All they saw was Verdi's legs that went on and on forever. My daddy loved his bourbon and now he had someone to share it with. She was so unlike my mama who never drank a drop and shrank from my daddy's rage. This woman kicked and clawed with her long fake nails, and she shrieked like a cat in heat. Daddy always backed off when she threw one of her fits. It was astounding to watch.

The whole bunch made me nauseous. Jed was disgustingly foul and must have never been taught any manners. Conner was creepy and kind, all wrapped together. He was always trying to befriend me and inquired often about my mama and how I must be missing her. He had an unusual way of getting me to open up about Johnny and how badly I missed him too. Conner seemed so genuine and yet so strange. It disturbed me how easily I would find myself opening up to him and spilling the secrets of my heart. Afterward, I would often regret it. I wondered how he was able to get me to say so much and why he even cared. I hated this about him, and yet I looked forward to his visits, even though his corny jokes were tiring. Every other weekend when it was poker night at our house, Conner and Frieda would bring me something. Sometimes it was just a Coke; other times it was more personal. They brought a woman's magazine once and a brightly colored scarf another time. The scarf was blue and green and brought out the color of my eyes. I tied it around my head and put on a pair of Verdi's white sunglasses, then acted as if I were popping gum over and over again. Conner laughed a little too loudly and said the scarf made me appear much older than I was. Frieda began to inquire about my private life and even offered me a babysitting job for the summer.

"Jade, you know my husband, Conner, lost his father at an early age?" He drowned in the Trudy River over in Crestwood!"

"Oh, Frieda, I wasn't aware of that."

"Yes, seems he can relate to you and what you are going through. I think that is why he makes such a fine stepfather to Jason."

She patted my hand and left to join the others in the kitchen. Conner had gone to fix himself a drink and had found a way once again to talk with me secretly. "So Jade, tell me how things are going? You like Veronica?" He rolled his eyes and made a gesture as to say he understood. I said nothing. His dimples looked like huge craters tonight and I wasn't in the mood for his wise cracks. "So what's up?" I uncrossed my legs and fidgeted with my bottom lip.

"I'm good Conner, how about you?"

"Why I guess the same as ever."

"Frieda's been nagging at me all day, but you know I can't really complain. I just get tired of her never wanting to do anything with me. It's all I can do to get her to come out here and play cards. I planned a boat ride on the river for us and she just complained, said she really hates boat rides. He made his voice squeak and squinted his eyes while he mimicked her. "I find them boring and it's so hot out there in the sun, Conner-- really?" He twirled his fingers in his hair in a girlish manner and batted his lashes for good measure.

"Cute, Conner, real cute. But a boat ride does sound fun. It sure beats playing cards," I said, halfheartedly.

He smiled then and said, "That is what I like about you, Jade. You seem like a gal that's not scared of trying new things. Frieda hates the outdoors and she sits in the house all day coming up with new school activities to do with her class."

Daddy yelled from the kitchen, "Conner we're going to get started without ya if ya don't get your hind end in here."

"Hold on, I'll be there in just a second, Albert."

"Anyway, I heard about this art show in town, crafts, and the likes. I thought women were into that sort of thing, but not Frieda. All she wants to do is lie around with her nose stuck in a book. She likes taking Jason to the park once in a while, and I do love the kid and all, but she doesn't take time for me. Jason loves science books and between the two of them being bookworms, I just sit there."

Conner talked on and on about his marriage and his stepson. The more Conner drank, the more he talked and it became wearisome. I couldn't get a word in, and I couldn't quite follow his thought patterns because they seemed to jump around from topic to topic, and then he'd tell a joke and laugh rather oddly.

I wondered if Veronica thought about me as a stepdaughter. I was a lot older than Jason and I knew she was just biding her time. She'd already removed nearly every memory of my mama from our home. She had pretty much run off my brother too. Now she just had to get rid of me and she'd be free! I glanced into the kitchen, at the room full of smoke and booze and the black matador that seemed to be saying, "It is time to thrust in your love!"

Chapter 10

I spent a lot of time alone after Mama died. I guess that was how Conner became someone I could lean on, someone who could fill a void in my soul. He told me things I had always longed to hear from my daddy but never did. He told me I was beautiful, on days when I felt ugly and overweight. He told me I was intelligent and articulate on days when I had given up on any future outside of Braxton. He told me the whole world was mine and that I could do anything I imagined or dreamed. It was as if Conner knew all the right things to say, at exactly the right time.

"Jade, I been thinking about a school up in Chicago for talented artists. Your dad told me you love pottery and painting and are quite good at it."

Although Mama had hung up one of my paintings of birds in the dining room, I wasn't aware my daddy had noticed any of my art, so now Connor had my full attention.

"Maybe Frieda could pull some strings. I hate for such a talented young lady as yourself to get trapped in a place like Braxton." Conner began to fill my head with dreams of fame. "You are so artistic, from your drawings I've seen, you should set up your own art studio."

I smiled and envisioned a new life far from Braxton and far, far away from the gum smackin' Veronica and my seldom sober daddy. Conner left me with daydreams of easels filled with paintings, all displayed and for sale in my art studio, a quaint little cottage. I pictured myself in a painter's smock and holding a brush, the sun cascading through the large windows of my studio filled with sculptures of beautiful women with flowing hair. I pictured a garden planted out back with plants and flowers peeking out at the people who would pass by on my cobblestone road. I would have business cards made up with my name displayed boldly. My mind continued to wander in and out of reality, and I began to look forward to talking with Connor. The anticipation for the next card game became stronger, as my small world came to include Connor.

We talked about our favorite movies and hit songs on the radio. He asked me what my favorite musician was, my favorite color and so forth. He gradually got more and more personal. He wanted to know if I had ever fallen in love. He asked me if I could live anywhere in the world where would it be. I pondered over each question, but especially the one about where I would live. I thought about a big city like Chicago or maybe Hollywood where all the movie stars lived, or I'd envision Nashville where musicians and artists hang out. Heck, I'd never been any further than Cleveport, Mississippi.

Conner said I had to think larger, like Paris or Greece or Italy. I wasn't even sure where they were on the map. He began to ask me about college and if I had any plans. I told him I was thinking about becoming a nurse so I could help sick people like my mama. I spilled my insides out to him, even confided in him about Dillon.

"Jade, don't rush things; there will be plenty of time for boys later on. Don't give yourself away. Take care of your dreams and your future first, okay?" He squinted his eyes and looked funny at me for a second. Then he said something that immediately erased all the kind things he'd spoken. "You ain't been kissin' on no nigger boy, now have ya?"

I could tell he was prejudiced like the rest of them. I could tell that my "no" answer was taken with an undertone of "good" as if he wasn't sure he believed me. Although there was something about him that really bothered me, even so he became a friend like I'd never had before.

It was a Thursday when he first stopped by to ask me to lunch. It was raining so hard I thought the windshield wipers would fly right off.

"Jade, how would you like to keep driving? We'll just head out and drive clear to the coast. Biloxi's got a nice beach. We could stay by the ocean and maybe do a little scuba diving. Hell-fire, I ain't never been scuba diving before!" He smiled and gave me a wink followed by a hearty laugh, and I wondered why my stomach felt strange by his comments. I suddenly wanted to be out of his car and far away from him. It was a feeling of icky.

He took me to a Chinese restaurant in Cleveport. I ordered an exotic dish I'd never heard of and a fancy drink with a little umbrella that floated on top. The waitress brought our plates out on a tray. The plates were inside silver platters with lids, that when raised up, revealed plenty of steam and a delicious aroma. My dish had a dark red sauce poured over chicken with sprinkles of sesame seeds. There was an egg roll and white steamed rice. Even though I felt that soft whisper inside that said I shouldn't be here alone with Conner, that Frieda should be here as well, I also felt I owed him something for all the nice things he had done for me. I knew how lonely he was and he said he always invited Frieda, but she was just a homebody. We laughed at this and knowing that he invited her too, I relaxed a little bit. After the lunch, we drove on back to Braxton.

This was the beginning of our times out together. In the last month of school, when the bell to dismiss rang in the afternoon, several times he was waiting in the parking lot as I came out to get on the bus. He would motion for me to come over to his car. "Jade, over here, come on, I'll give you a lift. I was just on my way to see your daddy and thought you might like a ride. Hey now, I got you a little something." He smiled and reached behind the seat and pulled out a paper bag. Inside was a brand new rock album and a bottle of Chantilly Paris perfume. It seemed odd and made me feel a little strange. Again, I was getting the "icky" feeling.

I was confused and felt mixed signals. I couldn't figure out what Conner wanted from me. I mean he was married and he was my daddy's age. I was just seventeen and I knew he only saw me as a child, but why did it seem so strange? The more he did for me, the more strange I began to feel about him. Suddenly I noticed myself inching away slowly from him and avoiding him like the plague. Had he noticed? At school, those last few days, I would look out a window and if I saw his car, I would go out through the back door of the cafeteria and cut through the woods to avoid him. I would go to see Miss Ellen in case he drove over to my house and found me there alone.

The weekend card game was coming up, and I was sort of dreading it. I hadn't seen Connor since the previous weekend and I was glad Frieda would be there. Veronica had asked me to help her clean and prepare for her guests. I loathed spending time with her, but I agreed to help out. She wanted me to make brownies and finger foods. I prepared pimento cheese and turkey sandwiches. I cut them in fourths and poked a toothpick in each one. I fixed a relish tray with carrot sticks, pickles, broccoli, and tomato chunks, and a bowl of Thousand Island dressing for dipping. One thing was certain, with Verdi's income of forty dollars a week, there was always plenty of food.

"Jade, can you wash the towels in the bathroom hamper and scrub out the tub?"

I mouthed a soft "yes" under my breath and kept stirring my brownie batter.

"Thanks, Jade, you sure are a doll. I have to do my nails still and roll my hair. Your daddy likes it curly you know."

I didn't know and I didn't care to know. I got the brownies in the oven, scrubbed the bathtub, and put the towels in the washer.

Conner arrived early that evening. He was bragging about all the weight he'd lost. I guess I hadn't really noticed but could see he did appear slimmer.

"Twenty more pounds and I'll be a sexy son of a gun!" He smiled at Frieda and Verdi and then glanced my way. He was wearing a new pair of Levi's and a blue sweater that seemed to match his eyes. Jed congratulated him on his weight loss and then looked down at his own protruded beer gut. Conner patted Jed's belly twice and asked him when the baby was due. Frieda rolled her eyes and lit a cigarette while Verdi slinked into the room wearing go-go boots and a skirt so short it screamed "stare at my legs" or maybe something worse. Everyone turned to gawk and Verdi drank it all in. I hated her more every day. Not because I was jealous of her or her legs that had no end, I hated her because of how easy my daddy had replaced the most beautiful woman in the world, my mama. She was not only beautiful on the outside but even more so on the inside. That was what was missing from Veronica Peyton.

At seventeen, the boys were starting to notice me. Sometimes I looked older than my age. I wasn't sure if it was because I'd lost my mama or because my daddy had aged me before my time, like he had Johnny. Whatever the case, I could pass for twenty or more with makeup on and my hair flowing free. But with no makeup, and my hair fixed in a ponytail, I could still look younger. My breasts were small but beginning to show. My freckles had faded almost completely, and they covered well with foundation and powder.

When I appeared that night to serve up the food, Conner looked me over and told Daddy he better be careful or he would have to beat the boys off of me with a big stick. Daddy just smiled, never looking at the daughter that reminded him of the wife he had taken for granted. I hung around in the kitchen making small talk, and then as the cards were dealt for the first hand, I decided to retire to my room and be alone. I was tired of the loud Saturday night poker games. The stereo was blaring a song.

"My eyes can clearly see,

That you are not the angel that you appear to be,

No, no, no, you are the devil underneath...."

I shut my door and crawled into bed. I was reading Mary Shelley and trying to concentrate on the storyline, but it was getting more and more difficult. Their thunderous voices rang from the rooftop, and I could tell they were getting wasted already. The card game usually ended early, and they often retreated outside and sat around the fire talking and drinking.

I had felt weird around Frieda that evening. It was almost as if I had betrayed her in some way. I thought about all the conversations Conner and I had together. Some of them were even about her. It felt strange to watch her at the kitchen table right in front of me. The small pecks he gave her in between jokes made me feel disgusted. It also made me feel relieved knowing this was his wife; he loved her and was truly only my friend. That was the underlying fear, that he possibly had another motive. I certainly hoped not because although he could be quite strange, Conner was also like the father I'd never had.

The confusion and the noise were making it hard to sleep. I couldn't seem to focus on my book either. I turned towards the window, wrapping my mama's quilt around me thinking about how badly I missed her. I counted the stars and thought about Johnny and wondered how he was faring with Uncle Ed. I guessed he was the lucky one in Kansas, and I was the one waiting for thc day I turned eighteen. My mouth was dry and I felt antsy, so I got up and went to the kitchen for a glass of ice tea. Veronica was dancing around the table singing to the lyrics as usual, and Daddy was looking at her legs with a lust that made me ill. My mama wouldn't have anything to do with him when he was drunk. I think that was what started most their fights, but with Verdi it was all different. Conner looked at her and rolled his eyes.

"What kind of dance do you call that, Verdi?" he said and then proceeded to cackle at her. Jed and Tillie had moved outside and the back door was standing wide open. I slipped back to my room and shut my door. I drank a huge gulp of tea and settled back down on my bed. I closed my eyes and felt myself drifting away in the peacc and safety of my own little space.

Chapter 11

When I woke, I didn't know what stirred me. Then I heard a soft tapping sound and turned over to face the door. I saw a flicker of light from the living room and the dark shadow of a man that seemed to be lurking above my bed. "Daddy?"

"It's me, Conner," he said in a soft voice. I felt an odd feeling and I could I hear the sound of him breathing heavily. "Whatcha up to? Thought I'd just drop in and check on you."

"I'm fine Conner, I'm sleeping," I said in a shaky voice. "What are you doing in my room?"

"I was thinking about how beautiful you looked tonight." He stumbled a little then sat on the side of the bed. The mattress sank with his weight and my heart sank with fear. I could see his features as my eyes adjusted to the darkness. He started to describe in detail how sexy I was. The air was getting thicker and making it hard for me to breathe. I felt frozen and betrayed. It felt like a knife stabbed me in my soul. He rolled on his side, and then the weight of his body was on top of mine. I pushed and thrust my feet towards his chest but to no avail. He placed a finger to his lips and made a shushing sound, as his blue eyes pierced the darkness. "It's okay Jade, I won't hurt you. I just wanted to talk to you for a minute, shhh, don't be scared."

I could smell his cologne, the whiskey, his scent, and I wanted to scream, but shock and disbelief had caused me to shut down. A lump was rising in my throat making it hard to swallow.

"You're so beautiful, like a porcelain doll," he said the words slowly, letting every syllable roll off his tongue seductively. His fingers ran along my cheek, down my neck and then back again. "You feel something for me don't you, Jade? I've seen how you look at me with those big green eyes of yours. You're always opening up to me about all your secrets and those sexy clothes you wear around me and all those curves just waiting to be touched."

His fingertips brushed along my neckline and across my chest, and I felt an excitement I didn't want to feel. It was one I couldn't contain. I felt like I was at war with my own body. "I can make you feel so good, Jade. Let me make you feel good. Don't you find me the least bit attractive?" His hand cupped my head and began to pick up pieces of my curls and twirl them around his fingers.

The truth was I had secretly found him charming in his own way. Not like Dillon, but like an uncle, or even a dad. It was a feeling of friendship; now the feelings were just plain creepy.

"I just want to see what it will feel like to touch your lips, just a small kiss, Jade. One tiny kiss to see if what I feel for you is real. Hmmm?"

I pushed as hard as I could, but he didn't budge. Part of me wanted to kiss him and part of me wanted to run from the room. I took my knees and squared his chest with all my weight. "Get off of me!" I growled. "What are you doing? Are you crazy?" I could feel the hardness in his pants pushing on my leg. Suddenly I couldn't breathe! My heart was jumping out of my chest, and I felt nauseous.

"Please Jade, I promise I won't hurt you. Please, I just want to be close to you."

I found my voice cracking, and I tried to protest…but, I knew I had no control over any of this. "Stop, Conner, please this is so wrong! Please don't do this. Please go back outside with everybody else and let's just forget this ever happened. Please!!" I was whimpering, begging now.

"Shhhsssh…just let me brush my lips on yours." And then he moved closer. I could feel his breath on my neck, in my ear, the calming shushing sounds and the trembling of his body. I felt frightened and special all twisted together in some sick way, and I wasn't prepared for what would happen if Frieda came in the room or even worse, my father! He'd kill me for sure. Or would he? Did he even care? Did anyone even know Conner was missing? I pushed with my hands again at his chest, this time harder with more force. He looked in my eyes with a plea that stopped me from moving.

"Oh, you're so beautiful and so innocent." His hands traveled down the length of my torso, running over my stomach then down to my thighs.

"Your wife's here…Frieda." I said in a scratchy voice that didn't sound like my own. "She loves you. You can't have feelings for me, I'm just a kid, for Christ sake! I'm half your age and my daddy is one of your friends. Conner what if someone finds you in here?"

"I don't care, Jade. Frieda is just some roommate, always has been. I've never had these feelings for her. She's so caught up in her own world, she don't care about me." His voice became louder. His speech was thick. "I'll tell them all about you. I don't even care anymore, I love you, Jade." And then his lips brushed mine.

I felt sick inside and confused. He reached inside the line of my panties and traced the outline of my skin. He said all he wanted was a kiss, so I couldn't understand why he was trying to take my panties off. He rose up and very slowly turned the door handle. I thought maybe he was going away after all. But he just peered out toward the kitchen area. I could hear the voices and the laughter over the music, "*My eyes can clearly see you're a devil* underneath..."

I was shaking and scared and just wanted him to leave. I was whimpering, "Please Conner, it's not right. Please go back in there!" I wanted to get up and run out of the room, but his weight was pinning me in place so I couldn't move.

In a flash, he pulled my legs apart and instead of kissing my mouth he was kissing my abdomen while he was exploring with his fingers in my secret place. It seemed so weird that my emotions went from fear and disgust to curiosity and excitement. I didn't like what he was doing, but in an odd way it seemed like maybe I did. My confusion made me queasy. I pushed and I pushed, but he wouldn't budge. I wanted to scream but felt frozen with fear and shame.

"I can make you feel good, see doesn't that feel good?" He was making me feel sick in a part of my stomach I never knew existed, and I kept shoving his head away.

"No, Conner, go away! I don't want you to make me feel good." I growled. "This is not right, I'm a virgin!" My voice was gathering itself again, protesting louder and stronger. My arms were pushing and my legs were aching, but it was almost as if he were in a hypnotic state. And then I felt it, hard and thrusting, shoving into me, searing, and tearing. I pushed and cried, screaming but no sound came forth from my mouth. I was whimpering, begging him to stop.

"Conner, please stop, please stop!" My words were muffled with sobs. Then, as suddenly as it started, it was over. He collapsed on top of me and he drew in several deep breaths.

As absurd as it sounds, he rose up swiftly and zipped his pants faster than I could blink. He ran his fingers through his hair and tried to gather himself. I could hear him trying to steady his breathing. He leaned over me and placed his hand on mine. It was like the hand of a monster. "I'm so sorry, Jade. I had no business acting like this." He took a deep breath and let it out slowly. I lay there completely still in a state of shock, frozen. His eyes looked so spooky and so frightening it reminded me of Mama or was it, Daddy?

"I just thought that maybe if I kissed you one time I could get over these feelings I have for you. I thought maybe I wouldn't feel anything for Albert's daughter, that maybe it was all in my head. I mean that's what you are, you're Albert's little girl, but to me you are a beautiful woman. And now I know that it was real, Jade. My whole body is tingling." He looked at me so serious, and then in a whisper said, "But I'll go now."

He stopped at the door then turned towards me, "You're so gorgeous, so full of life. I'm sorry, I never meant to hurt you. I just wanted to make love to you. I don't know what got into me. I won't ever bother you again." He dropped his head down, but then looked up at me like a small child who had been scolded.

I gathered all the strength I could find inside myself and thought about all the times I had watched my mama suffer abuse at the hand of my daddy and spoke with a forceful boldness, "I'm telling Frieda and Daddy that you raped me!" I said it so boldly and loud it almost shocked me. But deep inside I knew that I was much too scared and ashamed to tell anybody, especially them.

"I'll tell them for you, Jade," he said. His tone was flat and matter a fact, "I love you, everything about you! But how would you explain to Frieda about all our dates, the lunches in town, all those presents? And you were purring in here like a kitten. You did take pleasure in this, mark my words, girl, you loved it! Oh, and Jade, then there is Dillon. I think your daddy would not approve of his little girl and that *nigger* boy. No, he wouldn't approve of a lot of things, now would he?"

A chill ran down my spine, as an evil presence filled the room. He slipped out as quietly as he slipped in. He left me feeling like I was the one who did something wrong like this was my fault. He left me wondering if he really would tell them. I closed my eyes and prayed. I prayed to a God that I wasn't sure existed, a God who had allowed this to happen. I prayed to my mama and Johnny and the little girl inside of me that never would be the same. My insides ached and my head was pounding. There was a wet sticky substance oozing down my legs and a filth I knew I could never scrub away.

I opened the door and peered out into the hallway. I made my way to the bathroom. The scent of Conner's cologne was all over me. As nausea swept over me, I hovered over the commode and began to gag. Finally, my stomach ejected everything it had in it. I splashed cold water on my face. Gathering my strength, I ran hot water into the tub. I hoped the water would soothe the awful pain I was feeling "down there." As I eased down into the water and began to swirl it around between my legs, I was shocked when the water turned red. I was bleeding from what that low-life scum did to me. I let the water out immediately and turned on the shower. I began to wash with an intense frenzy. The water was scalding hot, and my legs felt wobbly and unstable. I scrubbed between them and I felt numb inside, hollow like my mama when she had become an empty shell.

"Dear God, if you exist, please take me home to be with my mama because I don't want to live."

Chapter 12

A couple of weeks went by and I didn't see Conner. On poker nights, I went and stayed with Miss Ellen Cotton. I told her frankly of Daddy and his rowdy friends and she was very kind to me. I actually felt safe there with her and Mr. Earl watching "*I Love Lucy*" and "*Perry Mason*." They were like the grandparents I never had. Although Miss Ellen always had plenty of food to offer me, it seems I was never hungry anymore. I had no appetite for food and much less for life. I started losing weight at a rapid rate. It was the one thing I could control. My heart hurt and I became so depressed it was all I could do to get through my days.

It was growing close to time for school to start, and even though I was in my senior year, I had little enthusiasm for it. Verdi took me shopping for clothes a couple of times. I didn't even want to do that, but I didn't let on. I thanked her profusely and tried to really mean it. I knew I needed to buckle down and press on toward graduating, but escape was always on my mind. I began to spend every free moment at Taylor's General Store, partly because I loved Miss Rita and partly because I didn't want to be home by myself during the day when Connor could come by unannounced.

Dillon took a step backward on that first day I came into the store. The bell jingled above the door as our eyes locked. Now that Daddy had Verdi and Johnny was gone, it was simple to sneak away to the store. It was easy to do just about anything now that my daddy's mind was occupied with Verdi's long legs and his bottle.

Dillon's voice was like a melody, a low soulful cure to my soul. "Jade, I was so sorry to hear 'bout your mama. How you been, girl?" I was captivated by his eyes, the deep honey skin and remembered a feeling of youth and a light-heartedness that had been missing from my life for some time now.

He said again, "I said, how you been, girl?" Dillon smiled broadly, his straight white teeth polished and shining sent another message, that he had missed me too. There was chemistry between us that I couldn't ignore, and it almost made me forget my worries about Conner.

"Oh, Dillon, it's so good to see you!"

I squeezed in a hug and inhaled his scent. Miss Rita spotted me from behind the counter and let out a squeal. "There's my girl!" She darted out from behind the counter and put her hands on my face, "I do say, haven't you turned into a beautiful young lady!"

I blushed and thought to myself, "Oh, Miss Rita if you only knew." I hadn't felt like much of a lady since Conner had stolen my innocence, but I was determined to heal.

I had a fresh letter from Johnny to show them and photographs of him and Ed. My favorite was one of Johnny and Uncle Ed leaving for work. They both had on matching blue uniform shirts with their names embroidered on the pockets, their lunch pails in hand and grins that shone straight through the lens and captured my heart. I thumbed through each snapshot making comments and passing them to Miss Rita and Dillon. I knew from the light-hearted tone of the letter that I could never confide in my brother about my problems with Conner and Daddy. He seemed so happy in Kansas that I had just led him to believe in my letters that everything was great back at home.

Miss Rita began to teach me how to quilt that evening and even called Verdi to let her know I'd be spending the night with them. She made banana nut bread and cocoa with marshmallows. She could sew and make patterns so unique and so beautiful that I was amazed. Her fingers hummed with the sewing machine and seemed as if they could stitch each piece even if she had her eyes closed. I brought a bag full of Mama's clothes with me to piece a quilt with the material. I loved the idea so much and was thankful I had saved what I had before Verdi had taken it all to donate to the Salvation Army. It would become an heirloom, something I could pass down to my daughter if I was able to have one someday. We found a stopping place in the work, and I decided to take a walk and clear my head. I told Miss Rita I was going home for a bit to check on Daddy and grab a few things. Dillon left at five each evening but seemed to be poking around a bit; it was about ten after.

"Where you off to, Jade?" He looked past me kind of shy-like.

I had no idea what made me spill out my next words, except for a fear of being alone and the urge to know him better. "Oh, I was just thinking about going down by Jupiter Lake and taking a stroll. It has been so humid and hot out today." I stuck the side of my thumb in my mouth and chewed all the skin around my cuticle, a nervous habit of mine.

"I guess it's a nice night ta go down by Jupita." He scratched his head, "Thang is, see, I was thinkin' more 'bout gettin' a cheeseburger. You houngry?"

"Well, I can always eat somethin'," I said and laughed nervously. I was seventeen years old, never had a boyfriend or even been on a date. I felt about as gawky and ungraceful as a girl could be.

Dillon looked down the road and then back at his car. "I don't want you to get into no trouble now, Jade. You knows how folks are in this town." Tiny beads of sweat were forming just above his lip. He seemed as awkward and nervous as I felt.

"I can take us down to my territory, Nathan's bowling alley. It's colored, though. You might feel uncomfortable, Jade? How old is you now anyways?" His eyes scanned me kind of discreetly. I was wearing a cream-colored sundress with a pale blue short jacket. I had my hair in a ponytail to show off my newly pierced ears, another gift from Verdi.

"I'm eighteen." I lied once more and then immediately started looking for more skin to chew, this time on my index finger. I didn't want to lie to him but knew what he was thinking. If my daddy went to the sheriff, he would go to jail just for having me in his car. I had never really been alone with him. We just always talked at the store. He opened the passenger door and motioned for me to get in. It seemed like he had weighed the possible penalty against the chance to spend more time with me and made his decision. I slid across the mahogany seat cushion and bounced on the springs. He told me of his plans to go away to college and showed me his class ring. There was a real sense of pride in his voice.

"How's your daddy been, Jade? I saw him with that Veronica woman last week. Is that goin' okay?"

I must have rolled my eyes or made a face because Dillon let out a laugh that was hearty and knowing. "She's something else, and Daddy's drinking again. I try to stay away from them and their parties they throw every weekend." My head filled with images of Conner and my throat constricted at the thought. I changed the subject quickly. "I miss Johnny so much, but I guess everything happens for a reason." No sooner than the thought escaped my mouth, I wondered the reason for Conner and his advances.

"Oh, girl, you is somethin' else. I had my stepfather Leroy, in my life for some time now. He been good to my mama, a little strict with me at times, but, all in all, a good man. Course he ain't never been one for the booze, nope, but he do like the ladies, the ladies be his downfall."

"I was thinkin' 'bout findin' my real father. I think every chile need ta know who his parents is. I looks at every white man I meet. I looks into his eyes and I say to myself, 'Dillon that could be your ol' man, right there.' The Negro man don't accept me half the time 'cause I ain't dark enough, and, course I ain't light enough for the white folks neither. I did hear though in places like New York, Michigan, and California that theys more acceptin'. They says that the bigger states and the Northern states is not as racist like they is here in the South. I's even heard tell all kinds of relationships occurs."

There was a silence in the car now. I didn't know what to say. I could picture kissing his lips. I wanted him to know that I had feelings for him before I knew it I blurted out, "Well, I'd date anyone outside my race if I liked them." My voice sounded strained, and I gave Dillon a matter of fact look, but inside I was scared.

Dillon looked at me with eyes that seemed sad and wiser than before. "Jade, you would have to put up with a lot of racism. You ever been called a 'nigga lovah'? Ever had people stare you down, try to make you feels dirty inside over the color of your outside? Did you know children of a mixed race are badgered and treated like trash? They git it comin' from both sides. They ain't black, they ain't white, so they is nuthin.' I was lucky to be dark enough to be okay, so to speak. But some folks have children and the babies are almost white, kinda yella looking with a light brownish color hair, but always nappy. People is cruel today. If any of the white boys in this town seen you with me, they wouldn't want nothin' to do with you and they'd beat me and maybe kill me, before they'd let a nigger have ya."

I thought about what he'd said and it seemed an answer to my prayers, "No man would want you if they seen you with me." But it was the last part I didn't like. I didn't want Dillon to get into trouble, but I wanted to make sure that Conner never wanted to touch me again.

I looked at Dillon as he pulled into the parking lot of Nathan's. It was very busy from the looks of things. He turned to me and said, "Jade, I brought you here because they's good people and you won't be humiliated here. I won't let anyone harm you, even if it were to cost me my life." He reached his hand under my chin and pulled my face up, looked into my eyes with a look that made me feel safe.

We grabbed a booth in the back and Dillon went to the counter and ordered. There was a jukebox in the corner playing Aretha Franklin and bright red-checkered curtains in the windows. I loved soul music because it seemed to carry so much emotion. Dillon set down two Coke-a-Colas and a bottle of ketchup. "Two double cheeseburgers and fries is on the way! Miss Jade, I hopes you got an appetite because Lenny makes the best around."

He smiled and his teeth looked like a parade of polished pearls. Dillon was something foreign to me, and I loved to hear him talk and tell stories. Before I knew it, darkness had fallen outside the red covered window. I wished I could stay with him forever, but I knew Miss Rita would be worried about me, and I didn't need her calling my daddy. "I best get goin' Dillon, it's gettin' late and I don't want to upset Miss Rita." Dillon reached in his pocket and pulled out a crumpled mess of dollars to pay the tab.

We didn't talk much on the ride back to the Taylor's store. I guess I was busy trying to figure out how to deal with the emotions I was feeling. I was terrified of Conner and not very sure of what would happen if he caught wind of me being with Dillon. I wanted more than anything for Dillon to somehow wash all the pain away. I wanted to know what his soft lips felt like. I wanted to make love with him and let him replace every fingerprint of Conner's and every piece of skin that he had brushed upon me. More than that, I wanted his spirit to cover all the evil Conner's had placed over my soul.

"Jade, I'm just gonna drop you off a little ways from the store. Don't want no static from the Taylors or with your pa. I'm not doin' you no disrespect. I've had a fine evening with you, Jade. Just don't want no worries."

I knew the concern was genuine. I knew we were treading on dangerous ground, but I welcomed the opportunity no matter what. I felt alive and more normal again. We got out of the car, and I could see the porch light of the store glowing down the way.

"Good night, Jade," he took my hand and kissed it. I reached up on my tiptoes and let my small thin lips brush across his warm full mouth. I felt a ripple of electricity and then a warmth that I never wanted to forget. He hungrily kissed me back with such intensity that I ran, ran like the wind and never looked back at Dillon. I carried the kiss all the way to the twin iron bed Miss Rita had fixed up for me. I replayed it over and over in my mind until I drifted off to sleep. My first real kiss.

"Dear God, it's me again, Jade. Thank you for making Dillon's lips so soft, and please help me to disappear. I still don't like the Earth you created and I'm sorry for that."

Chapter 13

The next morning I was up early. I got dressed, skipped Miss Rita's offer of breakfast, and walked home. Daddy had already left, and Verdi was about to go, too. "Hey, sweetie." Verdi smiled, while drinking the last of her coffee. I couldn't help but notice the hot pink lipstick all over the rim.

"Hello, Verdi."

"Tell me now Jade, how was your visit with Mrs. Taylor?"

I smiled back at her but didn't feel much affection for this woman, even though she had made several attempts to be my friend. I poured myself some coffee and told her about my quilting lesson and how Miss Rita was a good mentor for me to have. I was in midstory when she put her mug in the sink, grabbed her purse and keys and said, "Great darlin', see you tonight."

I took a shower and dressed and went over to Miss Ellen's. I had spent several days at the store and felt it was time to check in with her. Plus, I felt scared when I was alone at the house now, and Miss Ellen seemed to take my mind off my problems. I stayed with her through most of the afternoon. She was putting up blackberry jam and it was a job I could help with. We had a great time. She didn't pry or ask where I had been for the days when she hadn't seen me. I loved her for caring about me, yet giving me space I so desperately needed.

I had lost track of time and realized it was later than I thought. Daddy was probably already home, so I walked down the hill and at the bottom going toward our house, I saw Conner's car sitting in the driveway. I wanted to turn around and go back to Miss Ellen's but decided instead to face the devil. I walked into the house holding my breath.

I could hear him laughing and talking to Daddy. My stomach did a flip-flop and I took a deep breath trying to compose myself. It was the first time since the episode that he and I had been in the same room together. I decided that he was not going to win, and that I was going to outsmart him at his own game.

"Well, hello Jade, haven't seen you in a month of Sundays. How you been?"

"I'm doing fantastic, Conner. Keeping busy, you know." My mind wandered back to Johnny, holding that runt of a puppy and its crooning whines and suddenly I grew taller. I pictured my mama and her bent crooked trunk and I straightened my posture up to its full height. I looked evil in the eye and smiled at it with such power that I felt a little dizzy.

"What have you and Miss Frieda been doing, anything special?"

He sized me up and seemed to look a little awkward. "Oh, not much, just the usual things old married folks do." His blue eyes shifted and he ran his fingers through his thin hair.

"I see," I said, as I fixed a glass of sweet tea and talked to Daddy about staying at Miss Rita's for a week to work on mama's quilt.

Connor looked at Daddy and then back at me, and I saw an evil gleam in his eyes. "Does that there nigger boy still work over at Taylor's?"

He looked at me and grinned knowing that he had pushed a button. I was well aware of the signs posted over the bathrooms and water fountains, even the bus seats, but a change was coming, just not fast enough for Dillon and me. Because of people like Jackie Robinson, Rosa Parks, and Martin Luther King, President

Eisenhower had signed The Civil Rights Act of 1960 into law. I knew things were getting better for the black people in other parts of the country because the stench of hatred had been uncovered. I looked at Conner and burned with contempt for him. Only it wasn't because his outward color was white, it was because his inward heart was blacker than any colored person I'd ever saw.

"If you are referring to Dillon, yes, he still works there. He just graduated from high school this year and is getting ready to go to college." I smiled, exposing all my pearly whites and then said, "Did you ever go to college, Conner?"

I knew full well this redneck couldn't even spell "college," even if he was married to a school teacher. This always hurt his pride because her friends were always discussing authors, poets, and philosophers, and he had no clue what they were talking about. That's why he loved hanging out with Verdi and my father, blue collar workers who loved to drink. But Connor had walking around smarts and an ego that made up for his lack of class.

"No, Jade, I have something called common sense, and that there can't be learned in one of your school books. I just can't believe ol' Taylor has let that nigger boy work for him all this time, and man oh man, Miss Rita's no prize to look at. I don't know what he was thinking when he married her!" Conner stared at my breasts and then moved his eyes down my body. I cringed inside and told Daddy I was going to pack a few things and go on over to Miss

Rita's and I'd see him in a few days. I went into my room and hurriedly stuffed some things into my gym bag.

I could feel Conner's eyes watching me and traveling the length of me, as I opened the screen door and exhaled for the first time in what seemed like hours. I walked the row of honeysuckles and looked up at the hill Johnny and I had tried to cast down into the sea. It seemed like years had passed since that moment. How I wished I could crumple the pain up inside of me.

By the time I arrived at Taylor's store, I was a little sweaty but feeling better from the long walk. It seemed my daddy couldn't even look me in the eyes most days. I reminded him too much of a woman he never treated with love or respect. I couldn't wait until this next school year was over, and I had a driver's license and a job. I hoped that I could take Dillon's job when he went off to school, but I also dreaded him leaving. It was a thought that played in my mind constantly.

I wanted to feel safe and protected; I hadn't felt safe since the night I was defiled in my own room. I seemed to never be able to get Conner's shadow out of my bedroom. I washed my sheets and I bathed and I prayed, but the memory was seared in so deeply. The night sweats and the nightmares were so real. I couldn't seem to shake them, and sometimes in the night I would wake up frozen and unable to move my body. Other times I would scream out and then whimper. I was starting to realize now why my daddy drank. I just wanted to be held by someone that would never hurt me. I thought of Mama and how she would have been my protector and healer in all of this. I wanted to heal. I thought that if only I could enter a cocoon and wait until all the pain subsided and all the scars were covered, I could emerge a new beautiful creature, like the butterfly.

I began to notice things about men that I never had before. Every man, no matter what his age, noticed a good looking woman. Once my mama was walking into the church and I was coming along behind her. I noticed a white-haired man who had to be around seventy, he turned and eyed Mama up and down. Even our own pastor never seemed to look Mama completely in the eyes. Either he didn't want to look at those doe eyes that had been wounded, or he didn't want to look at her with lust in his heart. My mama had a presence about her. She was not even aware that she had an effect on men. She could cause a man to stutter and imagine what it would be like to kidnap her from my evil daddy and take her home with them to pamper.

It seemed to me that out of all the married couples I had met, only a small number seemed to be a good match. The rest reminded me of my biology teacher who was too smart for her own good and would often wear shoes that were mismatched, one black and one brown or one blue and one green. She would notice on occasion and look down at her feet in a most peculiar manner. Still these oddly matched couples seemed to tolerate each other and put on a good face in public. I wanted to make sure that I never ended up with the wrong spouse and that we became one in every sense of the word. I wanted a bond that could never be broken and a man who could only see me. His eyes could never look at another woman again in any way that was not pure.

It was past five, so of course Dillon was gone for the day. The door wasn't locked yet, and Mr. Taylor was there behind the counter straightening up. We spoke, and I went on upstairs to find Miss Rita. She was stirring up a skillet dish that smelled great. I realized I had worked up an appetite on my walk into town. I settled my clothes and things into the space Miss Rita fixed for me. Mr. Taylor came up and we three sat down to a quiet supper, the "slum-gullian," as Miss Rita called it was very good. I think it was a venison stew, potatoes and onions and carrots mixed in. I ate well.

Mr. Thomas retired to bed soon after our meal as Miss Rita and I washed the dishes and set the kitchen to rights. We sat at the table talking about the plan for tomorrow and what we might get done. I think Miss Rita was glad for my company, and I was certainly glad to be there with her. What little help I was to her, could never repay her for the void she was filling in my life.

As I lay down in bed, I thought about how I had stood up to Connor. It made me feel better like I wasn't weak. I was going to beat him at his own game somehow. I thought again about Miss Rita and Miss Ellen and how they were temporary shelters and how each one was trying to help fill the void my mama left behind. Whatever would I have done without the two of them?

"Dear God, it's me again, Jade. Please protect me and keep an angel close by. Also, God, I really miss my mama, can you tell her I'm fine."

Chapter 14

The next morning Miss Rita and I got busy right after breakfast. We cleaned out her kitchen pantry. First we removed the canned goods, boxes, and other food items to the table. We washed the shelves and put down new shelf paper, then cleaned all her empty jelly jars. Next, we cleaned out the fridge and gave it a good scrubbing. It made me feel good to be useful, doing the things my mama had done all her life for our family. We made grilled cheese sandwiches and tomato soup for lunch. I loved dipping the warm cheesy bread into the creamy broth. Afterward, we drank Coke-a-Colas from glass bottles that Mr. Thomas had brought from the cooler down in the store.

All morning while we worked, I could think of little else besides Dillon working downstairs. He was so close to me and yet he was like an artifact in a museum that was roped off, meant for viewing but never to touch. I had replayed our kiss over and over and couldn't seem to stop. I so wished we could go out again. I could almost feel his emotions. I wanted to run and find him and ask him to hold me until all the pain and fear had been forced from my body. I couldn't though. I had to instead act as if I had never shared a cheeseburger with him. I had to act as if the moonlight never had flickered through the open window draped with the red curtains. I had to consume myself with Miss Rita and her cleaning and her quilting expertise. If only I could go back in time and relive that moment.

"Jade, you doing okay? You seem to be off in space?"

"I know, Miss Rita. I just keep thinking about Johnny and how much I miss him, and, of course, my mama." I continued to lie. I couldn't tell her of the feelings of more than friendship I had for Dillon, nor the feelings of fear I had for Conner.

I was delighted when Miss Rita finished making Dillon's lunch – soup and sandwich same as what we had – and then gave the tray to me. I took it downstairs to him at the table in the back of the store where he took his breaks. I sat the bowl of soup down just as he slipped a tattered looking paper into my hand. I clasped the paper tightly and smiled at him, but neither of us spoke. I went back upstairs and made my way to the restroom to read my note.

Miss Jade,

I can't seem to erase the memory of our night together getting cheeseburgers. You have made it hard for me ta concentrate today on anything but your kiss. Would you like ta meet me at Jupita Lake? I will wait for you. If you don't come, I will understand.

Love, Dillon

I closed my eyes and felt wave after wave of emotion and wished to run away with him to a place where we knew no one. I held the note that looked as if it had been folded and refolded and possibly wadded up and thrown away, only to be plucked out again. I felt my heart beat faster, and then I tucked it deep inside my pants pocket and made my way back where Miss Rita had pulled out the quilting materials so we could do more cutting and sewing.

By the time five o'clock came, I was in a real frenzy inside. I couldn't even seem to get my hair to calm down. The humidity had caused it to frizz, and I was nervous about being alone with Dillon. Miss Rita peeked into the bathroom where I was fussing in front of the mirror. "Jade, what has gotten into you, girl?" Miss Rita asked. "You got a rash on your chest and you seem a bit nervous."

"Oh, I'm okay Miss Rita, just need some fresh air. I think I'm gonna go home for a while and come back later tonight if that's okay?" I grimaced as the lies flowed out of my mouth so easily.

"Of course, honey, you go do what you need to do. I'll be here. Me and Taylor aren't goin' anywhere. God knows I'd like to, but he is as much a part of this store as the furniture, and he doesn't like leavin'. It would be nice though if he'd take me out on a date sometime. But wishin' and gettin' are two different things." She chuckled to herself as if there was a secret joke in there somewhere. Then, she smiled at me and I felt my face flush.

"Okay Miss Rita, I'll see ya later."

I picked up my purse and opened the door and felt a stir of excitement inside. I had walked almost halfway to the lake, going down Mills road when I noticed a car following me. It was Conner. My feet instantly turned as heavy as concrete and my legs became numb. Each step was taken mechanically. He had taken all the air from my lungs and I hadn't even laid eyes on him yet. I could see his evil grin through the rear view mirror as he passed me ever so slowly, only to put the car in reverse and begin to back up. I stood frozen, my mind screaming, "Run, Jade, run as fast as you can." But my body stayed unmoving as I was picturing him running after me into the woods and raping me again. I wanted to melt and be absorbed into the red dust under my feet. He rolled the window down.

"Well, look who it is! I was just looking for you. Where you headed to on Mills Road, Jade?" He looked intrigued like he already knew the answer to his question.

"Just going for a stroll and waiting for Miss Rita. She and I are going to have a picnic. She's gettin' the food ready." The lies seem to spew out of my mouth more easily than ever before. I tried to imagine an iron wall around my body. I cracked my knuckles each one in unison with my fingers crossed and then proceeded to dig under my fingernails while looking at his car door. There was an uncomfortable silence and then my mouth opened to break it. "Where you headed, Conner," I said with my eyes on the gravel that was under my feet. A cow bawled in the distance, and Conner's evil eyes tried to swallow me whole.

"Just checking up on you Jade, and funny I just talked to Miss Rita and she said you were on your way home, but this sure ain't the right direction." His grin was so menacing it made me shrink in stature. "You meetin' up with that nigger boy, ain'tcha?" I cringed at his words and I could feel hives forming on my skin, but I gathered my strength again.

"Conner, I am certain it is none of your business where I am going, and if you don't mind I want to be left alone." My body was shaking inside, and though it was warm outside, I felt a chill like no other.

"Ahh. You are much too pretty to be alone, Jade. Why don't you get into the car with me and we'll go get something to eat or see a show in town." He looked at me with eyes that pled and for a moment he reminded me of a small boy who wanted to make a friend. He looked almost pitiful in some strange way.

"Sorry, Conner, but I can't do that. I feel sure Miss Frieda would not approve if she knew you were taking me to dinner. You are married and you are much too old for me, and, as I said, I don't feel like company." I waited to see if this response would sink in. I stared out at the field on my right and the cattle whose tails were busy brushing off flies. I dug my shoe into the gravel and held my breath.

"I won't hurt you, Jade, and I'm sorry for what happened. I never meant for that to happen. You believe me, don't you?" he pleaded with those blue eyes that had been so menacing moments before. "I feel sick inside, truly I do, about that night, but it's also a beautiful memory I treasure. If I hadn't been drinking and you weren't so breathtakingly gorgeous, well things would have never transpired. I love you, Jade, you know that. Now I want to make it up to you and tell you how sorry I am." His eyes searched me to see what I thought about what he had said. "Will you forgive me, Jade?"

I looked at him, shivered again and then numbly without any truth I mouthed a soft "yes." I didn't think I could ever forgive him. I knew I needed to because a bitter root had grown inside of me and it seemed to be taking over. Whether I ever learned how to forgive him, one thing I knew for sure was I could never forget. No,

I could never forget his skin and his fingertips and his breath stained with alcohol, nor his tongue that was like a snake that slithered and invaded every part of me that was sacred! I could never forget how like a snake he had wooed me with gifts, admiration and praise. How he had taken the death of my mama and the abuse of my daddy and used it to invade my spirit and invade my body and my soul with his lust and his evil pleasures. I might learn how to remove the bitter root I was choking on, but I would never forget.

He took that which wasn't his to have and that could never be given back to me. I knew he had stolen something sacred and holy that was mine to give, but not his to take! He didn't even seem to really see that what he did was not only a SIN, it was a CRIME. I wished I was brave enough to tell the police what he did.

"I gotta go Conner." I said and I took off running through the wooded path along the shoulder. I didn't stop or look back until I heard his car engine slowly grow silent. I felt my heart beating in my chest, my heart that had become so swollen and so hard. Each muscle rapidly pounded the memory of Conner into the earth with a gait of fury. I ran so fast and so hard that I felt the ground beneath me shake like a herd of wild horses. My heart was so full of fear, that even all the water in the river wasn't enough to wash it all away. Would anything good ever come to me? "It never has!" I mouthed inside my spirit.

I was panting hard by the time I arrived at the lake and spotted Dillon walking among the trees. I was beyond worrying about what he thought about me or my behavior. When I ran to him and grabbed him and whispered through heavy breaths, "Please hold me." I closed my eyes, felt his strong arms embrace me and I tried to let all my fear drain into those arms. I was beside myself.

"Jade. What's wrong, what happened?"

I couldn't catch my breath, let alone speak. Dillon held me and he placed one hand on my head, cupping it as a mother would cup her infant. I tried to melt into him as my heart slowly quieted to a more normal rhythm. I wanted to tell him the nightmare that haunted me and to confide in him, but I just couldn't tell anyone. What would he think of me if he knew the truth? Would he still want to meet me? Would he still want to kiss the lips that another had pressed so hard they were bruised? Would he find me soiled and damaged? Could I trust him? Could any man be trusted? I wasn't sure.

"I don't know if I can tell you, I want to. God knows I need to tell someone." I chewed the skin around my index finger and then chewed my bottom lip. "I'm so scared. I have never been this scared in my life. I have been carrying a secret around, and it's getting so heavy I can hardly hold it. It seems to grow heavier each day and I don't know how to get out of the mess I am in."

He looked at me and his eyes studied me for a moment before he spoke. "Jade, I am your friend, you can confide in me. Who am I gonna tell? We both know the white man is not gonna listen to me no how. We shared a kiss the other night, but I wasn't expectin' that to happen, and I don't want nuthin' comin' between our friendship. I am riskin' a lot just to see you, but it seems like there is a power beyond my control that just draw me to you. Now I want to help you. Your secret is safe with me. Look at me." That reminded me of my daddy when he would tell my mama to look at him, only Dillon's eyes were not like a wolf and they held truth that seemed purer than any eyes I'd ever seen. "I care 'bout you!"

I began to sob and bow my head with disgrace as I began to reveal my nightmare. I described the whole scenario leading up to the night he entered my room and the haunting nightmares that racked my sleep. I cried with such intensity that snot ran down my lips and my tears soaked my shirt. Dillon took out a handkerchief and held it out for me to blow my nose. He wiped my wet cheeks and lifted my chin up with his fingers so that my eyes were on his. Only I was scared to look into them for I knew that eyes don't lie.

"I am so sorry that you were treated with such disrespect and so vile by the hands of a man you trusted as a frien'. I'm here for you, Jade, and I don't think no different of ya because of this. Do you understands me?"

I nodded, still not wanting to look directly into his eyes. "Dillon, I'm worried about one thing and it's really scaring me bad." I twisted my mouth sideways and chewed a hunk of skin on the inside of my mouth until I tasted a faint hint of blood. "What if he planted a seed inside me and I am pregnant? What will I do? O God, what will I do?" The tears began again.

Dillon stared far off for a minute or so. Then, he spoke, "Jade, you tellin' me this has made me to know for the first time in my life what my own Mama went through. I have known for a long time that I may have been born of a white man raping my mama. A colored woman don't get to say a white man raped them; they jus' go on and keep quiet. I know from what you have said that my mama must have thought about what happened to her every time she laid eyes on her growing belly and every time she felt a kick."

I could see Dillon thinking and processing. Finally, he said, "Jade, it don't have to be that way with you. You can go to the police, his wife, and even your daddy and make this thing known. You know, Jade, I was once inside my mama because of rape, but she loved me and raised me anyways. She could have left me on a do' step at a church or put me out for adoption if anyone would be kind enough to raise a mixed baby. But she made it through, and I am here because of an evil act, but I enjoy life because my mama loved me. She has become a hero to me because of her strength.

You will get through this. But who knows, you might not be pregnant."

I didn't want to hear the word "pregnant." It felt like a death sentence, and I was not prepared for what it could do to me. I had been analyzing all the possibilities, all the places I could run off to, and what people would whisper about me. I just was exhausted from worrying about it. "I want you to do something for me, Dillon, will you?"

"Of course, Jade, I will do anything I can."

"I want you to hold me, just hold me until I heal." Dillon reached for my hand and then pulled me to him.

We laid down on the soft grass, and I buried my face into his chest and felt my breath become steady through the many tears I had cried. Then I felt his lips on mine and I was eager for him to replace all the fear and all the hurt. I ached for him to replace all the memories of my first experience. I wanted to be a virgin again and him to be my first, my husband.

I drifted off into my fantasy land as he kissed me softly and I responded. I felt his body against mine and his hands began to caress the secret places that were now ready to be touched with something filled with love, not lust and filth. I just wanted to be so close to him that we were one in spirit. I just wanted to replace every print of Conner's with Dillon's skin and his flesh and his lips that were inviting me to a new place of refuge. I cried out to God inside my spirit, "Forgive me, Father, for I am so scared and I just want to be protected and loved." I wondered if He would ever hear a prayer from my mouth again. I wondered if I had reached a place so dark and so filled with sin He might never take me back. I wondered if my mama could look down from heaven and see how I had forsaken His grace and given myself away. My life was nothing but broken pieces of shattered glass. I felt Dillon's body shudder with a blast of power and thought that he had planted seeds in me that were more powerful than Conner's. If Conner had any seed forming inside of me, Dillon's would overwhelm it.

Then, I was catapulted back into reality when Dillon turned away from me and I could feel that stickiness. It reminded me of another time when it made me heave over the commode. I felt a conviction that this sin might continue if something didn't change, if God didn't help me. I wondered if anyone had seen us. I knew Dillon would be hanged from the highest tree if anybody found out. If I was pregnant by Dillon, I would never be looked on the same and would endure the stares that spoke out silent judgments. I knew it would mean the end of Johnny speaking to me, the end of Daddy, and even Miss Ellen and Miss Rita Taylor. Yes, it would mean the end of a lot of things.

We walked down to a secluded area of the lake. The sun had set and darkness was falling. We jumped in the river in our under clothes and held each other in the peaceful night air. I felt like a million stars were filling me with a new light of love I had never dreamed of.

Dillon rubbed his hand on my cheek and tucked a strand of hair behind my ear then whispered, "I love you, Jade," in a soft tremble. I was swept up into his caramel eyes that melted my soul.

Chapter 15

My daddy was the first to mention it. He just kind of looked at me oddly one day and said, “Jade, if I didn’t know better I’d swear you were pregnant.” I felt my stomach do a flip-flop and the realization that a bad situation was only going to get worse.

“Right, Daddy and my name is Mary; it’s an immaculate conception.” I smiled a crooked smile while rolling my eyes and trying to control my feelings of panic and alarm. My head was racing and I couldn’t remember when I had my last menstrual cycle. Why hadn’t I been keeping up with this? I had that feeling that my life was never going to be the same, and I was no longer going to be a child. I was going to be a woman, and one with many difficulties ahead no matter who had fathered the baby.

"Oh, come on Jade," Daddy said. "You just look haggard and pale, that's all." Verdi walked in the kitchen popping her chewing gum, smiling at my daddy with a look that made my breakfast eggs come back up in my throat. I was feeling a little queasy in the mornings lately, but after the day got going, I got hungry and just about ate everything in sight.

"You've gained a little weight too, Jade." Verdi said as she smacked her gum and then gave me an evil smile. Daddy eyed me real slow like and made a face that looked kind of cross.

"Well, your mama was kinda plump when we started dating, come to think of it. Ha! Yeah, she was a tad on the plump side then, of course, she didn't stay that way." Verdi let out a long sigh as if to say "don't discuss her, you've got me now."

The whole conversation was making me feel more ill. I picked up my plate and walked to the trash can and raked the rest of my eggs and toast into the can. I placed my plate in the sink and poured a glass of milk. I walked to my bedroom and shut the door and placed my hands over my belly. I rubbed over the small protrusion I had been trying to ignore.

I looked down and pondered aloud, "Who are you, little baby? Are you Dillon's or Conner's?" I knew there was only a couple weeks difference in the dates when conception might have occurred. If only I knew the answer to that question.

Just the name Conner brought a chill and an image of a baby that looked just like him. A little shrunken man in a diaper with blue eyes that seared into you, with a frayed cigar hanging out of its mouth where a bottle should be. I then pictured the infant rising up out of his crib yelling, "Hell-fire!" and laughing uncontrollably. I thought Conner had said "Hell-fire" so often, he was just preparing for his future home.

Then I began to replace those thoughts with the alternative... what if this child is Dillon's? I rubbed my stomach with an emotion I could not describe. I pictured a creamy coffee colored baby with hair that had the texture of silk. I pictured Dillon looking down at our beautiful baby and me with such pride and joy in his heart. But I knew that was nothing but a death sentence for everyone involved. The only solution seemed to be an underground doctor with a rusty scalpel. I shuddered at the thought of that. I wondered if maybe I should just leave the state and go up north and have my baby and raise it alone. If only I had a job so I could support my baby and live away from my family and Braxton.

I reached under the bed and counted the roll of money Mama had given me. It amounted to one hundred and thirty-three dollars and sixty-two cents. I knew that was a lot of money, but I didn't know how long it would last. I remembered paying some of the bills for Daddy before Verdi had moved in. I figured a hotel room would be much cheaper. I wasn't really sure where to go or what to do. I didn't have a car or a license to drive. I had no friends really, save Miss Ellen and Miss Rita. They were the only true mother figures in my life, but I was positive neither of them would understand.

I pondered on whether to tell Dillon or Connor. I hadn't seen either one of them since the evening Dillon and I were at the lake. If I told him, it would risk his not going off to college and not finishing his degree that was so important to him. If I told Connor, it would just break up his marriage and cause him to be a part of my life forever. That repulsed me just picturing it. I wasn't about to let any man control me like my daddy controlled my mama.

Oh, how did I end up in this mess? I held my pillow over my abdomen and cried silent tears. I thought of my brother, Johnny, and how he had managed to escape Braxton and this farmhouse we had called "home." How would I ever be able to do that, too? I put the money back in the shoe box and bowed my head.

"Oh, Lord Jesus, the God my mama prayed to, how could this have happened to me?" I looked up at the cracked ceiling with the brown stain from a roof leak years ago. I clenched my teeth and said it again even louder as if He didn't hear me the first time. "HOW COULD YOU LET THIS HAPPEN TO ME? My mama served you and look at what her life was like. My daddy beat her and verbally abused her and treated her like she was nothing. Now you repay her by letting her daughter get raped? I hate you God! I hate you!" I fell over on the pillow and sobbed over and over, "I hate you, I hate you, I hate you, God," until it was a whimpering moan and I fell asleep from pure exhaustion.

The next morning, I got myself dressed, ate a bite and headed out to Taylor's Store. The walk in the morning air was refreshing. I wanted to see Dillon but had no intention of telling him about the baby.

He was holding his letter of acceptance into Lemoyne College in Memphis, Tennessee. He was smiling so wide I could just about count all his teeth. "I'm going to college, Jade!"

He ran towards me as I entered the store, seemingly unaware that people were watching him as he went to hug me. He was so excited that his feet were almost dancing down the aisle. I felt their stares, and yet I was so filled with a mixture of joy, heartache, and a giant fear that I would be left alone with this seed that had begun to sprout inside me.

"Oh Dillon, I couldn't be happier for you. That's wonderful news. When will you be leaving?" I waited, ready to calculate just how much time I had left with him, and if I would be able to keep my secret tucked safely away and wondered if I was even strong enough to do so.

"Semester start on September 8th, but I has to be there for orientation and gettin' moved into my dorm. I gots about a month, and I can hardly wait!" He smiled at me with those eyes that made me melt. I tried to figure in my head the distance from Mississippi to Tennessee, but I failed miserably.

"How far away is that Dillon?" I said, looking down and wondering if I would ever see him again.

"It's uhh, ovah three hundred miles. I never bins that far away from home in my whole life." He said, with eyes that held such excitement and hope, but also seemed to hold some fear. I admired his courage. I thought how I could use some myself. "I don't know how I'll ever make my way around without getting lost. Memphis is a big city and Braxton ain't even on the map."

He laughed, but I could tell it was nervous laughter. Still I was very happy for him. I knew he wanted to be a teacher, and I knew that he would change the lives of many students with just his heart. Dillion was smart enough to get a good education, too. This would open doors for him in the coming years, as the call for equality was going out over the whole United States of America.

Chapter 16

I didn't see much of Dillon over the next few weeks. He quit his job at Taylor's Store in order to get things ready for school. He was taking shopping trips to Cleveport and spending more time with his mama and other family members.

I began to settle into a routine, spending a big part of the day at Taylor's store and still avoiding Connor. Once in a while Dillon would come by and visit with the Taylors and me, but we were never alone.

Once he left for college, I turned my thoughts to how to escape my circumstances; but I fully understood that wherever I went, the circumstances would go with me. I felt like crying all the time, sometimes for no reason. It seemed to go along with the pregnancy. I was unable to control the tears and had to go to the ladies room so I could get a grip. One day was particularly difficult, so I told Miss

Rita I didn't feel well, and she had Mr. Thomas take me home in his pickup. For some reason though I didn't like being alone with any man, no matter how old he was or how long I had known him. I thanked him for the ride and prayed Conner was far away. It was nice and quiet there with Verdi and my daddy both at work, so I made a peanut butter sandwich and poured a big tall glass of milk. I walked into my bedroom and pulled the shoebox out from under my bed. I stared at the contents again like I had so many times, trying to make sense out of something, anything. The peanut butter was making me feel better, but I was also getting nervous about the pouch that was growing more each day. I finished taking the last bite and guzzled half the cold milk before sitting up on the bed and wiping my mouth with my hand. "Mama, I miss you." I looked up at the ceiling as if she could hear me. I took her Bible from the box and bowed my head.

"Lord Jesus, I want you to tell me what to do because I am lost. I am very sorry I said I hated you. I really don't hate you. Please, please forgive me." I hated the mistakes I made and the words I spoke. It seemed like I kept doing wrong and not right. Perhaps there was more of my daddy in me than I thought?

I closed my eyes and held my mama's worn out Bible, then reached my fingers along the edge and flipped it open somewhere around the middle. My eyes landed on this verse Luke 1:24-25: *"And after those days his wife Elisabeth conceived, and hid herself five months, saying, thus hath the Lord dealt with me in the days wherein he looked on me, to take away my reproach among men."*

I wasn't sure what that meant, but I was excited that it was about a pregnant woman who went into hiding. I thought God was trying to tell me to go hide, but I needed to finish school. I knew I couldn't finish school with my belly showing and the whole town gossiping. What could I do? I thought about telling Uncle Ed and Julie that I was raped. Maybe they would let me stay with them and finish school up there? But they would want to know who had done such a horrific thing. If I said it was Conner and the baby was born looking colored, it would make me look like a liar. Nobody would believe the truth about Connor ever. I also knew I would be pushed to put the baby up for adoption, and I wasn't sure that was what I wanted to do. I didn't know if I could part with my own baby. I knew if I looked in its eyes after carrying it for nine months, I would be hopelessly in love with it. I read the scripture again only this time more slowly.

"To take away my reproach among men." I couldn't figure out how God was going to take away my reproach when everyone would be disgusted with me if they knew I was pregnant at seventeen years old. Oh, how would I ever survive all this? How would I even get medical care? I wished so badly that Mama was still here, but then, of course, I would have never gotten into this predicament if she was still alive. If only I knew where to turn.

I read the first part of the verse again, about hiding for five months and wondered how many months along I was. If I was going to live to see this baby, I knew I would have to leave, but where could I go? I thought about taking a bus to Memphis and not telling Dillon, just going there and trying to get a job. I knew they had more jobs for women in the country music industry and that Elvis himself lived there. I could wait tables or perhaps get a job singing backup vocals until my due date got closer and before my belly swelled like a watermelon. I didn't have a clue what to do. I only knew I had to decide quickly.

I would take the money I had and I would go away. I needed to tie up a few ends here, but I knew the only way for me to survive was to get out of Braxton and away from Daddy. Conner had seemed distracted lately and getting as far away from him as I could, was the right thing for me. Why did life have to be so hard?

I closed the Bible again and thought I'd try one more time to open it and find direction. This time, I found a verse from John 15:7: *"If you abide in me and my words abide in you, ye shall ask what you will and it shall be done unto you."* I thought that verse must mean something different because I was sure my mama had enough Bible "words" in her to ask for anything, and she was dead. Then I thought maybe she asked to die? I shut the book, placing it back into the box. I laid back on my bed and was awakened as Verdi came in the front door. She turned the stereo on, blasting music loudly throughout the house. "So much for peace and quiet," I thought to myself. Then I turned my thoughts to the two Scriptures I had read. I felt some uncertainty and a feeling of disbelief, but I really wanted to believe like Mama did. I opened my closet and started looking through my clothes and trying to decide which ones would stretch enough to cover my stomach and how long I had until I wouldn't be able to fit into anything.

Daddy came home and announced he'd been given a raise and that he was taking Verdi out on the town to celebrate. "Guess you're on your own for dinner, Jade." Verdi smiled, showing her two front teeth smeared with the hot pink lipstick.

"That's okay I'm not very hungry anyways." I lied, knowing as soon as they left I would raid the cabinets and over stuff myself with more PB&J's, Lays potato chips, and pickle slices. I was always craving something and peanut butter had become one of my favorites. It seemed as soon as I would eat my stomach would protrude for a few hours, only now it was starting to stay extended and looking more round.

As soon as they left, I sat at the kitchen table and tried to devise more of a plan. I needed a clever scheme, one that wouldn't backfire. I figured the first thing I needed to do was pack, so that when the time was right, I could get out of here in a hurry.

I dragged a large canvas suitcase out from under Daddy's bed and opened it on my bed. I began filling it with clothes, shoes, sweaters, a winter coat, makeup, toiletries, and my journal. I packed all my letters from Johnny and the photographs I had of him and Mama. I added a few cherished items. One was a little china angel that Miss Ellen had given me. The little figurine had blonde hair, and she was kneeling with her hands folded, and eyes closed in prayer. Her white wings spread out behind her. Miss Ellen said she found her in an antiques store in Cleveport and immediately thought of me. She showed me the maker's name on the bottom and "Made in W. Germany." The original price tag was on it, too, $18.50, but Miss Ellen said she got a very good deal on it. Then she told me this angel was perfect without any flaw or chips or cracks. She said I should think of it as the symbol of my real guardian angel that God had given me when I was born. I wrapped the little figure in a clean washcloth and found a safe place for her inside one of my shoes.

The last item to place inside the trunk was my Mama's shoe box. I nestled it in and closed the lid. Then I went to the kitchen and got saltine crackers, peanut butter, and jelly beans, so I would have something to eat on the bus. I put all the food into my big tote bag purse, so I could get to it easily. Now, I had to get to the bus terminal in Cleveport without anyone noticing.

I got in bed then, feeling what Mama used to say, "Bone tired." I was so tired, in fact, that I had never known that someone could be this tired. I was seventeen years old and walked like a fat old lady. When I laughed there was no mirth. If I smiled it was a plastic pumpkin face going through the motions. Even my tears were tired tears that didn't have the strength to glide down my cheeks.

I sighed deeply, punched my feather pillow, making a mental note to take it with me when I left. It was one of the few "comforts of home" that I could say I ever had. I had the quilt Mama gave me, probably from Miss Rita at the store. It was a birthday present when I was about twelve years old. I decided I would make it fit into the big canvas suitcase, too. I smoothed the quilt with my hands and could see the patch work in the moonlight coming through my window. I closed my eyes.

"Dear God, I need help! Can you please hide me away for five months? Sincerely, Jade"

Chapter 17

The sun was coming up and I could hear Daddy and Verdi making a racket getting ready for work. The bathroom door kept opening and closing. I could hear Mr. Cotton's roosters crowing proudly. Daddy and Verdi moved on into the kitchen and started breakfast. I stayed right where I was. I was thinking about where I was going to hide.

I felt the butterflies in my stomach and with each flutter a little fear shot through my body. I heard Daddy's car start when he left. Then when I knew Verdi was gone too, I got up. I fixed myself a breakfast of eggs and toast with jam. I showered quickly, dressed and assessed what I had packed again. I folded my quilt from Mama and got it into the canvas bag. I put an extra pillow case over my pillow so I would have a spare. I would carry it in case I got sleepy on the ride to Kansas.

I decided to call a taxi to take me to the bus station in Cleveport so nobody would know where I went. But after counting and recounting my money, I decided to ask Miss Ellen to take me. I would simply tell her I was going to visit Uncle Ed and Johnny. She and Mr. Earl were not neighborly with my dad, and I knew I wouldn't have to ask her to keep my whereabouts a secret. She had seen him fly off the handle more than once. I was almost certain this plan would work. Plus, she had said after Mama died that she was here if I needed anything, and boy did I ever need help now. Only God knew how much help I was going to need.

I waited until nine a.m. and dialed Miss Ellen's number holding my breath and chewing the skin around my thumbnail. "Hello, Miss Ellen, it's me, Jade."

"Well, hello dear, how are you doing? I've been missing you for the past few weeks."

"I'm doing rather well, Miss Ellen. I've been learning to quilt with Miss Rita Taylor down at the store. But today, I'm excited that I'm going to see my brother Johnny in Kansas before school starts. I can hardly wait, you know it's been so long since Mama passed, and I'm so looking forward to catching up with him. You know he's working in a factory now with my uncle Ed and they say Kansas is just gorgeous in the fall…" I continued to talk excessively until Miss Ellen interrupted.

"My, you are excited! Well, honey, that's wonderful, I am so pleased. You must drop by before you leave; I insist. I'll fix us a lunch and we can catch up on your plans for school and what all is going on with you and your daddy."

"Oh no, Miss Ellen I really don't have time, but maybe when I get back. I'm leaving today for Kansas, and I was wondering if you could take me to the bus terminal in Cleveport. Daddy and Verdi have to work all day, and I don't want to be a bother really, it's just I don't know how I'm going to get there." And then, I began to cry. The hormones were kicking in, and I was a useless mess.

"Oh, my dear, please don't cry. You know I will take you. Why, I will take you anywhere you'd like to go, Jade. Now just take a deep breath and I'll pick you up as soon as I can get ready. Now, what time will your bus leave for Kansas?"

This threw me off, of course. I had never ridden a bus except the school bus. Heavens, I hadn't a clue as to even how it all worked and so I did what I had been doing a lot of lately, I lied.

"My bus will be departing for Kansas at eleven o'clock, Miss Ellen." I was so nervous I started to hiccup. I chewed a bit of flesh off the side of my index finger and then bit the inside of my lip for good measure.

"Well now, it won't take me but a minute or two to get ready. You get your things together and I'll be there shortly, and Jade, please don't cry, you're much too young and much too pretty."

"Thank you, Miss Ellen." I said. I was feeling better already. The first step of my plan, getting to the bus station, was working. I began doing as she said, inhaling and then exhaling. The hiccupping stopped. I thought it was odd that something as simple as remembering to breathe could calm a person's nerves.

I placed the phone in its cradle, pulled a sweater over my head, and grabbed my tote purse and shoved the roll of bills wrapped in rubber bands into the side pocket. I paused, thinking about Dillon, his eyes and smile that made me feel alive, more alive than I had ever felt. But of course, I was leaving everything and that included him. I walked through the only home I had ever known, where I had been raised and I began to study its contents. The black velvet matador pictures seemed foreign, and countless bottles of nail polish were lying about. A picture of Daddy and Verdi sat on the side table, replacing the one of Mama and him from the fair. This really was not my home anymore. This was Verdi's home, filled with Verdi's things. I walked to Johnny's old bedroom and looked at the racks of clothes, mostly mini-skirts and hot pink blouses. It reeked of Verdi's perfume and gave me a wave of nausea. I knew that room would never be a baby room and this house would never be a home for me again. I heard a horn beep and hurried to get my canvas bag out the door.

Miss Ellen had arrived as she promised, her long blue Buick eased up the drive and she helped me put my suitcase in the trunk. Her gray hair was beautiful as ever and in the daylight I noticed a fleck of blue in her eyes.

She smiled at me. "You sure have grown since I saw you last." I wasn't sure if she meant my belly which I was conscious of now, or just me in general. “You look just as lovely as ever. You’re becoming a fine young woman. Your mama was a very attractive lady, as well. I bet you miss her so much. She would be so proud of you, Jade.” She smiled at me and rolled the window down a crack to shoo a fly.

“So you’re off to see Johnny? I love that boy. Well, he isn’t a boy now; no, and he’s probably grown into a handsome young man at this point. But Johnny sure did give me the chuckles a time or two. He even caused me to laugh so hard once I got a belly ache.” She rolled the window up and continued to talk. Her grey eyes were sparkling and a tuft of hair had caught loose of her bun and was dangling along her cheekbone. I realized how I had come to love her and felt like she loved me, too.

“Johnny got ahold of one of our goats one morning and he couldn’t have been more than six or seven years old. Well Jade, it was the funniest thing I ever saw. He tied a rope around that goat and took it for a walk like it was a dog. He even named it. He had just learned how to count to a hundred and he never started at one, always started at zero. Anyways he named that darn goat Zero and the name just stuck. He was Zero his whole life. Johnny even brought him scraps from dinner. He'd stick corn muffins and anything he could get a hold of in his pockets to feed Zero with."

She turned towards me and chuckled heartily. I was laughing too. The more she talked about Johnny the more I missed him. I wished I could get a ticket to Kansas and just visit him and Julie and Uncle Ed, but I wasn't sure what would happen next. My belly would continue to grow and there would be no way to hide it. Life sure had grown complicated in a hurry for me.

"Jade, what's your uncle Ed like?"

"Oh, he's a big ole' bear type. He's always smiling and happy. Julie's a little peculiar, but she sings like an angel and plays guitar, too. She even writes her own music."

"You don't say? I'll make sure I tell your daddy when I see him that you got off to the bus station just fine. Don't you worry, Jade."

I almost panicked, "Oh no, no, Miss Ellen that won't be necessary. I already told him I had a ride. See if you couldn't take me, Miss Rita down at Taylor's store could take me. I just, well, I just wanted to see you. I hadn't had a chance to thank you for all you did for me after Mama passed away."

The lies seemed to flow like a river, a river I couldn't dam up. I had felt bad, even a little convicted at first, but it seemed the more lies I told, the easier it became to tell them. We pulled into the bus station parking lot and I felt sick inside with fright.

"Let me help you now and make sure you get on the right bus. You know you are going to have to get off and change busses before you reach your destination? Kansas is quite a ways from here."

I tried to soak in what was happening. I was leaving Braxton, and I was moving somewhere else to live but where I did not know. "I can do it, Miss Ellen. I'll be fine, you don't have to worry or wait around."

"My goodness, child, I am not leaving this bus terminal until you are on the right bus, and I have talked with the driver. I certainly won't leave until you are on your way, and I can see you off properly."

I couldn't figure out how I was ever going to get out of this mess I was in. I couldn't seem to talk her out of staying. I had even brought up Rosa Parks and how if she was okay after refusing to give up her seat, I was sure I would be just fine. I knew in my heart somehow, some way I would be just fine, yes, just fine and dandy.

Miss Ellen walked up to the ticket counter and ordered my ticket from the man in the blue cap. Then she opened her change purse and paid for it. I was so shocked and so relieved, I didn't know what to do. It was all I could do to keep from crying.

"Thank you, Miss Ellen, you didn't have to do that for me. Thank you. It is so sweet of you."

I looked into her gray eyes and detected again the hint of blue. I thought about my childhood years where there was quite a lot more love and peace than I realized at the time. Here was this little woman with her own children flown away a long time ago, but more than willing to be a shelter in the storm for Johnny and me. I thought about my guardian angel she had told me about. Then I decided in my heart, "She *is* my angel."

"Now, don't you go on about it, Jade, this is my way of helping you like your Mama would have wanted me to do. I am waitin' right here and makin' sure you get on that bus and that the driver looks out for you."

I began to wonder if Miss Ellen had surmised a lot more than I had hoped she would. I thought, "She knows." And then, I thought of Miss Rita. She knew, too. They were there for me as much as they could be, while leaving me with what little dignity I had left. I had branded that whole town of people as hateful bigots and gossips, but here were at least two people that were not.

I boarded the bus and found a seat by the window. As I smiled bravely and waved to Miss Ellen, my heart sank. I felt myself parting from one of the few people who had ever cared about me. She was waving frantically as I pressed my hand against the glass. A lump had formed in my throat. The bus lumbered slowly onto the highway, taking me away from the people I had known my whole life and the place where I was born.

I glanced around sizing up my fellow passengers. The bus driver had almost no hair and a long mustache and he had sideburns that came clear down his face. His eyes were friendly enough, but they were constantly moving, scanning the passengers, and our surroundings. I glanced around at the other passengers. There was a painfully thin pale girl, who looked like a model and a soldier wearing a dark green uniform. There was an older lady with a bag of knitting needles and multi-colored yarn. The older lady got on the bus after I did and sat down beside me while I was turned to wave to Miss Ellen. There were some empty seats, but she came right to the seat by me. I wondered why. I turned around after the bus drove away. Her face was kind and I was glad for the company. She had the scent of bath powder that women of her age seemed to like.

My seatmate spoke to me when I turned and we exchanged hellos. I smiled what I thought was probably an anemic effort at best. The events of the morning had drained my already low energy reserves. I leaned my head back against the seat and wondered if any napping and sleeping would be possible on this long trip.

I grabbed the bag of jelly beans and began to eat them nervously. I took out a letter from Johnny and studied the address: *348 Winsor Avenue, Topeka, Kansas.* I hadn't a clue how to find such a place or even how to read a map. I thought I'd call Uncle Ed's number from the bus terminal when I arrived in Topeka and hope for the best.

"Dear God, It's me, Jade. I really need you to help me. Everything's bigger outside of Braxton and I feel very small."

Chapter 18

"Better find something to do young lady or you'll be bored to pieces! These bus rides take the longest time."

My seatmate sighed and grabbed her needles and started knitting so fast I couldn't even keep up with her fingers. "You know how to knit?" She asked it as if I should, but I had only just learned the basics of sewing from Miss Rita.

"No, I-I- haven't ever had anyone teach me."

"Well, you're going to need to learn so you can make clothes and blankets for that baby!" I gasped wondering how she could know such a thing. I mean it was a secret and I wasn't even showing yet or was I? I looked down at my small protruding pouch and back at her fingers that seemed to fly across themselves.

"How did you…I mean who told you I was pregnant?"

"Well, it doesn't take much to see that. I mean look at you, you're young and scared and on a bus all alone and you keep rubbing your belly. Anyways, I'm what we call a 'seer.' I know certain things at times, secret things."

"You do?" I said sitting up with eyes wide with wonder, hoping to know what my future held.

"Yes, dear, and don't you go hunting for palm readers or fortune tellers 'cause them kind could put a curse on you and your baby. You see," …and then she stopped talking and knitting and looked at me with widened eyes.

"You are named after a birthstone." She gazed upward. "Yes, Lord Jesus, thank you Holy Spirit!" Her eyes looked as if she were speaking to a real, but unseen person. Her face appeared so peaceful as if she was listening intently.

"Go on!" I said. "What else do you know? My name is after a stone. It's Jade, you were right! Now, what else, what else!?"

"Calm down, honey, God don't answer in restlessness, no, no, child. God comes in the still soft voice. I stopped talking and bowed my head, remembering how I had told God how much I hated him.

"But, He's mad at me." I began to cry remembering how I'd screamed at him. I was suddenly terrified of the God my mama had worshiped endlessly. The words I had screamed just days before echoed in my head now. "I HATE YOU! I hate you, God!" I felt so ashamed.

I suddenly missed my mama terribly and the tears were trying to flow. I kept wiping them quickly and sniffling. Then, my fellow traveler reached into her bag and gave me some tissues. I calmed myself and waited as she seemed to be thinking. All the sudden this stranger was placing her hands on my belly and praying in some language I'd never heard before. Her eyes were closed and she looked serene and peaceful. My belly suddenly felt a warmth flowing through it, and I felt a peace I'd never known.

"Jade, this child has a gifting in music and the Lord is going to use his voice to set the captives free. Oh my, you have been wounded badly by someone! The Lord is going to heal you of that hurt. He says He is peeling you like an onion, layer by layer until the hurt is gone and you are free. He says, don't worry, He will protect you and open a door for you. But you must wait on His voice."

"It's a boy?" I asked, holding onto every word she had spoken. Set the captives free? What did it all mean? I couldn't seem to grasp what all her words meant, but I was intrigued by it all and listening intently.

"Yes, Jade, a fine baby boy gifted in music! Praise the Lord Adonai!" She said it with such strength and confidence, and such joy. She stretched out the same hand she had laid on my abdomen just minutes before, silently inviting me to clasp it.

"My name is Renée, by the way." Her voice had that southern drawl that made the word "way" linger on and on. "It means 'born again,' you know."

"Thank you, thank you." I thought Renée was a very appropriate name for her, such a vibrant and lively person. I wished I had a tape recorder to play back the words she had spoken over me and my unborn baby, but I knew somehow they were engraved in my heart. "I've been so worried and so scared about my situation. My mama died of cancer last year and my daddy is a real bad alcoholic." I stopped talking and wondered why I felt comfortable around this perfect stranger, and why I was telling her my whole life story. "My daddy just never could stop drinking. He tried over and over again, but he just never could. Then Mama died." I lowered my head remembering the last night I had held her hand and listened to what she wanted for my life. Before I knew it I was opening my mouth and spewing out all the evil that had transpired.

"One of my daddy's drunken friends…" I couldn't say his name. I didn't want to relive the nightmare, but something was telling me to let it all out. Something about Miss Renée and her sweet spirit made me feel I could let it all out. I studied her peaceful blue eyes and soft grey-blonde hair that was draped down her back and felt tranquility. She wore a long turquoise dress with a copper belt and she had the rosiest cheeks I had ever seen. They were more like two pink apples than cheekbones. Her glasses were held by a strand of beads and perched on the tip of her nose.

"Go on, dear," She nodded and repeated the words adding "you can tell me anything, and I will make sure it stays right here between the good Lord and us."

"Well, my mama was a mighty good Christian woman and she raised us in church. My daddy beat her real bad sometimes. He just -- the drinking you know, and after my mama died, he met someone else and all they do is party. Her name is Verdi and you should see her! She's a real live hoochie-mama!" Miss Renée and I both laughed in spite of the serious conversation we were having. "Well anyways, one night Daddy had his friends over to play cards, and one of his friends that I trusted, who is married, came into my room and raped me." I said the word "rape" in a hushed tone and I didn't go into any details. I just blurted it all out in one big long breath. Then I looked up at her again with my tears flowing.

"And this baby is a product?" I could see the concern and sympathy in her eyes.

"I don't know, Miss Renée." I realized how horrible that sounded now that I'd said it and began to sob rather loudly. The bus driver kept looking back at me in the rearview mirror and other passengers were staring boldly. Miss Renée eyed the bus driver with a look that seemed to say "Mind your own businesses." She stared the other passengers down too and cleared her throat as if to say "get back to looking out your windows." She leaned over and took me in her arms. Then resting my head atop her large bosom, she began to sing ever so softly:

"Why should I feel discouraged,

why should the shadows come,

Why should my heart be lonely,

and long for heaven and home,

When Jesus is my portion... My constant friend is He:

His eye is on the sparrow, and I know He watches me;

His eye is on the sparrow, and I know He watches me

I sing because I'm happy,

I sing because I'm free,

For His eye is on the sparrow,

And I know He watches me."

I spoke abruptly after the serene song had ended. "I'm not a whore. Really, I'm not, Miss Renée."

"I know you're not, dear, now take this handkerchief." She handed me a pale blue cloth. I wiped my eyes and blew my nose. She said, "I want you to keep this little hanky as a memento of our meeting on this bus and the way the Lord is speaking to your situation and your future through me."

"I want to explain this to you, Miss Renée. I only had sex with the person I loved to get the evil man's dirty finger prints off of me. I thought that if I was pregnant by the man who raped me, maybe the one I loved could replace his seed. I know it sounds stupid, but I was so scared and that horrible man was stalking me. I am in so much trouble. Miss Renée, you can't even begin to know how much!"

"It's okay, Jade, now take a deep breath and let it all out slowly. Where are you planning on going? Do you have a family you are going to stay with?"

"I have an older brother who left home when Mama died. He's been living with our uncle and aunt out in Topeka."

"Well, I'm headed to Topeka too, going to stay with my niece. She is having a baby right soon. But it's her third. Poor thing always gets the morning sickness and can't even get out of the bed. Her husband was recently deployed to Germany for a year, so I am going to help her out all I can."

I turned toward the window and looked out as the road moved under the wheels of our bus. The scenery had changed. I was feeling extremely drained. I found my pillow and put it on the window and began to hum the song Miss Renée had sung earlier. "*His eye is on the sparrow and I know He watches me*." Then I closed my eyes and drifted off to sleep.

Chapter 19

I awoke with Miss Renée shaking me. "Wake-up darlin', we're fixin' to get on another bus now." I felt so tired, it was as if this baby was using up all my energy. I tried to focus on collecting my purse and my pillow to follow Miss Renée, who also had several small bags besides her knitting. "Are you taking any prenatal vitamins, young lady?"

"No, what are they? I haven't seen a doctor yet." I looked at Miss Renée speculating what prenatal meant.

"Jade, prenatal means "before birth." It's vitamins you take so you and the baby can stay strong and healthy."

"Oh," I said, barely audible. I was shuffling my feet and looking down to the ground. There was so much for me to do. How would I see a doctor and how would I get these vitamins and how could I keep trying to hide this baby?

"Now, Jade, you're gonna have to go see the doctor, there ain't no getting outta that one. Who can you get to take you? Just what is your plan when you get to Topeka?"

We each got our large bags from the baggage storage area under the bus, and hauled them to the other bus we would be boarding. The driver helped us get them stowed away.

On the bus, I stood and waited for the lady in front of me to load her things in the rack above her head. I walked to the next seat and began to get situated. I wanted to chew all my skin around each finger to the bone. I was so nervous and so scared about how I was going to get through this. I couldn't deal with it all. It had grown too large for me to deal with.

"I can't tell my brother or my aunt and uncle about this baby or they'll kick me out, sure as I'm sittin' here, Miss Renée."

"Well, Jade, you got to tell somebody."

"I know," I said, "that's why I told you." I looked at her with eyes of hope that said 'please don't leave me. I need you more than you could ever imagine.' My eyes were pleading and I had stopped breathing, waiting for her reply.

"Yes, my dear that is truth, the Lord put us together for a reason, but what shall I do now?"

"I'll be eighteen in just three and a half weeks, so when the baby is born I'll be nearly nineteen, and I can get on my own. I won't tell a soul that you've helped me, and I won't ever bother you again."

"Now you listen here, Jade, you are not a bother. I will do whatever I can, but it's not my house, it's my niece's. Even though, maybe we can work out something. You would have to help out and when the baby is born, find work and of course, there would be rules, but I suspect you're not much trouble anyhow."

She pulled a notepad out of her purse and wrote down the address and phone number of her niece. She handed me the piece of paper which I tucked safely into my purse. "Now, you hold on to that in case of an emergency, alright dear?"

And before I could answer she said, "Honey, it's going to be fine, the Lord is already watching over you."

I wished I had the faith and trust she had in the Lord, but with my background it was hard. I had watched my mama praise and worship God, and serve Him the best that she could and what had it got her? She had nothing but trouble. She had a husband who drank and raised his hand to her, and then she died a slow painful death. I could still recall the smell of death in her room. If there was a God who cared about her and could be trusted, where had He been? Where was He when I was raped? Where was He when my mama was being beaten and my brother was becoming old before his time? Where was He when Verdi moved in my mama's house and took away her precious things? Suddenly I was screaming to myself in my own head, "HUH? GOD ANSWER ME, WHERE WERE YOU?" Anger rose up in me and I had to take a deep breath and try to get a grip on things.

The bus wheels raced over the miles, and we were approaching our destination quickly. I pulled Uncle Ed's address out of my purse and wondered if Daddy had phoned looking for me yet. I thought about Dillon and what life would be like if he were white and we could have married. I fantasized about situations that in my heart I knew were only fabricated tales of a life I would never know.

The bus pulled up to the depot in Topeka. Miss Renée and I looked at each other and quickly embraced before stepping off the bus. There were yellow cabs waiting for the departing passengers. Miss Renée's niece was standing on the curb with a child's hand clutched in each of hers. I looked down at her beautiful children; they were both girls and both dressed in paisley playsuits. Her niece looked ready to pop, her belly button poking out from her blouse. She had the same calm eyes as her aunt Renée only hers were dark brown, and I wondered where her own mama was. Miss Renée made the introductions, and I nodded and said hello to the little girls who smiled up at me.

"Well, we better go. Jade, you take care of yourself and remember, if you need anything." Her words floated off and I watched as they walked towards the car. I wanted to grasp hold of her and plead with her not to leave me but to take me with them, but I knew that I had to see Johnny first.

I approached a cab driver who took my things and opened the back door. "You got money, Miss Lady?"

He was rough looking with a beard and had an accent I wasn't familiar with. "Yes, I have money."

"Okee. Well, we starteen da meteir. Whey-er to?"

I looked down on the crumpled envelope and read off the street name as he pulled out of the parking lot. I held my breath all the way through town, past the town square lined with banks, a drug store, a couple of five and dime stores, a hardware, and a nice clothing store. Then we were driving down gravel back roads through farmland and wheat fields. It was lovely. The taxi pulled into a farm house that sat closer to the road than I thought it should. The house was white with green shutters and a green porch that was adorned with a hanging swing and two big potted red Geranium plants. I saw a storage shed and a bright red barn in back of the place. A scruffy little dog greeted me by barking and jumping excitedly. I collected my things, paid my fare and walked nervously towards the front porch. The front door was open and I tapped on the screened door frame. Ed's wife Julie opened the door and looked at me with a surprise and an expression of joy.

"Jade Gentry, what in the world are you doing here? Why just look at you, all grown up and pretty as can be!"

"Sorry to show up without any notice, but I just needed to get away for a bit." I bowed my head and waited for her to speak.

"Well, Johnny and Ed will be so pleased, now come on in and let's put your things away. Does your father know you're here?" I looked up and before I could respond she said, "Well, that's okay, I'll have Ed call and let him know so he doesn't worry. Jade, you can have the guest room, it's a little dusty, but we can fix that. There's a nice bed and a dresser for you to use while you're here. Are you planning on staying long?" She looked at me with a curious frown that I wasn't sure meant she wanted me there or she wanted me to leave.

"Uh, just a few days."

"Well good, we sure have worried about you since your mama passed away. You know Ed grieved for weeks over that. We just never would have thought of cancer."

"Yes, I guess we were all shocked," I replied. "Life sure hasn't been the same since."

"Oh dear, I shouldn't have brought up that sorrowful time." Julie hugged me, and I put my bags down on the floor. "You hungry, Jade. I was just about to make some dinner. Johnny and Ed will be here shortly and what a pleasant surprise you will be." She smiled and we headed to the kitchen where she chopped vegetables, then cut up a chicken to fry. The kitchen was yellow and had white starched cotton curtains. Julie had pictures of roosters on the wall and a white-washed pantry filled with all sorts of food items. Her dishes were red with white trim. The floor was cheap linoleum with tied rag rugs thrown about. I was so hungry and could hardly wait 'til supper, but realized that if I wanted to keep my secret for any length of time I had better lay off stuffing myself. I helped roll out the biscuit dough and made sweet tea. By the time it was all prepared my mouth had watered so much I felt queasy and hungrily pulled apart a biscuit and shoved it in my mouth when Julie left the room.

Johnny and Ed arrived like clockwork at five fifteen PM. The door flung open and boots were thrown off. I ran from the kitchen passing by my Uncle Ed and going straight for Johnny. His expression was beyond words and his arms made me feel so safe for a minute. He was tanned and his dark wavy hair was shiny. I couldn't stop looking at him and laughing.

"Sissy! I can't believe you're here! You ain't in no trouble are ya?" He looked at me smiling, but with concern in his voice.

"No, Johnny, everything's fine," I lied. Lying was starting to get more difficult, and I was beginning to wonder when the whole thing was going to blow up in my face.

"Get over here, girl," Ed said with arms open. "If you ain't the spittin' image of your mama. Let me get a good look at you." He pulled a strand of hair out of my eyes and kissed me on the cheek. "You make me miss your mama something fierce." He squeezed me again, and then gave Julie a peck on the lips. "So, what brings you to Kansas?" I threw my hands up in the air and made a face. "Beats me?" We all laughed, and Julie told them to wash up for supper.

I had been on that bus for a day and a half without a real meal and I was famished. We all gathered around the kitchen table. Ed said a blessing and bowls were passed, green beans, carrots, potatoes and chicken was divvied up on plates, and I felt like I had just entered a dream. The peace was like nothing I ever had in the home where I grew up.

Johnny and Ed talked about work and asked about Daddy and Verdi. I tried to refrain from rolling my eyes and kept my remarks short and to the point. Julie looked up at Ed and said, "By the way you need to call and let them know Jade's here, seems she left without anyone knowing." She raised her eyebrows and Ed looked at me with concern.

"Okay. I'll call as soon as dinner is over, but for now let's enjoy her company." He smiled broadly. I loved Ed, he was such a kind man. His eyes were warm. He looked like he had even lost some weight. Johnny was excited to show me his new guitar, and how well he'd learned to play. He had his driver's license now and was saving up for a car. The evening was perfect and several times I almost forgot that there was a life growing inside of me. I laughed and ran my fingers through Johnny's hair. Julie sang, "*I'm Sitting by the Purple River*" as Johnny played guitar. Ed and I watched with pride, him for his wife and me for my brother. I laughed and sang along, my feet tapping with the rhythm. Later Ed called Daddy and got an ear full. Ed held out the phone and said, "He wants to talk to you." I nervously took the phone and barely whispered "Hello."

"What in the hell do you think you're doing? Do you know how worried Verdi was about you? We been down to Taylors store looking for you. Had the whole town in an uproar. Connor's been driving clear across town trying to see if anyone's seen the likes of you!"

"I'm sorry, Daddy." I said almost as soft as I had mouthed "hello."

"Sorry don't cut it, you can keep your sorry ass there for all I care!" He slammed the phone down onto the receiver and my stomach did a flip-flop. I wondered what all this stress was doing to the life that was forming inside me. For weeks I had cried myself to sleep almost every night and woke up with the fear of what I faced. If this baby was Connor's or if this baby was Dillon's, it didn't really matter, both came with problems that seemed to have no solution. I was suddenly exhausted and decided to go lay down. I told Johnny to wake me up in an hour and retired to my room. The bedroom was small and cozy, and there was a window with a beautiful view of the country. It seemed the baby was making it difficult for me to stay awake and I was in need of those vitamins Miss Renée had told me about. "Oh, if only Mama were still here," I thought to myself.

Johnny woke me up from my nap, and we reminisced as we took a short walk just like old times. I wanted to tell him about all my troubles, but I thought if he were ashamed of me I wouldn't be able to go on living.

"Why'd you run off like that and not tell a soul, Jade?" He looked at me those piercing blue eyes watching and waiting for my reply.

"Just tired of Verdi, that's all. I'm just tired Johnny. I really miss Mama, and I wish I didn't have to stay there another minute."

"Well, maybe I could get us a place here and I could help take care of you 'til you finish school and can get a job of your own?" He looked at me waiting for my reply. "You sure you ain't in no trouble, Jade? You know you can tell me anything, and I promise I won't tell a soul."

I wished that Johnny's promise was true but the truth is you really can't tell everything to everybody, not without it changing how they think of you. I wasn't going to tell Johnny. I wasn't going to let on that anything was wrong. I was going to enjoy every moment with him and Uncle Ed and Aunt Julie, and then I was going to disappear.

Chapter 20

I had only stayed a week when I began to feel an underlying sense of tension growing between Ed and Julie on account of me. I knew they were starting to wonder if I was ever going to leave. They didn't come out and say it, but the small remarks and the eyes across the room that stared too long gave way to truth. I can't describe the emotions that were running inside my heart. I was a scared little girl with no one to turn to, but I had been a scared little girl ever since I could remember. Between daddy and Conner, I was certain I'd seen more than my years allowed for. Conner's evil grin haunted my sleep at times. And if that wasn't enough, I was about to be a mama. I was about to have a new little person in my life that would need me to be brave and grown up, not a shy, scared of her shadow little child. I told myself to shape up and get ready to make another move.

It was a Monday morning when I had them take me to the bus station. I knew I would miss Johnny terribly but what other choice did I have? I grabbed Miss Renée's phone number and address from my purse and clasped the paper in my hand tightly. I was sure that God had sent her to me. So, I decided to follow the open door. Mama used to say God opens doors that no man can shut, and he shuts doors that no man can open. I liked that. It made me feel better inside for some reason.

Johnny and Ed left me at the station. I told them I didn't want them to stay and watch me get on the bus, that it would be too hard for me. "You know how I hate goodbyes, Johnny!" Johnny smiled shyly, his black hair shining in the sunlight. He squeezed me tightly and so did Ed. We exchanged pleasantries and then I walked inside the bus station. It smelled like peanuts and leather and there was a faint scent of tobacco smoke in the air. I waited 'til Ed and Johnny were long gone and then moseyed over to the pay phone and dialed Miss Renée's number or rather, her niece's. It rang and rang and I held my breath. "What if she didn't answer?" About the time I thought I'd die of panic, I heard a voice faintly say, "Hello?"

"Uh yes, I was wondering if Miss Renée is there."

"This is she, speaking."

"Oh, hello, Miss Renée, this is Jade. We met on the bus going to Topeka."

"Well, Jade, how are you dear?" I could hear children in the background and music playing.

"I'm fine."

I didn't know what to say and I sure didn't know how to ask her if I could stay there. My mind was racing and I thought about how ridiculous it would sound to say, "Oh, by the way, I was wondering if you could feed, house, and care for another baby and me in a few months?" The whole idea made me shrink with fear of the tiny word "no."

"Jade, do you need me to come get you?"

I pressed my lips together as the tears literally squirted from my eyes. I managed a raspy, "Yes" and chewed my thumbnail, then exhaled sharply.

"Of course dear, now where are you?"

"I'm at the bus station, Miss Renée."

"Alright sweetie, I'll be there in just a bit, you hold tight."

"Thank you, oh thank you so much!" I hung up the phone. Tears were streaming down my cheeks and I felt my belly do a flip flop and began to rub it. "Dear God, help me get through this life, help me protect my baby."

Miss Renée arrived with the same little girls I had met at the station. One was named Tamar and the other was named Dory. It was a short ride from the bus station to their house. Miss Renée's niece, Alice, had her baby two days after Miss Renée arrived in Topeka. She and the newborn were lying down. Miss Renée said the baby was healthy, a beautiful baby girl. They had three daughters now, but she still wanted a boy. They named the new baby Evelyn. Miss Renée brought me through the hall to the bedroom and I got to catch a peek at the new baby. I had never seen fingers and toes so tiny. Alice was changing the baby. She put rubbing alcohol on the cord and with a dab of Vaseline. She told me the cord would fall off by itself in a week or so. I realized I had a lot to learn about babies. I felt better knowing Alice was alone and doing fine with three. Of course, she had Miss Renée there and a husband who was providing for them financially. I hoped that with a little help I could figure out my own situation.

The baby cried so softly and stretched out her tiny legs. Her lips were making a sucking sound and her olive brown skin was very smooth. Her hair was like black silk and I thought she was absolutely breathtaking. She smelled like powder and lotion and everything good babies are supposed to smell like. I wanted to hold her but was afraid I might hurt her. However, Alice persisted and

I took the little round ball wrapped in receiving blankets and rested her against my chest. A new life has entered the universe, a beautiful new spirit has been released. And I am carrying one of them inside myself now, I thought with wonderment.

I rubbed the baby's back and glanced around the room at my new surroundings. There was a bookcase filled with colorful books. We, Gentry's, had only ever had the Bible and our school books at home. There was one that caught my attention: "*The Old Man and the Sea.*" I studied the cover and read the summary on the back. Miss Renée told me I should read the book and that I could really glean from it.

The house was small but homey. Miss Renée led me to a room off the stairs that had a small door, almost like an attic area. The ceiling was so low I could only stand in the center of the room. There was a twin size bed, a small night stand, and a hope chest. There also was a tall chifforobe with drawers and some wall hooks for hanging my clothes. My first thought of this cozy little room was that it was like a little nest where my baby and I could rest for a while.

"This will be your room, Jade. Tomorrow we've got to find you a doctor. Now, I have been thinking about this and until we know whose baby this is there really isn't a way to contact the father. I will be praying for you and this child, and we will see what the Holy

Spirit will have us do. We must always be led by the Spirit. Now you put your things away and come down and get you some lunch."

I unpacked my bag and felt good about the things I had brought with me. I had made good choices. I hung dresses and my coat on the hooks, folded items that went into the chest. I arranged the shoes along the wall under the hanging clothes. At last, I took my little guardian angel figure out of the shoe and put her on the nightstand by the bed. I looked around and felt so grateful. Had God really found a place for me to hide for five months?

I walked into the kitchen and sat down while Miss Renée fried thick bologna and sliced onions. We had sandwiches with mustard and potato chips. The potato chips came in a can and tasted better than anything I'd had in a long time. For some strange reason, I felt at home here already, and by evening the two older girls were bringing me books to read to them and showing me their paper dolls. I loved paper dolls and felt like a child again for a moment. The fear of what the future would hold for me was worrisome at times. But I kept in the forefront of my mind the truth that I was about to become a mama, and, therefore, a woman.

That night, my first night with this new family, I lay down to sleep but there were so many questions still running in my thoughts that seemed to bother me and cause me to tense up. Would I see Johnny or Daddy again? Would this baby be Conner's or Dillon's? How would I take care of it? Would any man ever want to marry me with a fatherless son I was raising? Should I just give this baby up for adoption? Would I die giving birth? What if I had to get a Caesarian? I worried until I left chewing the skin around my fingers and had begun chewing the inside of my mouth until fever blisters started to appear. I reminded myself that I HAD to be brave. There was no other option. If only I knew what the future held.

"Hello God, it's me, Jade. Thank you. What you have done for me is unbelievable, especially after all the lies I've told! I am sorry, truly, and I hope I can get to know you. Also, why do people say "amen"?

I woke the next morning and opened my eyes, unsure of where I was at first. The sun cascaded through the small window and I heard a baby crying and then reality seemed to kick in. The baby sounded more like a bird cawing. I picked up the book *The Old Man and the Sea* and began to read.

"He was an old man who fished alone in a skiff in the Gulf Stream and he had gone eighty-four days now without taking a fish. In the first forty days, a boy had been with him. But after forty days without a fish the boy's parents had told him that the old man was now definitely and finally salao, which is the worst form of "unlucky."

I thought about "salao" and became deeply interested in the story. I read it every morning when I woke and every night before sleep. I finished in just a few days. Miss Renée told me that reading the Bible at night would give me great faith and that God could show me what to do and help me with my problems. She gave me a nice leather Bible. It reminded me of my mama's that I had safely tucked away in my suitcase. I just didn't understand how reading the book could help you? Mama read it all the time, but she never did anything to reverse the curse. Just thinking about Mama made my heart sad. I missed her terribly. But time had changed me, and I was having difficulty coming to terms with the fact that life has a way of throwing you out to sea and leaving you to scorch in the elements with not a fish in sight. I saw myself in the old man.

The doctor Miss Renée found for me looked like a lumberjack and his hands were as huge as one. I wondered what would make a man want to look at women in such a way day after day. I sunk down on the table and placed my feet in the cold steel stirrups. I closed my eyes but occasionally stared at the ceiling in shame. The thin sheet was not much comfort and his gloved hand reached so far and so rough that I couldn't help but fight back tears. I wasn't sure if they were from the pain or pure humiliation. My under arms had perspired so much the paper sheet was slowly becoming wet and pieces were sticking to me. He cleared his throat and said, "How old are you, miss?"

I had to think for a minute. "I'm eighteen," I said in a voice filled with fear. The problem was I looked about fourteen and no one believed me.

"And the father?"

I didn't know how to answer that, so I didn't answer. But I decided to find mama's wedding ring that I had secretly taken off her hand and place it on mine for all future visits.

"Do you recall the date of your last period?" I wasn't prepared for that question, so I shook my head, no, and then said, "But I know when I got pregnant more or less. It was the week of May 20th. Just a while before school was out."

He had a little sliding wheel paper thing. He moved the center part around. He took a measuring tape and ran it across my stomach and then made some notes on the chart.

"We are going to give you a target due date January 28th give or take a couple of days. See you in six weeks," he said and looked at me with disdain that I could see and feel.

I told him thank you as if he had done something to help me. I guess he had because I was able to get a big bottle of vitamins for free and a pamphlet on how to take care of newborns. The brochure went over all the steps of the labor and delivery process. It told me how to properly feed my baby and bathe it. The text went over something called colic that seemed to upset a baby's digestive system. It also had illustrations of taking care of the cord. I read it several times, but still felt uneasy about the whole thing.

I wondered if I'd ever run into Ed or Johnny. We lived in the same city, just on opposite ends of town, but one could never be too sure. I wondered if Miss Renée could get in trouble for having me here. She didn't seem to ever worry about anything; it was as if worry wasn't a part of her vocabulary.

Alice on the other hand was always stressed over something. I had begun to venture out of my room and try and get to know these two distinctively different women to whom the Lord had led me.

We got home from seeing the doctor and found Alice about to diaper the baby. "Can I help you with anything, Alice?" I said it with stooped shoulders, uncertain of what I could do.

"Sure, you want to practice diapering the baby?"

I didn't know where to start, and felt certain that somehow I would completely mess up. I pictured the diaper pins puncturing her tiny little girl's skin.

For whatever reason, Alice had coined the new name "Eva" for Evelyn. So they had been calling her "Eva" all week. She looked up at me with widened eyes and a certainty that I didn't know what I was doing. My nervousness had spilled out into the air and I could hear her whimpering begin to grow louder as I uncomfortably clasp her two stick-like legs together to lift her body and pull the wet diaper out from under her. I placed the dry diaper under her bottom and sprinkled the baby powder. I was feeling better about how things were going until it was time to poke the diaper pin into the folded cloth. Alice took my hand and showed me a trick where the only thing I would stick would be me. I sighed with relief and little Eva seemed to relax with me, as if she sensed I was going to make it through this thing called motherhood. Once I had gotten Eva's diaper changed and her little peach gown pulled down, I looked up at Alice for approval. "Well, Alice, I think she's all dry and ready for you. Did I get the diaper pinned tight enough?" "You sure did," Jade. I knew you were a natural." She smiled and I felt my body relax.

I was so scared knowing I was bringing a new life into the world. I wondered how many mistakes I would make and if this tiny little life would love me half as much as I loved it already. What if I became something to my child that my daddy had become to me? What if my child grew up to loathe me? What if my child fled in the night and left no return address? What if after all the diaper changing, breast milk and rocking in the night, the child I loved outgrew me and ran as far as I had? I wanted to be the best mama I could be, but what if my child reminded me of a monster that took my virginity in the night? What if my child reminded me of something cruel and evil? What if I became the shell my mama did? I pictured her hollow eyes and hollow trunk, walking stooped over in despair. A big shiver went down my spine.

"What's wrong Jade, you look like you just watched a frightful horror film? Are you okay?" I wished I had only watched it and not lived it.

"Yes, Alice. Thank you for letting me practice being a mommy with little Eva. I only hope I turn out to be a good mama like you." I smiled painfully.

"You will be an excellent mother." Alice said. "You don't have to worry about that, it's a natural instinct all women are just born with. You'll do fine, just fine!"

Chapter 21

Miss Renée motioned for me to come and sit next to her on the sofa. "Jade, I'm going to need you to be strong and brave. I know you are worried about this baby and who the father is, but God already knows. He knew this baby before it was in your womb, according to His word and He also knows your thoughts from afar off and even when a hair falls from your head. Now don't you think you should trust such a mighty good God?"

I knew I should, but my mama trusted God and all it got her was a ton of bruises, verbal abuse, and then finally, six feet under. I nodded, though, not wanting to admit my doubts. I decided He had led me to Miss Renée and Alice or at least it felt like He had. I was finally safe from Braxton and any gossiping country folks with their disapproving eyes. I was thankful that I was far from Daddy and

Verdi and even Conner. I was actually safer than I'd ever been in my life. Ironically, it took a real evil circumstance to bring it about.

"I'm so scared," I said, my lip trembling.

"Now, now, dear. Come here." Even though I was already sitting next to Miss Renée she pulled me closer and snuggled me. I laid my head on her shoulder, and just for a moment I remembered Mama comforting me when I needed support in days gone by.

As the days went along, Alice gave me all her baby's hand-me-downs. There were newborn sizes and three to six month onesies that Eva had outgrew faster than I'd ever imagined. She gave me her maternity clothes too and several receiving blankets. With this being her third baby, she had a big stash of baby things. She told me I could use Eva's bassinet while I was there because Eva would be in her crib by the time my baby was born. Miss Renée crocheted a beautiful baby afghan for my baby. Eva's was finished about the time I got there. Both were done in the softest yarn I ever felt. The one for my baby was a lacy pattern of white and blue and I loved it.

I looked at Alice with her pretty olive skin so different from her Aunt Renée. Her hair was dark brown and her eyes were just as dark. She had a little mole on her left cheek that was quite sexy and she slinked when she walked like a cat, yet her posture was perfect. Miss Renée told her if she got any prettier she would end up doing nothing but having babies because her husband wouldn't be able to keep his hands off her when he came home on leave. They were firm believers that birth control was a sin. Her husband, Carl, was from a strict Catholic family. He had three sisters and five brothers, nine siblings in all.

"Do you have any names picked out, Jade?" Miss Renée asked.

"I hadn't really thought about it too much. I didn't like my mama's name. She being named after a state and all, but I wanted to give her a strong name if it was a girl. If it was a boy I thought I would name him Charles. I liked the name Charlie and thought it might be even better for a girl. I could name her Charlene and call her Charlie, maybe if I give her a boy's name she'll be tough enough to stand up to their wiles? I really don't know." I shrugged and looked at them for suggestions.

"Well, you should give the child a good strong biblical name like Ruth, Esther, Jeremiah or Noah. Perhaps David, a man after God's own heart? But I believe the "prophetic word" I gave you is true. It will be a son." I thought Miss Renée was right about a Biblical name, but none of those names sounded right to me. Miss Renée brought an old Bible from the top of her closet. It was very thick with gold lettering and pictures of saints galore. There was a whole section in the back with a list of names. I wasn't even aware that Alice had named all her daughters from the bible, even Evelyn had turned into Eva or Eve. I listened as she read names and I played with them in my mind. Then she came to boy names and each one rolled off her tongue with such ease, but most I couldn't even pronounce. Then she said Jonah and I knew that was a name I liked. It reminded me of Johnny and yet it was unique. "Jonah," I said it over and over again letting it roll slowly over my tongue. "I like that one."

"Well, have you ever read the book of Jonah?" Miss Renée asked.

"No. What's it about?"

Miss Renée told me it was a short story, only a few pages long and that I should read it for myself. So that night I lay in my small bed in my little nest bedroom and began the story of Jonah. Jonah's character was something puzzling to me. He claimed to be a righteous man but when the Lord asked him to witness to the sinners of Nineveh he ran and hid on a ship at sea. I wondered why I kept getting stories about men at sea and fish. This story had a fish so big it swallowed Jonah up and kept him in its belly for three days and three nights. Darkness and slimy stomach gasses caged him in as he traveled to the bottom of the ocean's floor. All it took was for God to whisper in that large fish's ear and tell him to spit up Jonah on dry ground and it was done.

I thought about how if God could whisper to a fish, He could surely whisper to me. I decided to believe that He really did speak to Miss Renée about my baby and that it was going to be a little boy and one with great musical talent. I decided Jonah did not fit my son's personality and began to search the Bible for a man who had a great voice and even greater character. I wanted a son with integrity. I wanted a son who would never shatter a woman with his hands or his words but would realize a woman's worth and realize she was formed out of him. I closed my eyes and prayed.

"Father God, if you can whisper in a fish's ear and cause him to spit up Jonah, maybe you can whisper in my ear and tell me what to name my baby." I closed my eyes tightly and waited to hear the sound of thunder and rushing waters boom in my ear the name of my first born. But just like the mountain that didn't move at my command, I heard not a thing.

I picked up the Bible and opened it up randomly and my eyes landed on this scripture, "His name shall be John." I was stunned and read it again. My brother's name was John, and who better than Johnny to name my baby after, but that wasn't good enough, I wanted to know if he had any musical talent. I wanted to know that he had a voice. I continued to read, "A voice of one crying in the wilderness" and then I knew that God really did hear me! He really could speak to me and I thought perhaps He had even whispered my brother's name on the pages before me, a book that had words from centuries before.

I had asked both Alice and Renée to give me their favorite name picks for the baby if it was a boy. Since Renée was certain she had heard from the Lord on the matter, I didn't inquire about girl names. Miss Renée told me that she would pick the name Isaac. She said the name meant laughter, and just like Isaac who brought his mother Sarah joy, this child of mine would bring me more happiness than I could ever imagine. I wondered how that could be considering the child so far had cost me everything. But still, there was a mustard seed of hope in my heart.

Chapter 22

Sunday morning came and Miss Renée told me to get ready for church. Baby, Eva, was now old enough to be taken out in public. I dressed in what was the best attire I could find that would still fit. The maternity clothes Alice had given me were still too large and I intended to hide my belly as long as I could although it was clearly visible.

"You ready Jade?" Renee yelled up the stairs, as I hurried to brush my hair. "Coming!"

I wobbled down the stairs and first noticed the girls in their dresses, tights, and shiny white shoes. They were smiling up at me gleefully. We loaded in the car and Renee sang gospel songs all the way there.

The church was simple yet beautiful and the people seemed jovial. They greeted one another happily, hugging each other like family. Introductions were exchanged with several folks, as we made our way up close to the front. I was pretty much invisible due to all the attention Eva was getting with her soft coos and pretty smiles. The song leader had us all stand, and we began singing a song called, "'*How Great Thou Art*.'" The people raised their hands and many began to speak in some foreign language like Miss Renée had done on the bus when she prayed over me. I was a bit uncomfortable, never having experienced anything like this in our church in Braxton. Pastor Caldwell was much more reserved and collected. This pastor prayed a prayer that was so booming and loud I wasn't sure what poor little Eva thought as she squiggled in Alice's arms. I looked at Alice to see what her reaction was to such a service, but she just shrugged her shoulders and smiled crookedly.

The pastor's name was Brother Jonas and I thought it strange that I had just read the book Jonah and him having such a similar name. His prayer went like this: "Father God in heaven above, have mercy on us, O Lord, and save us from our wickedness, cleanse us, search our hearts and humble us. See if you can find one wicked thing, and bring revelation. We lift you up and exalt your son Jesus Christ, our Lord, our savior! We cry out against the enemy and we say take your hands off our sons and our daughters and we speak to our seed and we decree and declare they will serve the Lord. Come on Church!" He shouted so loud I thought heaven and hell heard him and everyone in the church began to pray loudly. I felt so uncomfortable I began to shrink down and fumble with the hem of my skirt. Then Pastor Jonas started up again, "As for me and my household we will serve the Lord!"

I sat down wondering what this man would preach on and what I could learn from this experience. I remembered how God had whispered in the fish's ear, and felt like God didn't need us to yell so loudly in order to be heard.

I remembered a story my mama told me about Hannah in the Bible who prayed for a son because she was barren and how she prayed silently, only her lips moved and the Lord heard her just fine and gave her Samuel. I liked that name Samuel, but I also liked William and Robert. So many names to choose from and still a person, such as myself could acquire a nickname and never use it. I thought I would call the baby Jonathan Isaac. Miss Renée eyed me as if she knew my mind was a thousand miles away from Brother Jonas's sermon and I quickly turned my eye to the podium.

"Peter was in prison, Herod wanted to take his life. Oh, but the people prayed, and it says without ceasing. When was the last time you prayed for someone without ceasing? Do you know what happened? I'll tell you what happened, a great and mighty angel of God showed up in that prison and Peter's shackles and chains were loosed, the iron doors and gates to the city opened and he walked right through them. Maybe you feel like you are in a prison cell, shackled and in heavy bondage today? God wants to set you free. How many want to be set free today? I raised my arm in unison as he continued to discuss all the different types of bondage many fall into. Then he said, "You know what happened to evil king Herod?" I didn't, but I sure wanted to.

"He sat on his throne and the people praised him as if he were God. He didn't correct them and point to the true God, the maker of heaven and earth and God struck him dead and worms ate him! It's right there in the scripture, read it for yourself! I tell you, we need to always make sure we give God all the glory for everything in this life! I want anyone who is here today and you feel like you are in a prison cell stuck in chains of bondage and grief to stand to your feet. God wants to open the iron doors and release you today.

I wasn't sure why but I sprung upward and then instantly regretted it because the people were now focused on me and not brother Jonas.

"That's right, now anyone else who feels this way gather down here in front of the altar. We have some ministers who are going to lay hands on you and pray. Yes, just like the people prayed for Peter and you are going to get set free today. He who the Son sets free is free indeed."

The congregation kept hollering "amen, praise the Lord, hallelujah." I walked slowly down to the front and so did several others. I felt like my mama with her stooped over shoulders and I was secretly wishing I could crawl under a pew and hide. The pastor took a bottle of oil and put the sign of the cross on my forehead. He prayed for peace and freedom to come forth in my life. I was scared at first, but then it was as if when he spoke the very word "peace" over me, I felt waves of peace and calmness flow through my body.

Then he looked at me and asked a question I had never heard before. "Do you have the baptism of the Holy Ghost?" "I was baptized in the river in Braxton at ten years of age." I mumbled and told him it was after I had asked Jesus into my heart. "You need the Holy Ghost!" he said. What was a Holy Ghost? I thought ghost were spirits that needed to find rest. He looked at me again and asked, "Do you speak in tongues?" I shook my head "no" and felt suddenly more frightened than I ever had in my whole life. "Don't be afraid. I am going to lay hands on you and I want you to just relax and lift your hands in the air and began to praise the Lord in your English language." I thought, what other language does he expect me to praise him in? It's not like I speak French or Hungarian?

I lifted my arms and began to say quietly "Thank you, Jesus. I praise you, Jesus" and then I felt his hand push against my head, "Be filled with the Spirit! For out of your belly shall flow rivers of living water, take the baptism in the Holy Ghost." It felt as if all the peace had been sucked out and fear was replaced.

Then he looked at me and rather calmly said, “Just begin to say anything that comes to your mind but not in English.” He began to speak and it sounded like this, “Has sata me tee ah tee autta yonda la to kianta sheetiana hosintiana.” I was very confused! About that time Miss Renée walked up and escorted me back to the pew. I felt the eyes of the people on me and tears ran down my cheeks. "Jade, don't you mind him or any of these people. You hear?" I nodded and wiped the corners of my eyes.

I felt so different and so unholy. I thought if I could only be as close to God as them, He would give me a beautiful language. But because I had committed fornication, He must be very angry with me and be withholding such gifts meant only for the very elite of Christians.

I suddenly wanted to crawl under the pew and make my way outside. I felt more in prison when I left the church than I did before I started. I couldn’t seem to understand all the mumbo jumbo, and I knew Miss Renée was there to protect me. I was thankful she whisked me away to safety. I just would have to remember to never stand up again for prayer but try and blend into the congregation. I would have to come up with some sort of funny language to speak or either pretend to be sick on Sunday mornings. Yet, how could I do that with Miss Renée? It was as if she could read my mind with that prophecy gift she had. How could I ever bring a mixed baby to church without being condemned? I wanted to cry, but my stomach kept reminding me that someone else very tiny would weep with me, and I couldn't stand the thought of putting him through such turmoil. As soon as it was over I made my way outside at breakneck speed.

I got into the car and waited for Alice and Miss Renée to pick up the smaller girls from Sunday school. I slinked down in the seat and hungered for the car to pull away to safety. Miss Renée turned the radio on and to my surprise she put it on country music. Hank Williams sang a song that my daddy loved to play and suddenly I was back on the porch with Johnny, Mama and the man in the moon. I closed my eyes and escaped to a happier time in my life.

When we got home I went to my "nest" to lay down and promptly fell asleep. I dreamed a dream so strange. I was in a jail cell and daddy and Verdi were staring at me with disgust. Suddenly an angel came and opened up the door and told me I was free. I walked out of the cell and into a beautiful meadow away from everyone. The sun was shining down on me and I could feel the warm rays soaking down into my soul.

I was left with a tingling feeling all over my body. It was something I had never felt before. It was a feeling of extreme wellness, safety, and peace. I was pretty sure the God I had been seeking had actually found me.

When the two little girls came up to my room to tell me lunch was ready, I still felt like I was in some kind of marvelous glowing bubble. I felt no pain, no fear, no anxiety, just a wonderful feeling that everything was going to be just fine. I had a sense of being pardoned and made okay from what had happened to me. I opened my mouth and thanked God for this beautiful dream that He had given me that was surreal. It was as if the sun shining on me had brought a spiritual peace that I had never felt before.

I got up and went down the stairs to a nice meal prepared by my friends. Alice commented that my nap must have been good for me because I looked more glowing than usual. I smiled and felt a bit of joy bubble up in my heart. I wanted to tell my dream to Miss Renée and Alice and see what they thought about it, but I felt I should keep quiet and ponder it myself.

Chapter 23

On Monday morning, Miss Renée took me to an educational center where they did testing to see if I could pass my GED. She said I needed my education, and I knew I did with a baby to bring up by myself. I had already conjured up another lie to tell the doctor and anyone else who looked at me sideways. The idea came to me after hearing Alice talk about the war in Vietnam and how she hoped Carl would be able to stay clear. It was 1966 and things were changing in the world. I had just been living in a sheltered part of the globe in Braxton. I had almost no knowledge concerning politics or war or anything much really. The world had become just about me and my own combat. But I figured telling people that I lost my husband because he was a brave soldier, sounded better than being raped or being a whore nobody would want. I knew lying was wrong, but it seemed to be the only way for me to function without pure and utter shame.

"Jade, it's getting late now, come on we gotta get you to the school."

"Okay, Miss Renée," I said as I hurriedly brushed my teeth and my hair.

"Have you thought about a career or what you want to do with your life?" She pulled her long hair to the side of one shoulder and looked me directly in the eye.

"No, I really haven't thought about it much. I love to draw and paint, but what kind of job would that get me?"

"Why Jade, you never told me you are artistic. You can do a lot with that talent. You could even get a job illustrating children's books or selling your own paintings to the public."

I thought about how exciting it would be to own my own shop and sit around painting pictures of people and landscapes and sunsets. I loved painting horses with unusual colors. I painted a purple horse once with a yellow mane and I made the trees blue and the sky green.

"Maybe we can get you an art set today and see what you can do?" Miss Renée smiled. "We've got to get you living life again!" She honked the horn as a car pulled out in front of us and then pulled up to the curb of the GED building. "See ya later," Jade. Now you go do your best. It will all be fine." I struggled to believe her, but walked in through the double doors where a small sign on a stand said, "Pretest for GED Second Door on the right."

The test was mundane and mostly the questions just made my brain hurt. There was one that went something like this, "Daisy is driving from Marysville to a county fair in Yorkville. After driving two hours at an average of fifty-five miles per hour, she still has eighty miles left to travel. What is the distance between the two towns, in miles?"

I was sure my grade level would not surpass that of a sixth grader when it came to math. Achieving any activity on the left side of my brain was almost nonexistent. I knew the only thing stopping me from getting the GED would be math or Science. I tapped the pencil several times and looked around the room. My eyes shifted to a dark headed man who looked to be in his thirties and then back to my paper. I was stumped on the next question, but didn't want to draw attention to myself by calling the teacher over.

Mr. Richards was volunteering his time to help those who were slow in certain subjects. He was young and went by the name Mark; although, Mr. Richards was what he had written in chalk on the board. I instantly liked him. He had blonde curly hair that was disheveled and pale blue eyes with a hint of green. He was tall and slender and had terrible posture, but a bright smile. He took great length trying to show me how to make the mathematical word problems into numbers, converting them into an equation. For whatever reason, my brain just wrapped up like a twisted pretzel and I felt more dim-witted after his explanation than before. He told me not to worry, it would only be a small part of the test, maybe two or three problems.

"Jade, have you decided what you want to do after you get your GED?" This seemed to be the question of the day and I apparently needed to make a decision.

"No Mark, I haven't a clue. My life has become rather complicated and I am not sure what my future holds." I lowered my head and fumbled with my pencil.

"Well, you are very articulate and intelligent. I feel you can do just about anything you put your mind to."

Suddenly, I felt sick at my stomach, and instead of Mark it was Conner who was mouthing the words. Conner had said everything Mark was telling me. All the lies and all the schemes had started with, "You can do anything you put your mind to." He had tried to make me feel so good about myself, all because he wanted to take my virginity. I hated him and with a passion that seemed to intensify after the doctor's appointment and the humiliation he had forced me to endure due to his wicked lustful desires. I should be at home finishing school with everyone else my age, I thought. Then bile started rising up in my throat and the sweet water pouring into my mouth while I tried to swallow and make it go away.

"Jade, are you okay?" Mark put his arm around me, and I was reminded of when Connor sneaked into my room and put his arm on me that night. There were other students waiting for Mark to help them with the subjects they were struggling with, but he followed me out of the room. I ran quickly into the restroom and began to hurl into the commode, and then I heard Mark's voice.

"Jade, I'm going to get you some help."

The next thing I knew a young girl from the class was knocking on the stall door. “Excuse me, are you gonna be okay?”

“Yes, I’m fine,” I said, spitting into the toilet. I was embarrassed to come out and re-enter the room knowing Mark would wonder what had happened.

“How far along are you?” the girl asked from the other side of the door.

I felt humiliated. I thought I could cover this pregnancy for its entirety. What a fool I had been. I looked down at my belly which was clearly visible to everyone but me. Mark must think I am trash. I didn’t want to walk back into the room, but my purse and study manual were still on the desk. I stood at the lavatory and rinsed my mouth spitting out the water several times. I splashed water on my face.

“You gonna to be alright?” She said it with the twang only a Topekan could. I wanted to crawl away in humiliation, but instead I looked up at her and smiled and bobbed my head up and down. “Good, we were all worried.” She left the restroom, her hair perfectly in place, her fuchsia pink lipstick reminded me of Verdi, a memory I was trying hard to forget.

I looked once more down at my protruding pouch and then at my frightened eyes.

I went back into class with a posture that resembled Mark's, my shoulders bent over. Then I realized I was becoming my mama and immediately pushed my shoulders back and held my head up. I was going to get through this if it was the last thing I ever did.

"Are you okay?" His eyes looked concerned. I nodded and apologized for the disruption.

"No worries Jade, you just take care of yourself. There is plenty of time to work on your pre-test. I think you will pass it with flying colors."

"Are you a real school teacher?" I asked rather bluntly. I knew in my heart that he wasn't Conner and I really wanted to get to know him. He seemed caring.

"I am in Grad school, my last year and this is all part of my curriculum, helping out here. I want to teach English and be a writer one day."

"That's neat," I said. "What types of books do you write?"

“I write fiction; mostly science fiction, but sometimes I write contemporary fiction.”

“I just read, *The Old Man and the Sea*. It was wonderful.” I said a little too quickly.

“I love Hemingway!” He started naming other novels he’d read that I was unfamiliar with. “You’ve read "*For Whom the Bell Tolls*", haven’t you?” I looked embarrassed and suddenly decided to come clean.

“I just recently discovered his books and want to get a hold of as many as I can. So, no, I haven’t read much, just a few books in high school and the Bible.”

“The Bible, huh?” He looked at me rather funny and shook his head. “You really believe the Bible is true?” I looked at him for the first time in a different light.

“I can’t say I know for certain, but I am trying to figure it out. I do know that hundreds of years before Jesus was born the prophets wrote about Him and that there are many other things in the book that have come true. My mama sure believed every word of it, but she never lived much of anything but misery up until her death.”

"Oh, Jade, I am so sorry."

"She passed away last year and life has been completely different without her. Sometimes I wish I could just call her up and talk to her."

Mark looked down at my stomach and then back at my eyes. "The father?"

I couldn't decide whether to go with the war hero story or the truth and decided to go with neither. I shrugged my shoulders and lowered my head.

"Ahh, Jade I'm so sorry; I didn't know. It's none of my business."

"It's okay Mark, I just don't want to discuss it yet." I stacked my books and picked up my purse.

"See you next week then," I said it matter a fact like.

"Yes, Jade, and don't worry about the pre-test. I am very confident you've got this. Listen, if you are interested in some of the books I told you about, I can bring some to class and you can borrow them."

"That sounds great! Thanks Mark for all your help." I waved and walked outside into the sunlight and made my way back to Miss Renée's. I decided to walk the four blocks and check out the town I was hiding in. The square had a dry cleaners and a community bank, and one florist with a window full of décor dressed in spring daisies. There was Jake's Deli and a clothing store. I kept an even stride and wondered how my future was going to turn out. A car pulled up to the shoulder and Miss Renée beeped her horn and motioned for me to get in.

"Well, how did GED class go?" Her pale blue eyes penetrated me. Her long hair was pulled up in a twist, wrapped around and around in a roll that looked like a cinnamon bun. Every time she looked at me like that I thought she knew some deep dark secret about me because of her spiritual gifting. Sometimes it made me think harder about the fact that God did know everything about me including my thoughts.

"Fine, just fine." I opened the door and placed my books into the bucket seat then slid in.

"You got errands to run?" I asked looking at Miss Renée.

"We are going to Hamilton's Art Supply Store in Finleyville. I have decided that painting will be good for you and the baby." She smiled at me and I felt like I could never repay her for all she was doing.

"I don't have much money left for art supplies." I said, "and plus you and Alice have already done so much, I don't know how I will ever be able to repay you!"

"Jade, you don't have to repay me. I don't want anything from you. Just accept it as a gift from your Father, Daddy God. He loves you and this baby so much and He is going to show up and change your life. I know it may look like a mess to you now, but God makes all crooked places straight. Remember that, Jade."

I wanted to believe her. Truly I did, but at that moment I felt like things were getting more crooked and less straight. I had lost my mama, my virginity, my respect and my family. I had lost so much.

"I have checked into some coffee shops in Topeka and a boutique that sells baby items. They are willing to take a look at your work and may even display it and pay you a commission if it's good enough to sell." She smiled at me and winked. Her bright red and orange shirt was decorated with summer fruit and her dangling ear bobs were even brighter orange. I loved her. I knew she was a mother that every daughter needed, strong and sure and full of unselfish love.

"Oh, Miss Renée, that would be so exciting!" I could picture it. What if all my artwork hung in the town of Topeka and people purchased it and placed it on their walls? My creativity becoming a signature in their homes. It was more than I could hope for, something good coming to me. How would I be able to accept it? I was used to bad things. But good things? "I hope I can still paint; it's been a long time since I actually picked up a brush."

"I have a feeling that you haven't lost your talent." Miss Renée said with a reassuring look. We pulled into Hamilton's and I looked at all the pastel pencils and colors of paint. The paint brushes with their firm bristles and the blank canvasses that cried for color made my heart merry. It was like going to the candy store.

We bought several canvases and a box of acrylics. I picked out a paint brush set that was lined in rows, inside a box with a tray to mix the colors. I was very excited, yet trying to control my impulses since I was spending someone else's money. I asked Miss Renée how much she wanted to spend. She quoted me a very generous figure, and I stayed well under that mark. I couldn't wait to get home and start painting!

On the way home Miss Renée sang. Her voice was soothing. I leaned my head back and I felt my baby kick for the first time. It was a scary feeling and almost bewildering. There was life inside me. Just as I was once inside my mama's womb, now a new life was inside of mine. What would he be like? What would he look like? What kind of smile would he have? There were so many questions.

I told Miss Renée that I felt the baby move. She got tears in her eyes, and said, "It's a miracle, Jade. Though millions of women have done this before you, it is a miracle every single time." I felt a happiness inside that was growing right along with the baby. In spite of my fears and bitterness, I was finding something to live for that I had never known before. That something was a tiny life, my baby.

We walked in the door and I immediately put all my art supplies away. Then I lay down for a nap. The baby was draining me even with the vitamins and good food. I was still extremely tired. I closed my eyes and placed my hands on my belly. "John Isaac, you are going to be a strong man. You are going to sing songs the whole world will sing along to. I love you and we are going to make it. I will try to be the best mama you could ever have. I am going to take care of you and shelter you from the darkness that hides inside the world of light. God will make all our crooked places straight." I said "amen" and closed my eyes.

Chapter 24

The first picture I painted was of birds. They were all sitting in one tree and they were all red bellied. The tree seemed to catch the sunlight and cause the leaves to sparkle. The leaves were purple, yellow and green. The birds were soft-eyed and looking into an imaginary lens only I could see. Miss Renée loved it so much. She just couldn't stop telling me how talented I was. It made me feel so good like I wasn't totally useless.

Alice wanted me to paint portraits of her children. I never had really tried to paint people who were real. I had only painted the ones that I had conjured up in my mind and they were more abstract. I painted features in extravagant rainbow shades such as lime green hair and violet eyes, but I thought for Alice's sake I'd give it a try. We never could get the girls to stay still long enough for me to attempt it, so she gave me a photo of them. It was black and white and only had the two oldest girls in it because it was taken before the baby. The girls were dressed for church and had sun hats on. It looked like an Easter picture, so sweet. I went right to work on it.

I didn't have an easel, so I propped the canvas against my bed and sat in the floor. I painted both girls using black and white paint only. I shaded with gray and tried to match each shadow. Their tiny teeth were hard to get just right at first, but their smiles ended up looking almost identical to the photo. The only colors I used were pale pink and red to paint their Easter hats. I placed an Easter basket beside the tree where they stood and gave the eggs bright colors of pastel blue, green, yellow and red. I stood up and walked to the door, turned and eyed the finished work. I felt good. I felt creative again. I picked up the portrait and made my way down the stairs. Alice and Miss Renée were in the kitchen doing dishes. I held up the canvas and waited for their response.

Miss Renée sucked in air and Alice exclaimed, "That is breathtaking! You are so good! That looks just like the photo!" I smiled and felt a warm glow escape me.

"We are going to have to get you more canvas." Miss Renée exclaimed with a shout. "Little girl, you got talent!" I soaked in their compliments and for the first time in months felt like I was worth something.

By the end of the week, Miss Renée loaded up the five paintings I had completed, and we set out for the coffee shop and the boutique. The Coffee shop was cozy and inviting. There were books on a shelf and a large rug. Plants were scattered about and tables with red chairs filled the room. The dessert case was filled with delectable treats. The lemon bars, fudge brownies, and coconut cream pies made my mouth water. The owner, a large redhead named Suzy, greeted us. She wore a green apron and she had more freckles than Mama and I put together. She walked out to the curb and Miss Renée opened the trunk and began to pull out my paintings. There was the tree filled with birds, a cat asleep in a chair, the portrait of her grandchildren Tamar and Dory and two of the ocean, her proud waves crashing and the sun setting in the horizon. Suzy seemed to ponder the paintings and then looked around. The wheels were turning in her head.

"How much are you asking a piece?" I wasn't even sure what pictures sold for, let alone original artwork.

Miss Renée must have sensed my uneasiness and lack of knowledge. "She's asking twenty dollars each."

Suzy studied the work some more. "Well, you sure are talented, young lady. I would be taking twenty percent of all sales. Is that acceptable?"

I looked at Miss Renée who seemed to know what I was thinking. "We'll take it!"

"Okay, well let's get these inside and hung on the walls."

We got them hung up, with Miss Renée arranging them in an order that was more eye-catching. The last one, the one of her little grandnieces, she set in the front window. Suzy got a piece of paper so Miss Renée could write: "Original Artwork by Jade Gentry. Let her paint your children or grandchildren." She added her address and phone number to the paper. Then she taped a small card on the top of Dory and Tamar's picture that said, "Not for sale."

"This is free advertising and when they call, you can go to their homes and paint for them and charge even up to a hundred dollars if they're wealthy. That way you don't have to pay anyone commission. Once you start making money, you can help out with groceries and that will make you feel less needy and more like a part of the family. I know you would feel better if you were contributing."

I couldn't believe it; there in the window was my artwork, with my name on it. I stood on the sidewalk and gazed into the window just as a couple walked by and admired my painting. I listened to their positive remarks and felt that "sudden" happiness I had been sensing lately. Suzy brought a handwritten agreement to sign stating that she would receive twenty percent of all sales. I signed it. Since I was mostly out of art supplies, we headed back to the supply store. I picked up five more canvases. This time, I paid for it out of the money Mama had left me. I was beginning to see that God had a plan for my life. If I was a failure in the eyes of my family and they didn't ever want to speak to me again after finding out about the baby, I still had worth. I would make it. Miss Renée was talking to me about Suzy and the things she knew about a person was almost mind boggling at times.

"Suzy's hiding behind layers of guilt. She gets nervous and shoves food into her mouth. The more her family talks about her weight problem, the more she eats. I saw her in a vision sitting on the couch eating handfuls of food, just shoving it in her mouth and then crying. We must pray for her.

"Okay, Miss Renée, I will pray."

"Jade, I mean we should pray right now. We cannot say we will pray for someone and then forget to. We must pray as if we were praying for our own selves."

I said "okay," but didn't know what to say. I mean we were driving down the highway.

"Father God, we come to you…" Miss Renée began to pray as she drove. It was the most natural thing for her. She could be standing in the drugstore and start praying out loud. She had no fear of man whatsoever.

"Lord, heal Suzy. Lord heal her heart that has been wounded. Take away her cravings for food. Lord let her begin to walk instead of eating, and let her begin to love herself so she can love others."

I kept saying, "Yes, Lord. Yes, Lord, help her."

Whenever Miss Renée prayed there was a presence that filled the air. It was as if I could feel God's spirit. Sometimes when I was around her I seemed to have a healthier fear of God. I felt drawn to Miss Renée. She had a charisma about her as well.

She patted my arm and told me she was proud of me. We pulled into the driveway and I opened the trunk and removed the clean white canvases.

"He has given you a clean white slate, Jade, just like those canvases. And He is going to let you begin to paint your new life with Him!"

"Thank you, Miss Renée. You have helped me so much. I don't even know where I would be right now. I am so glad you were on the bus that day." I hugged her with my free arm. I smiled into those kind eyes and she looked back at me with so much love. I felt like crying over it, but I held the tears back.

"God led you to the bus station and to me. He is a Father to the broken hearted. The steps of the righteous are ordered of The Lord, Jade. It was Him who led you to me."

I couldn't understand why she thought I was righteous. I saw myself as pretty wicked, doing bad things and then lying to cover up. I was pregnant with no husband, too. I didn't understand.

"God is merciful and true and His mercy is made new every day, Jade." She said it as if she could read my thoughts.

"Yes, you are right. His mercy is new each morning!" I was remembering my mama quoting that verse to me. Perhaps, I didn't deserve such mercy, but I was glad He had given it to me.

Chapter 25

It was Friday and I had to take my GED test that morning. Mark was sure I was prepared, and he said the test took roughly two hours with a break in between. I had studied and studied the night before. Alice and Miss Renée had gone over fractions and algebra with me until my brain felt like mush.

"Johnny, you would be so proud of me," I mouthed to myself. I was going to get through this test and I was going to pass. I could feel it.

"Good morning, Jade," Mark said, as his eyes glanced at my protruding stomach. "How are you feeling today?"

“I’m good Mark, getting bigger every day, but I feel good.” I patted my belly and smiled at him. For some reason, he didn’t make me feel bad or uncomfortable about my pregnancy.

“Are you ready to take this test then?”

“Yes, I am! I think I’m as ready as I’m going to be.” I smiled and looked around the room. There were only five of us there to take the test, two more young ladies, and two men. I sharpened my pencils and sat down at the table. Mark passed out part one of the test. It was mostly English and reading comprehension, and there was an essay to write at the end. He looked at his watch to mark the starting time.

“Please remove everything from your desktop and everyone is to keep their eyes on their own paper. If you get stumped on a question go to the next one. This is a timed test. Good luck. You may begin.” He smiled at the class and sat down at his desk in front of us.

I went to work quickly answering the questions and giving the definitions to a number of words. Some were way beyond my vocabulary, but, all in all, I felt good about it. I then began a section called, "Reading Questions." Each section had a short story to read and then a set of questions to answer to test comprehension. The last story captured my attention, it was called *The Tell-Tale Heart* by Edgar Allen Poe. I had never heard of him. The story was a dark and chilling tale of a murder most vile. This was the part that really captured my imagination: Edgar Allan Poe wrote, "*It is impossible to say how first the idea entered my brain; but once conceived, it haunted me day and night. Object there was none. Passion there was none. I loved the old man. He had never wronged me. He had never given me insult. For his gold, I had no desire. I think it was his eye! Yes, it was this! He had the eye of a vulture --a pale blue eye, with a film over it. Whenever it fell upon me, my blood ran cold; and so by degrees --very gradually --I made up my mind to take the life of the old man, and thus rid myself of the eye forever.*"

The story continued with the man killing the blue-eyed old man and hiding him under planks in the floor of his room. The police arrived and the killer is haunted by the old man's heart. He thinks he can hear the heart beating and pulsating in his ears, louder and louder until he becomes insane and tells them what he has done. He confesses his crime.

I began to wish Conner would become haunted with such insanity that he would confess his sins. I began to daydream of him going completely insane. Hunting for me and searching to find me and wondering if I was dead and he was to blame. I wished guilt and sickness upon him and that his wife would find out what a pig he was. I yearned that his crime would become so tortuous that even God himself would make him relive his sinful lust and he would hear my cries for help and my words of pleading for him to stop. I hoped sleep would escape him.

"Jade, are you okay?" Mark startled me out of my daydreaming and back to the reality that I was being timed. I looked over the questions.

1. Why did the narrator want to kill the old man?

2. What caused the narrator to go mad?

3. Is the old man aware of the narrator's plot?

I continued to the next page and began answering questions about another short story and then a poem. The essay was on the last page and we could write on one of three topics: A. What has been your greatest accomplishment in life? B. What has been the happiest day of your life? C. Is it difficult to change one's life? I pondered on which one to choose and decided to write on topic B. What has been the happiest day of your life so far?

This is what I wrote:

The happiest day of my life so far happened just yesterday. I can think back over cheerful memories of family, especially my brother Johnny, but yesterday was the first day I realized I could possibly change my future. It was the first day I didn't have to force myself to hold my head up. It was the first day in a long while that I didn't fear what the future holds for me.

I have felt for months now that I have been drowning in a sea of mistakes. I have felt like loads of bricks were strapped to my back and that the weight of them could only be lessened in the water, and yet the water was covering my mouth and I had no voice. It was a dark place that held no sunlight. But yesterday the sun's luminosity shimmered down on me as God's grace seemed to illuminate and remove my fears. I felt light, like a feather floating in the breeze. Even my feet seemed to spring forward and want to dance.

I completed some paintings I had been working on, and now they are displayed in the windows and on the walls of a quaint little coffee shop in town. Yes, my artwork and creativity is on display for the world to see. Well, the world of Topeka anyway. It was a good feeling and people were complimenting me. I felt like I had worth for the first time in a long while. I could picture my painting being hung in houses clear across Kansas and people coming to visit and saying, "Wow! I love your painting, where did you get it?" And my name being spoken; my fingers creating and moving colors from brush to canvas, from white plain pockets to colors bursting with emotion. Yes, yesterday was the happiest day of my life thus far!

I reread the essay and then Mark said it was time to turn in section one and take a fifteen minute break before going to the science and math portion. That was the part I loathed. Numbers and I just didn't mix. I walked outside and talked to one of the girls who was nervous about passing the test. Her high pitched voice was annoying, and I wondered why so many people seemed to bother me. Maybe it was just my hormones and the pregnancy. I took some peanut butter and crackers out of my purse and ate a couple, then went to the bathroom before going back to my seat. Mark has a stack of fresh new tests to hand out. I noticed he seemed tired. It was his last semester of school, and he had a lot going on.

I didn't know why I felt safe with him. It was not like how I felt when I was with Dillon but a different kind of safe. I sure missed Dillon and even Daddy a little, but I was becoming more used to life in Kansas, and more used to the idea of having this baby alone. I knew I had the support of Miss Renée and Alice. Miss Renée was helping me realize that God has everything under His control and nothing happened by mistake.

The first section of the test was pretty simple, but the last part was very difficult. Mark gave us all scrap paper to work out the math equations. I filled the front and back so quickly that I had to ask for more. By the time the test was over, I was exhausted. I couldn't wait to get home and lie down and eat something.

After Mark collected the tests he told us our results would take a few weeks and not to fret. He tried to reassure us that we all did well. Then we were dismissed. I was putting my things away and collecting my purse and books when I looked up to find Mark there, standing beside my desk.

"Jade, how are things going for you?" He smiled but looked concerned. His curly blond hair and peaceful eyes were quite attractive. I could see concern and kindness there.

"I'm good just really tired; this baby is draining me."

"When is the baby due?"

"His due date is in January, right after the holidays."

Mark smiled and looked up quizzically, "And how do you know it's a boy?"

"Oh well, that's a kind of strange story. Have you ever met a prophet or prophetess?"

"No, Jade, I can't say I have? Is that like a fortune teller?" He wrinkled up his nose and waited to hear my reply.

"It's kinda like that, but they get their answers from God directly. Fortune tellers get their answers from the evil one. At least that's what Miss Renée said. She is my godmother, sort of. She took me in when I had nowhere else to go. I live with her and her niece."

"I see, do you have any family here?"

"No, not really, Mark. I have a brother on the other side of town, but he doesn't know I'm here."

"Lot of secrets you're holding onto, huh Jade?"

"Yeah, I seem to have my share of secrets, what about you? Any skeletons in your closet?"

"Me?" He shook his head and grinned. "I think my life is pretty dull. I'm an only child. Never had many friends in school and never played sports or seemed to like the things other young men my age did. I was strangely content with a room full of books and a quiet evening alone listening to music or watching the television. I've been told I have an old soul."

"Old soul, huh?" I knew about those and was surprised at how fast I had grown to like this guy. "How old are you?"

He smiled and looked up at the ceiling. "I'm twenty-four going on forty!" I laughed and knew exactly what he meant. He continued, "My parents had me late in life. I was the only child in school who everyone thought was being raised by their grandparents. I never seemed to fit in anywhere and so I just kind of kept to myself. Didn't do much for my social life. To this day, I haven't had a girlfriend unless I count Mandy, who at the age of five got a kick out of playing "house" with me. And then there was Carly, who kissed me at the Junior Prom." He chuckled and I could picture him, a little boy with a head full of golden curls and big almond eyes playing with his little friend Mandy. "I guess we have had very different backgrounds."

"Yes, Mark it seems that way. My mama got married young and my daddy, well, he was handsome and carefree, but after the Korean War he was never the same. Drinking just took over his life. After my mama died, my daddy met a new woman faster than I could have ever imagined. The whole thing was horrible. The endless parties and drinking became tiresome. My brother left me to deal with it all and started a new life out here with my uncle."

"That sounds pretty tough for you, Jade." He looked at me with such sincerity. "It sounds difficult," he said again, as he waited for me to agree. But instead I felt my heart racing and I felt overcome by the memories of Conner and his filthy voice mumbling in my ears, "shhhh I can make you feel so good, Jade."

And then for no reason at all I blurted out, "My daddy's friend raped me."

After I said it we just stood there in an awkward silence. An uncomfortable look came over Mark's face. He cleared his throat and walked back to the desk to collect his things. I felt so stupid for opening my big fat mouth, and I wanted to hide under a plank in the floor like in *The Tell-Tale Heart*. Then he turned back towards me and looked straight at me and said, "Jade, that is so horrible. I am so sorry that happened to you. I'm sorry that your first experience with sex was something so violating and frightening. I want you to know I am here for you. I promise I will never tell a soul, nor will I ever place a hand on you. You can trust me." His eyes looked so hurt as if he could feel my pain.

Suddenly, I wanted him to hold me. I wanted him to make all the pain go away more than anything. Without thought, I was walking towards him and waiting for him to open his arms and he did as if it were the most ordinary thing for him to do. As if we had known each other a lifetime ago and Mark was the strong man who could make all the pain go away. I cried and laid my head on his chest, but as quickly as I had allowed him into my space and my secrets, I turned and ran. I grabbed my purse and took off down the sidewalk with him calling for me to wait. With each step, I tried to pound the pain away as I had before. With each step, I pictured Conner's face and my big feet stomping him. I was so afraid that my baby came from him. It was a constant torment. I would be relieved to know once and for all whose baby this was. I was starting to realize that it wasn't because I loved Dillon that I slept with him, it was because I wanted someone to hold me and make the pain stop. I needed someone to help my heart heal. I slowed my pace and exhaled, trying to forget the night Conner had stolen my peace. Under the planks of my tell-tale heart was another tiny heartbeat and me trying to figure it all out.

"Dear God, it's me, Jade, Do you think you could hold my heart in the palm of your hand for a bit. It won't stop bleeding."

Chapter 26

The letter arrived on a Monday. That was the day Suzy had called to tell me she had sold the two ocean scene paintings. I was excited that they had sold so quickly and realized now that my GED was out of the way. I needed to get back to painting.

The letter was addressed to Miss Renée, and I guessed the truth was coming out. I could not stay hidden in the darkness with my deep secrets forever. Ed and Johnny had written inquiring about me. They wanted to know if I was living there and what was going on with me. Daddy had been calling and they were trying to piece it all together. Ed's wife, Julie, had spotted my artwork at the coffee shop and told Johnny and Uncle Ed all about it. They wanted to know if they could come by and talk to Miss Renée about the situation. Miss Renée held the letter and looked up at me.

"Jade, you are an adult now. You do not have to tell your family a thing. This is between you and God. If you think this is going to cause more anxiety and stress on you and the baby, well, I would wait. But you have to make your own decisions."

I lowered my head and waited for the spinning to stop. I had already replayed each scenario in my head: Johnny and Uncle Ed wanting to know who the father was, daddy calling me a two-bit whore, and Verdi popping her gum, nodding her empty head in agreement. I was so over all the drama. All I wanted to do was live in a cave until the baby came. I had to decide if adoption was for me. Could I hand my baby over to a complete stranger and live with that decision? Not knowing who was taking care of him? I just couldn't decide what to do next.

"I don't know Miss Renée. I don't think I'm ready for all of this just yet. I'm sorry if I have caused you any trouble with my family."

"No, no, Jade its fine. We will get through this and you have less than three months till the baby comes anyway."

"I don't know if I want to keep the baby," I said softly.

"Not keep the baby? Have you lost your mind? That's a gift from God."

"Is it?" I looked up thinking about Conner and his evil smile, his breath on my chest and in my ears, and his fingers that invaded spaces not meant for him. "How is rape a gift from God?" I asked rather boldly, considering I needed a place to live.

"Jade, God makes all things work together for good, even bad things like rape. God is forming this baby in your womb. This baby could be the next president of the United States, this baby could find a cure for cancer or start a new movement that changes the world and the way we see it. He could be the next Martin Luther King. This baby has worth."

"Miss Renée, you said God was in control. Well, how in the heck is He in control of everything if I am allowed to be raped?"

She studied me for a minute and then said, "Jade, you listen here, I will only say this once. The steps of a good person are ordered of the Lord. His word says if you keep His commandments and if you fear Him and walk in His ways, then you will abide under His shadow. Your daddy didn't keep the Lord's commandments or he wouldn't have had that women move in the house like he did, and he wouldn't have had his drunken friends there in the first place. Drunkenness causes nothing good. Drinking a drink isn't wrong, but drunkenness just leads to shame. Take my word for it. I ain't always been a Godly woman. You don't know what all I have done in my past. Why do you think I never judged your situation? Have you ever thought I might have been you once upon a time? And besides that, God let's life live and in this world we will have problems."

She made sense, but I still knew bad things happened to good people. Most the good people I met at her church blamed all the bad on Satan, but then quoted verses about how if you resist the devil he would flee. I couldn't argue with her. Daddy had opened the door and said, "Hey devil come on in." The devil wore a mini-skirt that day. I felt like I was drowning.

Two days went by and I kept to myself in my room. I read the whole gospel of John and prayed to a God that once again felt a million miles away. I painted pictures of flowers and fields of sunflowers. I painted landscapes and I painted people I didn't know. One canvas displayed women with dark eyes draped in veils, their eyes peeping out from behind a sheer fabric. I painted pictures for the baby boutique of clowns and teddy bears with pink and blue hues.

Then on Monday I received another letter. This time it was from Congress and had a golden seal stating I had received my GED. I was excited and relieved. Along with that envelope was a personal letter from Mark:

Dear Jade,

Hope this letter finds you well. I took the liberty of taking your books home with me and you also left your journal. I can drop them off to you or you may come and pick them up anytime. My address is 1671 South Millard Street. Apartment 3. My phone number is

228-3451. I hope that you will let me know when the baby arrives so I can meet him.

Your friend,

Mark

I couldn't believe he had written me. I suddenly felt like going to his house, but I had no idea how to get there and I didn't want to tell Miss Renée. I was so lonely, and I longed for companionship. But what could Mark possibly see in me? I was getting bigger every day and my freckles were multiplying from the summer sun. I hadn't taken a notion of fixing my hair or applying makeup in months. I sighed and looked into the mirror over my dresser. It was hopeless. I decided to write Dillon a letter and give him my address. I wanted to see how he was doing and how college was treating him. I missed him and his smile. I was torn between what to do and who to allow into my life.

Dillon,

Hello, I hope you are enjoying school and that things are going just perfect. I miss you.

I marked out I miss you and put this.

I'm living in Topeka with Johnny. It's nice here, but I miss Braxton. Will you be going home soon to visit? I am painting pictures and selling them in shops around town. Life is great.

Love Jade." …I marked out love and put, "*Your friend.*"

Chapter 27

The following day I showered and put on makeup. I cleaned the whole house and organized the kitchen cabinets. I watched the children while Miss Renée and Alice went to the grocery. I curled my hair and then anticipated their arrival so I could see Mark. I picked up the phone and set it down. I picked it up again and dialed the number nervously.

"Hello"

"Uhh hello, Mark, it's me, Jade."

"Well, hello Jade, how are you?"

"I'm fine and you?"

"Good, I see you received my letter?"

"Yes, I got it a couple days ago and I passed my GED too."

"That's great Jade, I'm so proud of you."

"Did you want to come and pick up your things?"

"Yeah, that would be good," I said a little too fast. "When is a good time for you, Mark? I don't want to interfere with your plans."

"Jade, you know I don't have any plans. I'm a loner remember?"

I chuckled. "Well, how do I get to your place?"

"It's easy Jade. If you need a ride I could come and get you?"

"Really, okay well, I'm babysitting right now, so in about an hour. Would that be okay?"

"Sure," he said, and then there was an awkward silence. "Okay. So I'll let you get back to the children, and I'll see you in about an hour."

"Okay Mark, see you then." I hung up the phone and felt rather nervous but a good nervous.

Miss Renée came home and looked at the house and the children I had bathed and the kitchen that sparkled. She seemed rather pleased.

"I'm goin' out for a bit tonight."

"Oh really, where are you going?

"I'm going over to my GED teacher's place to get my things."

"Oh, do you need a ride?"

I thought about that for a minute and suddenly realized that if Mark was picking me up he could just drop off my things and then there would be no need for us to be together. "No, um, he's picking me up."

"Oh really." Miss Renée's eyes widened and I wondered what secret God was telling her about my heart and what secrets she probably already knew about Mark.

"Jade, is this a date?"

"No, Miss Renée, why would a man want to date me? I'm pregnant and don't even know who the father is?"

"Now, Jade quit beating yourself up. You're a lovely girl and many a man would want to spend time with you. My concern is that it may be too soon."

I wasn't sure what she meant by that, but I just shook my head and started putting the groceries away. Alice walked into the room and looked me over. "Well look at you, don't you look lovely."

I said "thanks" and then felt rather stupid as if I was trying to impress Mark with my makeup and hair curled. I felt as if I needed a veil like the women I had painted, something to hide behind. I finished unloading the bags of food and waited for Mark to arrive. The doorbell rang and I sprung up and grabbed my purse to leave.

"Now, you just wait a minute, Jade. I want to meet this fellow." Miss Renée eyed me with her eyes of wisdom, and I knew she would get some kind of feeling about his character.

She opened the door and held out her hand, "Hello. I'm Renée, and you must be Mark."

"Yes, nice to meet you," he said nervously, his shoulders slumped down and his lanky frame towering over Miss Renée. He had my books in his arm and he handed them to me.

"Oh, thanks. Well, I guess there's no need for you to take me to your place, thanks for bringing these back. I guess I had a lot on my mind that day of the test."

"Yeah, I know what you mean. But I was wondering if you might like to go out for a bite to eat or get ice cream and just talk." He lowered his head almost shy-like and I said I would love to, again a little too quickly.

Miss Renée told him to be careful and that she would see me later on. I knew that meant don't stay out all night. Be a lady. Her eyes always gave her away.

Mark opened the car door for me, and we drove downtown to the ice cream parlor. I ordered a strawberry shake, and he got a plate of French fries for us to share. The weather was perfect and before I knew it he was talking about my essay paper. “I have a confession to make,” he said. “I read your essay paper on the GED test.”

“You did?” I wondered what he thought.

“I loved it!”

“Really?” I was shocked that an articulate writer with his education would find it the least bit interesting.

We finished our shakes, and he wanted to show me where he lived. It wasn’t that far from Miss Renée’s really, only about four miles. The apartment was small with hardwood floors and a super tiny kitchen as the entrance. We walked through the kitchen into the living room and Mark put his hands over my eyes. “I have a surprise for you, Jade. No peeking until I say so.”

I got a giddy kind of feeling about the same time the baby stuck its foot into my rib. “Okay, Mark.”

“Now!” He said. Then he turned me around facing the back wall, and there above his couch hung my two ocean paintings. I stood there in awe. He had bought them.

“Wow!” I said. “You like my paintings.”

"Yes, after I read your essay I had to check them out and I just fell in love with these two. You are really talented."

I blushed and thanked him. The paintings matched his room, and I felt special that even after knowing about Conner and my whole troubled background he still wanted to be friends. I walked over to his bookcase and discovered there were more books in it than I had ever seen in any home. There were books stacked on coffee tables and end tables. It was like being at the library. I found myself reading the titles and wanting to take some home.

"You're welcome to borrow any books you see, Jade."

"Really?" I smiled and looked up at him.

"Yes, really." He chuckled and said, "You might just be the loveliest pregnant woman I've ever seen." His eyes pierced mine, and I felt a wave of emotion flood me.

"Uhh, well, that's kind of you to say, Mark, but pregnant women aren't really very attractive. I mean, they are big, and not very graceful, not to mention dumpy."

"Jade, look at me." I suddenly remembered my daddy's voice telling my mama to look into his eyes so that he could hypnotize her and feed her lies. I shifted uncomfortably and bent down to read more book titles.

"Jade, you have a beautiful life inside of you and you glow. I know you don't trust men and I for one don't blame you, but I'm sticking with my thoughts on this one, you are beautiful."

I wanted to run. I wanted to scream. I wanted to let him hold me again. I was such a basket case. There had been too many men who had destroyed my trust and my worth and had left me with scars that ran deep. I knew that much. But could I trust Mark? I looked at him and felt that feeling again of safety.

I walked over to the couch and sat down next to him with a stack of books on my lap. I read the titles out loud, *The View from Pompey's Head, Don't go Near the Water, and The Scapegoat*.

"What's a scapegoat?" I quizzed Mark.

"A scapegoat is someone who gets the blame for something

other people did. They are innocent, but they take the fault and often the pain that other people give them."

I looked down at my belly and saw a connection. I thought "what if I wasn't pregnant and Mark and I were dating?" But then I would have never met him because I would still be in Braxton.

The sun was setting, and I knew I had better get back home.

"I have to leave shortly, Mark." I looked at him and he looked at me and there seemed to be some sort of chemistry there, but I still felt so worthless. There was still a part of me that felt like a whore. "Thank you for everything, and thank you for purchasing the paintings." I smiled at him and felt good about the evening. All in all, it had been nice.

"Jade, I would have bought these paintings even if I didn't know you. The paintings are just spectacular. I mean that." He offered to lend me some books to read.

"I don't want to lose them or damage them in any way."

"Jade its fine, I have lots of books, and anyway, it will give me a reason to see you again." I found myself blushing more and more at his compliments. He didn't seem like he was only twenty-four years old but much older and much wiser.

We rose from the couch and I made my way to the restroom. I had to empty my bladder which was constantly being squeezed as the baby grew larger each day. The bathroom was painted tan and there were men's soaps and razors on the sink. The shower curtain had a black and brown stripe and there was a picture of a funny penguin on the wall. In the corner was a basket with newspapers and magazines, "More reading material." I thought to myself.

We drove back to Miss Renée's in silence, but it was a good silence. I was happy that he had not tried to kiss me or touch me in any way, but then it made me sad too, for reasons I didn't understand.

"Thanks, Mark. I had a terrific time," I said as I opened my door.

"Wait just a minute." He hurried around to my car door, took my hand and helped me out. Then he walked me up to the porch and said goodbye. It was very gentlemanly and yet it was strange. "I had a great time too, Jade. See you again?"

"Of course," I replied. I opened the door and watched his gangly body mosey to the car and drive slowly away.

Chapter 28

I opened the new diary I had purchased at the store. It was black with gold edging and in gold calligraphy letters said, *"Diary."* I found myself needing to venture back to where I came from, to realize who I was becoming and where I was headed. I wanted to write down my goals and dreams for the future. I needed something to work for and #1 on my list was a home. I longed for my own place. This was probably not what most eighteen-year-old girls thought about, but for me it was a constant nagging. I never, not even as a small child, felt like I had a place called "home." I was perplexed when I heard other people say things like, "I can't wait to get back home" or "there is no place like home." I wondered what that felt like? I thought it must mean safety, warmth, and a comforting feeling of being where I belong. A place, where I am wanted. I had never had that in the house where I grew up and found myself dreading the summer breaks from school.

Even as a young child, the main emotion was anxiety. I feared Daddy and his hands and voice that seemed to hurt everything he touched. I feared the screaming and the fighting. I also was made aware of every morsel of food I ate and how much water I used. Daddy was always making me feel bad about how much things cost. I wasn't allowed to take a bath every day. He said we used too much water. We spot washed most the time with a little water in the sink. I didn't eat anything extra, and there were no snacks. I made sure my dab of shampoo and toothpaste were as small as possible. There was always a feeling inside my soul that said, "Jade, you don't belong here, you are not welcome here and this isn't your space, you have to leave as soon as you can because your very presence makes them unhappy. They already are lacking and you are just one more reminder of that lack." I hated feeling like that and instead of saying things like, "I can't wait to get home" I said things like, "I can't wait to leave home."

Now that I lived with Miss Renée, I still had by no means learned to relax. I had never sighed with relief. Oh, I sighed all the time, but not that one soft long sigh that resonates peace throughout a body, a sigh with no guilt or shame mixed in. One day I'd get a place, and it would be filled with my artwork and I would be in control. I longed for a place with soft air that I could easily breathe in. My mama and daddy's house had leprosy in the walls and air so thick it caught me in the throat and strangled my voice. I longed for a home where I had the authority to say who could and could not enter. I had yet to experience that, but I desperately wanted to.

Miss Renée and Alice had been saints to me and had let me stay there when I had nowhere to go, and I knew I must repay them for their kindness. The forty dollars I had gotten from selling the ocean paintings to Mark would be a start. I was weary of eating food bought by other hands, and the money Mama had left me was quickly used up. Funny how money seems to always find you just about the time you'd given up on it coming at all.

I stopped looking for any letters from Dillon, as it had been weeks, but then one arrived in the mailbox. I was afraid to read it for some reason, so I sat it on my nightstand and left it there most the day. By six o'clock I had made peace with the outcome and was ready to read his words. I opened the envelope and pulled the letter out. It was written with the neatest penmanship I'd ever seen and his words started out very joyfully:

Dearest Jade,

I sure hope this letter finds you well. I am enjoying school and learning so much. I have a part-time job at the college doing janitor work and the rest of the time I spend studying. I pine for Miss Rita and the store and especially you. I have replayed the last night we spent together over and over again in my head. You are beautiful, Jade, and timeless. I hope this doesn't hurt you none, but I do need to be most honest with you.

You see, Jade, I've met someone and she is very special to me. I want you to meet her. Her name is Judy and she is going to school to be a nurse. Many Negroes are entering colleges now and the times is changing drastically. I still get upset over hatred of my people but things are changing for us. I hope you are okay. I was glad to read the postage and to know that you are safe from Conner and that town. I hope you know that I love you Jade, truly I do, but we can never be. This world would not allow us to be happy. This world is too cruel and too ignorant to realize love isn't about color. I wish nothing but the best for you.

Dillon

I held the letter and then I raised it to my nose and sniffed the paper. I could still smell the scent of him. "Judy." I said the name silently and then out loud, "Judy, Judy." I sat and stared out the window and felt a single tear travel down my cheek and drip atop my now very protruding belly. I decided not to write Dillon back, but to just let him be. Time and circumstances change us all, and I was sure his life would flourish without my drama. Besides, it was my fault he'd slept with me. I was the one trying to cover all of Conner's evil fingerprints with his good ones.

It was Thursday and I had a fresh canvas and a desire to paint fish and water. I wanted to cover the canvas with dancing fish that were more colorful than any tropical fish I'd ever seen. I desired to paint the old man in his boat who was unlucky and Jonah who was even worse off. I would paint a large fish with his mouth agape and Jonah's legs dangling out of the side. I felt hungry to paint as if getting it all out on canvas would wash Judy away, like dipping my paint brush in the water and removing the color red to dip in green. I would paint until my soul was eased, and I could erase the memory of a man whose caramel eyes had held me still, and whose voice had soothed me and gave me hope in men.

Dillon had taught me that all men weren't as evil as my daddy or Conner. He had given me a belief that possibly somewhere there truly was a man that could respect and care for me. Maybe I was carrying that man in my belly. I could raise him to cherish women and treat them with respect.

It was a warm day, so I decided I should take advantage of it and sit on the front porch in the fresh air. I pushed open the front door and sat down with a grape soda and the Bible Miss Renée had given me. My method of reading was not to Miss Renee's liking. She said I needed to start with the New Testament and read through, but I just kept flipping through randomly. I laid the Bible atop my knees and opened it up to a random spot and began to read Judges 4:21.

"Then, Jael, Heber's wife took a nail of the tent and took a hammer in her hand and went softly unto him, and smote the nail into his temples, and fastened it into the ground: for he was fast asleep and weary. So he died."

I pictured Conner, smiling at me with those lustful eyes, rubbing his filthy hands on me, closing his eyes softly and dreaming about my soft skin. I had a huge nail, almost like a stake and a hammer made of steel with a huge ball on the end. I would pat his hair and smooth it back from his face and whisper shushing sounds in his ear just like he did to me before he raped me. Then I would hover over his head and raise the nail and drive it through his temple. It made me shudder that I could think such things. I heard a child giggling from inside the house as Alice and Miss Renée were playing with the girls. I couldn't keep thinking such evil thoughts while carrying this baby. I had to forgive him for the sake of the tiny heart that was beating inside me. I looked around at the small houses that lined the street, with their potted flowers on the porches, and again, wished I had one that belonged to me.

"One day, Jade, you will have one bigger than any of these and it will overlook the sea and you can watch the wave's crash upon the shoreline while you paint beautiful pictures to sell to the tourists." Yes, I was going to affirm my future until it became reality. I smoothed my hand over my tummy and said, "And John Isaac you will play beautiful music on the piano while I paint and you will be as your name, "Laughter."

About the time I had said it, a car pulled in front of the house, and to my dismay there stood Johnny and Uncle Ed. I looked down at the bump that could no longer be hidden from anyone and I felt my heart slip down to my shoes.

"Jade, what are you doing here?" Johnny said with a perplexed look.

"I live here Johnny. This is my home now." I pushed strands of hair behind my ear and waited with fear for their expressions when they noticed my condition. Johnny and Ed walked up the sidewalk and up the first four steps that led to the porch. I didn't get up but kept my Bible over my lap wanting to prolong the moment.

"Jade, why didn't you tell us at the bus terminal that you didn't have any…" I stood up and stopped Uncle Ed in mid-sentence. As he finished up the rest of his thought ...notion of going back home?" He said in a slow calculated manner, all the while with his eyes glued to my tummy. He looked at me sharply and then looked away. Johnny's eyes became rounded with shock, then his pale blue eyes seemed to say more than words could.

"Should I even ask who the father is?" Ed said this with a look of hurt, or maybe it was repulsion. About that time Miss Renée walked out front and her presence enveloped the air, as it had a tendency to do. It was as if she carried an authority about her, an inner power none of the rest of us had learned how to access.

"Well, hello gentleman, my name is Renée, can I help ya'll?"

I spoke then, nervously, "Miss Renée, I'd like for you to meet my brother, uh, this is Johnny and this is my Uncle Ed. This is my friend, Miss Renée."

"Pleasure to meet you both," she said. She smiled as her blond hair was catching the sunlight and giving her cheeks a rosy flush. Her eyes, blue as the cloudless sky, twinkled and smiled along with her. "Would you two like some iced tea? I made it fresh just a while ago."

Uncle Ed spoke first, "No, we just came by to see about Jade. We saw her paintings in the window with this address listed. We just wanted to check on her. Her Daddy's been awful worried about her. He's beside himself, you know."

Ed looked at Miss Renée as if she did know, and then at my stomach and then quickly he allowed his eyes to settle on mine before he looked away again. This time, I knew it was disgust and not hurt. Miss Renée's voice began to boom, not with loudness, but again with that air of priesthood that only the Lord could ordain. Her voice held a power that I had never felt. She looked at Ed and then at Johnny and studied their eyes before she said, "I wasn't aware her father was worried about her. The way I see it, her condition is due to his addiction problems and the company he allowed around Miss Jade. Now if ya'll have some words of encouragement, please have yourself a seat. But, if you don't, then please see yourselves safely off my property." Miss Renée looked intently into Ed's eyes and then Johnny's. I saw their countenance change and even their posture. I was speechless and thought "Boy oh boy, she can drive tent nails just like Jael." I never had felt the emotions I was feeling. No one had ever spoken up for me or on my behalf with such force. Johnny looked down for a minute and shook his head and then walked up to the porch and sat down next to me. "You okay, Jade?" I nodded my head unsure of what I was feeling. He then leaned over and gave me a hug. "Well, do you got a name picked out yet Sissy?"

"I sure do. I'm naming him after my favorite brother, yep, gonna call him John." I waited, hoping he'd be proud.

Johnny smiled, his lips showing joy and his powder blue eyes gleaming. My heart sunk a bit as I was reminded that this child may be darker skinned than Johnny. Ed seemed to take Miss Renée's words to heart. I believe he thought about his dead sister for a minute and the hell my daddy had put her through and decided to take it easy on me.

"We want to help in any way, Jade. If you need anything for the baby or just anything at all, don't you hesitate to call us?"

"Thanks, Ed, that is very kind of you, and now that you and Johnny know where I am staying, please do come by anytime." We talked on a few minutes about my paintings and other safe subjects. Then, hugs all around and they were gone.

I glanced shyly over at Miss Renée who was pulling dead leaves off her flowers by the porch. She was pulling up weeds that had grown in the bed and were trying to choke her plants. I loved her so much, even if I did feel like a burden to her at times. I knew she was a woman of power and might, a special gift from God and I knew she loved me. She raised her hands in the air and she looked up at the sky and said, "Thank you Holy Spirit, thank you, Jesus, yes Lord, yes Lord, I see you've got your gaze upon me."

I shook my head and grinned, then found myself looking up at the same sky to see if it looked different. One thing about Miss Renée was she was in her own world. Even when she cleaned the house or was in the shower you could hear her talking up a storm. She'd say things like, "The Lord rebuke you Satan, oh no, you can't have my seed, O the Lord is good and faithful, a very present help in times of trouble." Then, "haseete ana, honia ana see ti ana, shadalangia, hosentianan shactaceandala." And on and on she went. Sometimes she laughed out loud and again she'd say, "Yes, Holy Spirit, thank you, Jesus!" It was as if she had her own safe place she lived in. If folks thought they could step on her toes, they had better get some mighty big shoes. Her charisma and power were amazing! God had given me a new mama, although my mama could never be replaced. Miss Renée was becoming the person closest to me and just like the weeds she was pulling up out of the flower beds, she was pulling up weeds out of my life, weeds that had tried to choke me and strangle my very breath. “Thank you, Holy Spirit,” I said out loud with a smile. Then I picked up my bible and walked inside the house.

Chapter 29

Miss Renée and Alice had taken little Eva to get her booster shot and a monthly check-up. It didn't feel like I had been there for a few months, and I guess that was a good thing. I watched Dory and Tamar while they were gone. After fixing them breakfast and putting their hair in pigtails, I started cleaning up the kitchen and washing the dishes. The girls were good natured and played well together and rarely were any trouble. They loved playing with their dolls and tea set. I was beginning to get used to living here but knew it would not be long before Carl would be returning to his wife and to his home, and then what would I do? I had to try to get through one day at a time. If I thought too much about the future, I would go crazy. The phone rang and I hurried to answer it.

"Hello."

"Well, hello there stranger." It was Mark and I must admit I was happy to hear his voice.

"Hi, Mark, how are you?"

"I'm good, Jade, how are you feeling?"

"I'm about ready to pop." I looked down at my belly and I wasn't exaggerating, I was huge.

Mark chuckled. "Well, I was wondering if you would like to go for a drive. Maybe go down to the diner and share some fries again?"

"I'd love to Mark. How is school coming along?"

"Funny you should ask because I just turned in my thesis paper, and I'm completely finished."

"Wow, that's great! I'm really happy for you."

"You know, Jade, you should think about going to school. You would really do well, I think."

"I don't know about that Mark, but it does sound exciting."

"More and more women are getting jobs in the workplace, and more and more secretary positions are opening up. I think you could do well for yourself and the baby, but I guess we need to wait until after the baby gets here."

"Yeah, I only have a couple months left. But Mark, I have to admit I'm a little scared to have a baby."

"Oh Jade, I'm sure you will be fine. Women have babies every day, and you are going to be a great mother."

"I've thought about putting the baby up for adoption again lately. I just feel overwhelmed at the thought of raising a baby on my own."

"Jade, that's a huge decision, and one that must require a lot of prayers."

"I didn't think you believed in God, Mark?"

"I never said I didn't believe in God; I just have doubts, at times. That's all." I knew what he meant. Many times I had doubts, but as soon as I began to sink into my unbelief Miss Renée would bring me back to my faith.

"Well, what time do you want to go?"

"How about I pick you up at around six?"

"Sounds great Mark, see ya then."

I hung up the phone and went to check on Tamar and Dory. They were acting out a scene from Cinderella, and Dory was trying on shoes, her mother's high heels. Each time she would slip the shoe on Tamar's foot she would say, "No, it doesn't fit." She threw her hands up in the air and said, "Where is the princess?" They were so cute I had to giggle.

The day dragged on and Miss Renée and Alice returned with Eva who slept for almost an hour before awakening with a scream and a leg that was swollen from the shot. Alice said she had a fever, and that was normal. She gave her some medicine and she went back to sleep not long after. There was so much to learn about babies. I wasn't sure I would be able to get it all down.

Once they got home and I was relieved of my babysitting job, I went to work on what to wear, what to do with my hair, and whether to do makeup or go natural. I pressed a dress Alice had given me. It had plenty of room and I liked the color, a green turquoise with a white color at the neck and a white ribbon with long tails that gave an illusion of being slimmer. I fiddled with my hair, not long enough for this, not short enough for that. I went with the straight pageboy look which was hard to achieve with my fairly curly hair. I put mascara on my lashes and a nice coral lipstick, not too dark.

By the time I was finished, Mark arrived and Miss Renée once again met him at the door. This time, she invited him to church on Sunday. He seemed a little bit hesitant, but then smiled and said, "Sure, I'd love to go." We walked outside and I could see that his curly blond hair was turning even whiter from the sun and his eyes were soft and kind.

I looked at him, then said sarcastically, "Going to church, huh?" We both laughed and he poked me gently in the belly.

"Well, I might as well see what all the hype is about."

I wondered why he would even waste his time with a pregnant girl, who didn't even know who the father of the baby was. I knew I was going to have to come clean about sleeping with more than one man, and then what would he think about me? I was sure that would be the last of him. Only the thing was, I had grown to enjoy spending time with him. He was not easy to figure out and that was something I appreciated. Now that Dillon had Judy I knew I needed to let him go.

We pulled into the diner, went on in and found a booth next to the wall. There was a jukebox playing an Elvis song. There were not a lot of patrons that evening. I saw an older couple in a booth by the door. The counter had red leather swivel seats and there were several girls giggling and talking. Two had pigtails and wore skirts. The other one had frizzy brown hair, and she was wearing her brother's Levis rolled up high on the bottoms. She also wore "Cat Eye" glasses which I found quite sophisticated. In another booth, there were three young men, having a meal and eyeing the girls. They were probably too old for them, and when the girls finished their frosted Cokes, they left without the boys even talking to them.

I thought to myself that I should be one of those girls right now and not a mama at my age. But then I remembered that even when I wasn't pregnant, I was never like them.

I felt uncomfortable with my swollen belly and no wedding ring. I had tried wearing Mama's ring, but my fingers were as fat as pork chops now. I wondered if Mark ever felt embarrassed by the fact that the waitress and patrons probably assumed it was his baby and me sitting there with no wedding band on my finger. "Why do you ask me out?" I said it so quickly I wasn't even sure I was going to ask until it was too late.

"Why wouldn't I?" He said it so matter of fact. It was as if he were oblivious to the people's stares or the assumptions they may have.

"Well, for starters, aren't you embarrassed to be seen in public with a pregnant girl who has no wedding ring on?"

"Jade, first of all, I don't know these people and even if I did, it's none of their business. Second of all, you're pregnant, and for all they know your fingers are so swollen that you can't get the damn thing on!"

I lowered my head.

"Jade, you-hoo!!" I looked up at his eyes that were so kind, so loving and wondered how he could be so carefree.

"Yes, Mark." I smiled sideways and waited for his words.

"I am not embarrassed to be seen with the most beautiful green-eyed women in the room, who is carrying the most beautiful life inside her. And, any way you make me smile. I am actually leaving my apartment, which is a huge accomplishment for someone content to not talk to anyone for days. Now let's get a cheeseburger, some fries, and a shake and see if we can find something else to talk about."

My face was beet red and flushed from the compliments he'd given me. I knew I had some explaining to do at some point before this baby came because who knew but God what color his skin would be. I sighed and picked up the menu and pretended to read it, but my head was busy replaying the words he'd spoken. Was I really the most beautiful girl in the room?

Mark made me feel beautiful, even if I wasn't. He seemed so convinced of it. He didn't even seem to notice that my figure resembled the back end of a bus. We ordered our burgers and stayed to finish our shakes and talk. He went on about his plans to teach school and how he wanted to write a book someday. He talked a little about his growing up days and always feeling different. This much we really did have in common, the part about no school friends and burying yourself in school work. I guess because he was being honest, I felt like I could let down some, too. I told Mark about Johnny and me and how bad it was for me when he left so soon after Mama died. I told him about Miss Ellen and Miss Rita, how they each had been a hen's wing I could rest beneath. I told him how God had engineered my bus trip so that Miss Renée would find me and "adopt" me. I told him my fears and my hopes. I didn't reveal anything about Dillon. I just couldn't yet.

The evening wore on in that magical way that time does when people get to know each other. Each one peels off a layer of themselves, to reveal something to the other. Some of it was just facts, like birthplace and hometown, some was funny, some was not too pretty and quite a lot was working on being sad. We shared in a matter of fact sort of a way, no tears or bad regrets cropping up. Each was sympathizing and sometimes identifying, with the other.

Time whizzed on by, the supper crowd came and went, and many of them seemed to know one another. The dinner hour was almost like a big family eating together. When we got up to leave, we realized we were the only people left in the diner. It was late. They stayed open 'til midnight and as we were walking out, a couple of police officers were coming in. I remembered the old saying about finding a good place to eat if the cops or truckers frequented the eatery.

It was passed ten o'clock when I got home, but Miss Renée was lying on the couch waiting for me. Mark came inside with me, and she was up on her feet in an instant making sure all was well. I thought if I had this at home, Connor would have never gotten a hold of me.

Mark said goodnight, and when I said goodnight to Miss Renée and went toward my room -- my little mama was right behind me. She wanted the whole scoop about where we went and what happened. I told her how we talked and shared our life stories and plans for the future, really getting to know each other. She smiled and laughed with me as I shared the highlights. She remarked that every couple should date like this, getting to know each other's minds before they start getting acquainted by Braille.

I laughed at that and said, "Now, you know we are not really dating."

Her expression changed to serious as she nodded, "Oh yes, of course, I know that." Then she told me to get to bed, gave me a kiss on my cheek, and disappeared into the shadows of the sleeping house.

I lay down in bed reminiscing over the evening with Mark.

"Dear God, thank you for sending me to Topeka. I never knew life could be so exciting! I love you. Sincerely Jade."

P.S. "Tell my Mama I miss her."

Chapter 30

Johnny and Uncle Ed must have spilled the beans about my current living situation. I can't say I was completely shocked the day Daddy and Verdi pulled in front of the house. My first inclination was to run and hide, so that is exactly what I did. It felt just like the old days when Johnny and I would run to Cottonwood Farm; only now it was just me, and I wished Johnny were here to save me. I happened to be looking through the linen drapes of the front room window and saw them pull up. Verdi emerged smacking that gum hard as she could go. Daddy was frowning and red in the face. I figured half of Braxton already knew I was knocked up and the other half would know before it was over. I wondered how long it would take for Dillon and Conner to find out, and what their reactions would be.

I fled toward my room as I heard the doorbell ring and Alice answering it much too quickly. I could hear my daddy's muffled voice growling out demands, and I could see Miss Renée coming into the living room with baby Eva in her arms. At this point, I was hiding on the top step peering down on the situation.

"I don't care who you are or where you've driven from. If you use that language again in front of my nieces, I'll have the police escort you off my property!" Miss Renée was in high form and I was starting to shake and not just on the inside, but on the outside, too.

"I want to speak with Jade now. I am her daddy and I have a right for you to let her know I'm here!"

"Mister, the whole street knows you're here! So, if you don't mind holding your horses for just a second, I'll see if your daughter wants to see you." She spewed out more of that authority that I admired so much.

I eased back up the steps and held my stomach as if to protect my baby from the stress that was coming upon me. I heard the steps creak and then Miss Renée's beautiful voice calmly say, "Jade, honey, they're here, and I know you already know that." She was peaking around the corner and could see me. I nodded my head and stared at the floor.

"Jade, you can face them now or you can face them later, but it has to be done. At some point, you are going to have to confront the issues." I knew in my heart she was right. I could prolong the truth and hide the one I was carrying, but it would just continue to feel like I was carrying a load of bricks.

"Will you go with me?" I said, as I wrinkled up my nose and squinted at her.

"You know I will." Miss Renée's eyes looked at me with such strength. Her hair was shining in the light coming through the window and her skin looked so smooth. She held her hand out for me to take and led me down the steps and out to the front porch where she had left them waiting.

I opened the door and walked outside. Verdi looked down at my stomach and shook her empty head. "I told ya' Albert, I told ya she wasn't nothin but a little whore." Verdi popped her gum and stood there in her mini skirt with her bleached blonde hair. It looked like she had gotten a really bad dye job and the color was more yellow than gold.

"Nice to see you, too, Verdi!" I bellowed out with sarcasm.

Miss Renée spoke up, glaring at Verdi. "You sound like a hussy, but I'm sure you are not one, so you won't be calling names while you are here, not to Jade, not to anyone." It looked like Verdi swallowed her gum, and I was hoping she would choke on it.

Daddy eyed my belly, and then looked into my eyes half way before darting into the yard. I could smell him before he even opened his mouth to speak. He reeked of alcohol and tobacco. He turned around to face me and said, "Oh, Jade, look at ya. You done went and got yourself knocked up. Your mama would have cried a river." He then looked at me with such sadness I felt sick at my stomach.

"I'm sorry, Daddy." I said it in a tiny weak voice that was barely audible.

He walked back onto the porch, looked at Miss Renée and said, "Well, are you the boy's mother?"

"No sir, Mr. Gentry, I am most certainly not!"

"Well, then what are you doing here, Jade. Who are these people anyway?" Alice and the girls were standing at the door peering out at Daddy and Verdi and taking in the whole drama being acted out.

"These are my friends Daddy, and I am sorry I have let you down, but there's more to it than you realize. I don't feel like going into that just yet, so if you'll excuse me, I'm going back inside. This cold air isn't good for me."

"Oh, you wait just a dad-burn minute, young lady. You ain't goin' nowhere until I say so." I sighed and wondered how long this exchange could go on. Miss Renée stood rocking the baby and waiting to see the outcome of the situation or until I dismissed her.

"Daddy, what do you want from me? I have been gone for months. I'm no longer a child and I'm no longer in Verdi's house. That's what it has become since Mama died. Yes, I've left you, and now you and Verdi can live happily ever after. I'm not in the way and I'm not going to ask either of you to babysit; you can rest assured on that." I could tell they both had been doing more than drinking. They seemed a little more agitated than normal. I wondered if the marks on Daddy's arm meant Verdi had introduced him to a new drug. She looked thinner and paler than ever.

"We want to know what you did with all that money you took." I stood now in complete shock.

"This is about money?" I said, my jaw dropping.

"Jade, we know you didn't get bus fare free, and we heard you were buying paints and canvas and making a good amount off your work. Now we want the money you stole, and don't lie about it." I was taken aback, my daddy had driven all the way to Kansas to get the money Mama gave me. "I talked to Johnny, I thought he had given you money but he said no, that you had a stash from Mama, but that wasn't yours to take."

I couldn't believe what I was hearing! I felt the angry red rising up my face from the chin up. Miss Renée stepped in just in time.

"You should be ashamed of yourself, driving all the way here, and finding your daughter in this condition, and not even concerned about her or this baby, just concerned about mammon!"

I didn't know what mammon was, but it sounded like something bad. I turned and peered into Miss Renée's blue eyes which were as cold as ice. "Another thing, Mr. Gentry, I bought Jade the paint supplies and the money she makes is hers. She's eighteen now, and if you don't have any other business, you need to hightail it off my property." Miss Renée's face was red now, and she was starting to get hives on her chest.

Verdi took one last drag off her cigarette and stubbed it out under her high heel shoe. "I told ya Albert, told ya she ain't nothin' but a whore and a thief."

Miss Renée made a little squeaking sound in her throat, turned and handed Eva to Alice. She whirled back around and caught Verdi by the arm and hauled her off the porch and back to the car. Oh, but she didn't go quietly. I couldn't stand watching it all. I was angry and hurt and wanted to scream that it was all Daddy's fault anyway.

Daddy just stumbled down the steps and out toward the car. He turned around and took one last look at me with those bloodshot eyes that I had grown accustomed to, and shook his head. He grabbed Verdi away from Miss Renée, and they were both gone in a flash.

I made my way past Alice who tried to console me, but I just needed to be alone and get myself back together and try to collect my thoughts. I brushed past her and made my way upstairs. In a minute, Miss Renée knocked on the door and asked if she could come in. "Yes, it's unlocked," I said, in a sobbing voice. Miss Renée sat down by me and put her arm around my shoulders.

"Jade, it's going to be alright. They don't deserve to be in your life or even to be a part of it. I know it hurts, but you have a Father -- a heavenly Father – who loves you more than anyone ever can or ever will." I wanted to believe her, but it was so hard to believe in something I couldn't see or hear. "I have a scripture for you to read, Jade."

Miss Renée opened the Bible on the table and turned to a passage in Isaiah, *"Fear not, for thou shalt not be ashamed, neither be confounded; for thou shalt not be put to shame: for thou shalt forget the shame of thy youth, and shalt not remember the reproach of thy widowhood any more. For thy Maker is thy husband; the Lord of Hosts is His name;" (54:4—5).*

She told me to read the whole passage. I did read it and I must admit it made me feel better. Then she laid her hand on my belly and began to pray. "Father, we thank you that you have good and perfect plans for Jade and her baby, plans not to do her any harm but to give her a hope and a future. Lord bless this child and bless this mother and heal her heart from all the scars and heal every wound."

Miss Renée rose up off the bed and slipped out of the room pulling the door closed behind her.

I thought about how I had made it through Johnny and Ed and now Daddy and Verdi, so that only left two more. I finally let it release and the ocean of tears came spewing out. I cried until my whole being felt spent, then I fell into a deep sleep.

Chapter 31

The first time I met the Kapolei's was by telephone. It was only about five weeks before my due date, but they were insistent. They had seen my work in town at the coffee shop and wanted me to paint a portrait of their son, and they were willing to pay handsomely for it. This would be my first commissioned work. Even though I was enormously pregnant, I decided that I could not say no. I needed the money desperately.

The day of our first meeting, they sent their driver to pick me up. I opened the front door and there stood a man smartly decked out in a chauffeur's uniform complete with the hat. "Hello there, I'm Henry, Mrs. Kapolei's driver. I've come to pick up Ms. Gentry." I nodded, my eyes as big as the white wall tires on the car.

"Well, did you ever?" Behind him was a long, low black Mercedes limo at the curb. I knew I was definitely going out of my element now.

Henry gave me his arm as he escorted me down the walkway. We drove across town into a neighborhood like nothing I had ever seen before. After driving through an ironwork gate, I saw we were on the grounds of a bona fide mansion. It was way fancier than anything a country girl from Braxton had ever laid eyes on. I only knew of such places in the movies. Henry opened the car door and gave me a hand as I hauled my pregnant bulk out of the comfy back seat. He retrieved my equipment, and by this time Mrs. Kapolei had opened the door herself and was greeting me. Her husband Francis was working, she said.

She explained he owned a large and apparently very profitable trucking company. I stood in awe of their home and their wealth. Their estate was filled with art, sculptures, paintings, and shiny décor. There was a large beautiful vase on a marble stand, Persian rugs, and golden framed mirrors. Mrs. Kapolei was quite delicate and her skin reminded me of flawless china. Her eyes were a pale blue and expressed sadness. Her hair was rolls of soft, blond tufts that fell down her back and draped her body. She talked just as softly as she looked, and when she smiled she reminded me of a statue. "If only I could give my baby to someone as affluent as the

Kapolei's," I thought to myself, looking around at all they had to offer a child growing up.

We were seated and the maid came with fresh glasses of lemonade and some tea cookies. She rushed off and then reappeared with the child, who was the subject of the proposed portrait. His name was Freddy, or Fredrick, as they called him. He was only three. Freddy was nothing like his mother but had taken after his father, Francis. The strong jawline and sharp cleft in his chin gave way to eyes, too huge for a boy his size with eyelashes most girls would covet. His hair was dark and his spirit was too rambunctious for a mother of such delicate constitution to deal with. He was easily drawn to me, my canvas, and palette of colors. I told him if he sat still for me until I was finished sketching him, that he could paint a picture if his mother would approve. His mother's first name was Adeline and she nodded that this would be okay as long as Fredrick changed his clothing and sat outside on the patio. Little Fredrick was sitting cross-legged in a red velvet Queen Anne chair. He had his hair parted on the side and a bow tie with a striped shirt gave him a "silver spoon" appeal. I gave him a dry paintbrush to hold to occupy his mind for a bit as I outlined his silhouette.

I took several photos of him and told Mrs. Kapolei that I would have the finished painting within a couple of weeks. Then, I took Freddy by the hand and helped him out of the chair. The nanny appeared and took him to change his clothes and after several minutes brought him outside to a table where I had paper and watercolors ready for him to use. He was a well-mannered little fellow, and I wondered if Adeline had plans for more children. It seems lately I had become more stressed out over what to do once the baby arrived. I had no home, no real income and no means to support the child. The surroundings were causing me to question everything! Plus I was terrified that I wouldn't be able to even love the baby. If the child reminded me daily of a man who forced himself on me, stalked me and terrified me, how would I get over that?

Adeline came and sat by me. "May I ask how old you are?" She was obviously interested in my condition.

"I'm eighteen, and my baby is due in five weeks on January 28th."

"Oh, I see," she said, staring towards the lake. "I can't have any more children. You see, I almost died giving birth to Fredrick. The doctors said my tubes were tattered and that I needed a hysterectomy. I would love to have another baby for little Fredrick, but of course it would have to be by adoption. My husband, Frances, has been leery of just jumping in and not knowing anything about the parent's background or their medical history. I'm sure you understand our position." I nodded as she continued to talk.

My heart literally leaped inside my chest at her words. Could it be a divine appointment that I was here? Renée was always telling me that my steps were ordered of the Lord. Perhaps this is God's way of allowing someone else to raise my baby. I looked up at Adeline, as she continued to fill me in on her desire to have more children. Her child-like demeanor didn't help the heaviness that still lingered from her words of barrenness.

"Oh, I'm so sorry to hear that."

Her blue eyes looked even sadder than before. Her pain was thinly veiled. "Are you married?" she asked shyly.

"I'm widowed." I lied. I knew I'd have to confess on Sunday, and Mark was supposed to be going to the service, but I just kept rambling. "My husband died in the Army."

"Oh, dear, how dreadful, and you are so young. You must be terribly frightened about giving birth so soon without the father." I suddenly felt queasy, but the lies kept flowing. I surveyed the pool house and enclosed area that led out toward the lake and boat dock. I thought of the money they would probably be willing to pay for a baby and the opportunities of a good education they could offer a child.

Adeline seemed to sit up straighter and carefully study me.

I decided to confront Mrs. Kapolei. "Well, Adeline, I have thought about adoption, but I'm not really sure how that sort of thing works. I know there are many people who are longing to have children and can't. Finding a couple that I would trust enough to hand over my baby to would be difficult at best. I don't want to have any regrets. I think you understand my fear."

Fredrick was busy painting strokes of red all over the paper. I cleaned his brush and dipped it into the blue for him. He was having a fine time. I was waiting to see if Mrs. Kapolei was interested in me and my baby. Suddenly she began to open up more to me about her wishes.

"Jade, Mr. Kapolei and I have often talked about adopting a little girl or boy but have been waiting for the right timing. We just would prefer an adoption that allows us to become more personal with the mother in order to learn more about her family history, mental and physical health issues and background. We just want to make sure we find the right fit for our family. You understand our concerns I'm sure. As I said before, Francis is leery of taking in a child whose parents we know nothing about.

I nodded and wondered how she might feel if she knew my child might be labeled as "half-breed." I kept quiet about that, of course. I knew I couldn't give this child the things the Kapolei's could, and for that I was hopeful that perhaps this was an open door. Adeline continued to probe me about my upbringing and social status. She seemed to be thinking out loud, as I continued to give her partial truths. Instead of disclosing the dark home life I endured under my father's abuse, I described Ellen Cotton and her home filled with light and love. I described friendly dogs cuddling up and lulling me to sleep and sunflowers waving from the window sill.

"Jade, if you decide that's what you want to do, please let me know. I mean we might consider. You are a beautiful, gifted young lady and many couples would be honored to raise your child. So, do let us know." She continued to study me and delve deeper into my life in Braxton prior to Topeka. "Jade, I'll speak to my husband and perhaps we can discuss this further."

"Yes, Adeline, thank you. I will let you know." I collected my paints and brushes and made my way through the foyer. I still had so many questions in my heart. If I were able to give my baby to this family would I get updates or pictures? Would it be antagonizing and painful, ultimately turning me into an inquisitive detective who secretly spied on this family? After bending down and shaking hands with Fredrick, I was escorted by the driver to the big, black shiny Mercedes. As we drove through the gated area I wondered what it would be like to live in such a mansion and have servants who waited on me. I could hardly believe that such wealth existed, after being raised as I was in Braxton. Living in that spirit of deprivation, I couldn't even fathom such a life. The car circled into the driveway and once again I was helped out and given my art supplies. The driver raised his cap and wished me farewells.

I was happy to be back at Alice and Renée's where it was comfortable and cozy. The rooms were not filled with fragile artifacts from around the globe but instead were filled with laughter and light and a peace I had never known. I marveled at what life would be like growing up with such privileged circumstances. I wondered if I could even give Conner's baby away to such a sanitized, stiff world, knowing that the baby also was a part of me. I knew it was time to come clean with Mark and tell him the whole truth and nothing but the truth. I had told so many lies to so many different people, I couldn't seem to keep the stories straight. I walked up the steps and wondered what fate awaited this baby and me. Each step up, with each added pound, it all seemed to keep getting more difficult. I sighed.

"Dear God, it's me, Jade. Do you think you could whisper in my ear like you did to the fish who swallowed Jonah? I don't know what to do about this baby."

Chapter 32

Mark arrived early and he was a little overdressed, but in a nice way. I was so big and miserable at this point finding anything to cover me was an achievement. Alice had given me a blue dress that brought the green out in my eyes. I had to admit that even though my calves were swollen and my face was just as puffy, I had a sparkle in my eyes I hadn't seen in a while.

"Hello, Brother Mark," I said with a smile. Accentuating "brother."

"Well, good morning, Sister Jade."

"Are you ready to meet Pastor Jonas?"

"Am I ever!" He smiled and his charming personality had a way of making me forget that I had any problems.

Miss Renée said, "We can't all ride together with the girls and all, so Mark, I guess you can just follow us." Mark nodded and I reached for my Bible and followed the train of little girls outside. He walked to the passenger side and opened the door for me as I waddled to catch up with him.

The choir was already singing by the time we arrived, and the song was about a tree planted by waters that couldn't be moved. The chorus repeated, "I shall not be moved" over and over again. Mark seemed to be taking inventory and soaking it all in. Some of the people were saying, "That's right Lord, I shall not be moved!" Others were raising their hands in the air and just singing quietly. Dory and Tamar were in Sunday school class, and the baby was being held by Alice. I wanted to just hold the baby and block out the service. If I held the baby, I didn't have to participate in raising my hands or singing or even listening to Pastor Jonas. I could escape and patiently wait until it was over. Besides that, my heart was racing due to sitting this close to Mark and how handsome he looked. I also knew that I had not gotten over last week's episode at the altar about speaking in a language called the "Holy Ghost."

Pastor Jonas had everyone open their Bible to Job chapter 38:4-11 and stand for the reading. "God is speaking to a man named Job after he has lost his health, children, and riches over a test with the devil.

God said to Job,

'Where were you when I laid the foundations of the earth?

"Tell me, if you know so much.

Who determined its dimensions

and stretched out the surveying line?

What supports its foundations,

and who laid its cornerstone

as the morning stars sang together

and all the angels[a] shouted for joy?

"Who kept the sea inside its boundaries

as it burst from the womb,

and as I clothed it with clouds

and wrapped it in thick darkness?

For I locked it behind barred gates,

limiting its shores.

I said, 'This far and no farther will you come.

Here your proud waves must stop!'"

Jonas looked out at the congregation and said, "How many of you can answer such questions? Stand and look at the ocean and feel its strength and depth and let me know if you could ever create such glory? No, brothers and sisters, we couldn't even create the sand it sits on. I believe creation has to have a Creator. God asked Job if he gave the peacock its beautiful iridescence feathers and if a hawk flies by his wisdom."

Look around you at His handiwork!

I sat listening and I must admit he had my attention. I turned towards Mark who seemed to be engrossed as well and waited to see where Pastor Jonas was going with this. "You either believe it or you don't. You either believe God is all powerful and all mighty or that we evolved from apes." I wondered if Mark was struggling still with whether there was a God or if Pastor Jonas was convincing him otherwise.

His voice was rising higher and louder with each question. Sweat trickled down his forehead and he wiped it with a handkerchief. I sat and stared ahead thinking about how Pastor Jonas was making me think about how amazing a peacock looked with its iridescent turquoise feathers. I wanted Mark to like the sermon and I wanted him to have faith, faith that my daddy never could grasp and faith that my mama let slip through her delicate heart.

"You either believe that Mary was a virgin and conceived by the Holy Spirit, or you don't. You either believe Jesus is the son of God or you don't. You either believe He died a horrible death on a cross for your sins or you don't. You either believe He rose from the dead on the third day or you don't." The church was silent. There were no "amen's" or "hallelujahs," only people engrossed in the sermon. No one that I could see was even moving around.

"You either believe that He is coming back again with ten thousand of his saints or you don't. You either fear him or you don't. But I have news for you today, my friends, it doesn't matter if you believe or you don't. One day every knee will bow and every tongue will confess that Jesus Christ is Lord. Are you ready to make him Lord of your life?" There was brief silence and everyone sat nervously. Mark shifted uncomfortably in his seat. I held my breath for fear that Pastor Jonas would start talking about a fiery lake and us all burning in it.

He looked around the sanctuary, and his eyes seemed to fall on each one of us and hold there for a second before passing. "Hear me, church, I'm only going to say this once. You either believe that the Lamb of God was nailed to a tree and that His blood was poured out for your sins, or you don't! Now if you do, it is time to confess with your mouth, and believe in your heart, and repent of your sins and make that Lamb, Jesus Christ, Yeshua Hamashiach, the Lord of your life. He already is Lord of heaven and earth. But He wants to make it personal for each one of us. Now, everyone think hard on what I have been saying here."

I was thinking hard, and wondering if I had been born in India or Africa, China even, what god would I be seeking? Would he believe in sacrifices or washing in water in the river? Jonas continued his sermon, "No one looking around, and nobody leaving. If you were to die today, and you don't know where you would go from this life, I want each of you to slip out of your pew and make your way to this altar in front. Quickly, come quickly." I wondered where Buddhists went when they died or Muslims? Did they believe in streets paved with gold or fiery flames that licked your skin forever? I caught myself daydreaming and looked back towards the front. "This will be your public confession of taking Jesus as your Savior" Jonas boomed loudly. "Jesus said, if you are ashamed of Him and deny Him, He will deny you before His heavenly Father. This is your public admission that you belong to Jesus."

I wanted to cry because the truth was, whenever he had an altar call I felt like I should go up front. I never really felt forgiven because I knew I had sinned greatly by being with Dillon, and now the lies I had told seemed to be weighing on my mind. Before I could think enough to talk myself out of it, I rose up out of my seat and made my way to the front. To my surprise Mark followed behind me and reached for my hand. I had never held his hand before and for whatever reason it seemed to help. I felt like we both were doing something together that pleased God. I began to cry over my sins. I told God that I was unworthy to even have Mark come down with me. I had not been completely truthful with him and I had done so many things wrong. Part of me wanted to believe that He was a loving God who was merciful and forgiving. Everything in my life seemed to be speeding up in full throttle. Pastor Jonas began to pray for us, and I closed my eyes and thought my Mama would be proud.

It seemed that Mark and I were making a covenant together before God. As I prayed from my heart, holding the hand of Mark, it seemed my heaviness began to lift. My heart felt better. All the weight of Daddy and Verdi and Johnny and even Conner and Dillon seemed to dissolve and melt away. I felt freer than I ever had.

After we prayed, everyone in the congregation came forward and began to shake our hands and hug us. Many of them were crying with us. It felt like a giant family reunion that was the opposite of a funeral. It was happy and alive.

I felt different when I left church that day. I really couldn't pinpoint it. I just knew I was changed. Mark and I walked out holding hands. Miss Renée caught up with us and hugged us both one last time. She was beaming from ear to ear. She told Mark, "This is the beginning of a new journey." I really didn't understand what she meant, but Mark responded with a big smile and a whispered "Thank you." His eyes were glistening.

Mark and I drove off from the church parking lot and he let out a long sigh. "Wow, that was really something," he said.

"Yes, it was! So, you like Pastor Jonas?"

"Honestly, Jade, I was so caught up in his sermon all I could think about was why I had been pushing God out of my life. I think partly because I never had really experienced His presence. My parents believed in God, but we rarely went to church. After my mother passed away I just didn't have anyone in my life to remind me that there was a higher power so to speak until you came along. And I had never said I believe Jesus is my Savior, until today, but I still think there is more."

I looked at Mark's kind features. His long slender fingers that held the steering wheel and his curly pale hair that blew softly across his forehead. He was strong and masculine, but gentle and kind, as well. I wanted to remember this moment forever. And here I was dressed in my Sunday best with my belly that gravity was pulling downward. I wanted to remember the elated feeling I had that God had allowed me to meet this kind gentleman. I thought how happy Mama would be to know that he didn't drink, and he wasn't scared to walk down to an altar and humble himself in the sight of a God that he knew existed somewhere out there in the vast universe. The baby kicked and I placed my hand on what felt like a foot.

"Oh, dear baby, whose are you and do I keep you?" I said inside my head.

Mark brought me back to the house and took my hand again, helping me out of the car. "You are an incredibly beautiful woman, Jade Gentry, do you know that?" He smiled and brushed my auburn hair back from my face.

"Right Mark, and have you had your eyes checked lately?"

He looked at me sternly and said, "Practice with me, ready? Say 'thank you.'

Come on, mouth the words." And then he repeated them over and over. "'Say thank you', Mark."

I replied, "Okay, thank you, Mark." I smiled up at him as I waddled up the porch, turning sideways and displaying my huge silhouette and kicking a leg out in a flirty manner. "Thank you, Mark!" I yelled out as I opened the door and went inside.

Chapter 33

Christmas had snuck up on me. I was heartsick and also excited. Whirls of hormones and emotions seemed to twirl and flutter through me like the snow in the chilly air. Mark was sitting at the table helping me watch the little girls while Miss Renee and Alice went to get the turkey.

"What would you be doing today if you were in Braxton with your daddy?"

I sighed and shrugged my shoulders that were already too big from carrying the weight of this baby.

"Jade, what was Christmas like before your mama died?" He looked intently at me, waiting.

I knew he wanted to get to know me better, but it was my first Christmas without mama and Johnny. My heart was heavy. I picked up one of the peanut butter cookies I had just baked and shoved a hunk in my mouth, before answering. "Well, Mark, what would you be doing if both your parents were here?" I grinned sideways, bouncing the ball back into his court.

"Oh that's easy," he said, "making popcorn balls and watching, "*It's a Wonderful Life*!" My mom absolutely loved that movie. We always made popcorn balls with caramel and then ate them hot and gooey while watching the movie."

"'Every *time a bell rings, an angel gets her wings*!' " I said, smiling.

"Okay, your turn." he said, eyeing me with a grin.

"Mark, sometimes Christmas was the most horrible time of the year. I dipped part of my cookie in the glass of milk and glanced at Dory who had fallen asleep on the floor with a pillow beside us. If my daddy was laid off, times were pretty lean. Small amounts of gifts or food, but if mama had her way about it, we always had a little something to open and a homemade jam cake with butter pecan icing. Miss Ellen Cotton, our neighbor, bought me a real nice doll one year with a bright red suit. She made her doll clothes after that for gifts and also crocheted me purses. She never forgot my brother either. If my daddy was off the bottle, he would sing carols and we would always go to church with mama for a service about baby Jesus and the Wise Men. If Daddy had a good week, he would build a nice fire and mama would make cocoa with tiny marshmallows. We would decorate a tree and hang stockings. My mama would read the Bible story and we would open our gifts. It would be a little something we secretly wanted, and somehow they'd manage to get it."

"Thanks, Jade, I guess I just needed to envision it. I want to try and get to know every part of you. Does that make sense?"

"Yes, Mark, just its hard this year is all. Daddy and Verdi are probably partying, and Johnny, well I miss him something terrible!"

Mark looked deep into my eyes and then glanced away. "How would you like to take a drive and pay Johnny a visit? I could take you?"

My eyes lit up immediately but then dimmed. I knew bringing Mark would only make them think he was the father and there was too much to explain. I'd just wait until things calmed down. "Thanks, Mark! That's really sweet, but I don't feel like it's time just yet."

He nodded his head and placed his hand in mine. A habit he had started after we went forward at church that Sunday. He still hadn't kissed me and I couldn't blame him with my swollen body and unattractive big belly, but he seemed like a man who was falling in love.

I wanted him to. I needed him to. I just had to make sure it was not for all the wrong reasons. I knew I had already done that once with Dillon.

Alice and Miss Renee came home with a huge turkey and bags of groceries to be put away. Mark trimmed the lights outside and placed a wreath on the front door while we baked. The night dragged on and I was ready to escape to my attic bedroom and prop my feet up and read.

After Mark put the boxes and unused lights away, he sauntered into the kitchen and said, "I guess I better get on home before the sleet starts. The weatherman is calling for snow on Christmas day." His blonde curls had grown out and were hanging in his eyes, and I thought he was the handsomest man I'd ever seen.

"Thanks for all the help young man!" Miss Renee called out.

"Not a problem, was glad to help."

"Take care of my Jade!"

He looked at me and winked, as I walked him to the door. "Good night beautiful; get some rest for you and that baby now. Go on, get in the bed."

"Okay Mark, please be careful and thanks for everything." He hugged me as best he could. It was more of a sideways pat due to my big baby belly.

I watched him walk down the sidewalk and get into his car. Once it started, I made my way up the stairs. I considered collapsing in bed fully clothed from sheer exhaustion.

"Dear God, Help me make the right choices. I want to be a good mother, but I'm scared. Show me what to do about this little life inside of me."

Chapter 34

It was raining the next morning, and the sound of it falling softly on the roof and blowing into the window pane awoke me. I was tired and the baby was pressing on my bladder something fierce. Only a few more weeks and this life would no longer be inside my body, but separate. After coming to terms with the fact that this baby wasn't planned, but one brought out of defilement and hurt, I feared I hadn't bonded properly with the tiny life forming inside me. I knew that if the baby were Conner's, I would always have him haunting me with memories of that hideously dark night, or worse, appearing wherever I moved to if he ever learned to count up nine months. And, if the baby were Dillon's I would live a life of pain trying to protect him or her from the evil world of discrimination.

The decision to give up the baby came abruptly in the night. I had tossed and turned and slept restlessly, waking from awful dreams of me opening a door and stepping through only to find myself standing on a cliff, losing my balance, falling and yet never crashing to earth. The more I replayed my life with the baby and my life without the baby, the more I thought about what would be best for this child.

The sounds of Dory and Eva, and all the commotion downstairs, let me know that Alice's day had started early. I had decided that even though Miss Renée thought I should keep my baby, I had to know deep inside my own heart what would be best for me. I lay there in bed and thought long and hard about the situation. Who was I kidding? This "nest" with Miss Renée and her niece was only a temporary arrangement. How could I ever go to school, paint pictures and do all the things I wanted and needed to do to support myself and this baby? How could I take care of myself, let alone an infant? I thought about all that Adeline could offer a child. Yes, she was delicate, but Freddy would enjoy a new playmate and maybe, just maybe, Adeline would keep me posted on my son or daughter. Miss Renée said it was a boy, but I had also learned that Miss Renée was not always right about her words from God or maybe she really did hear, but the person had stepped out of God's will, therefore altering the course. Of course, there was one problem, if it were Dillon's baby I knew the Kapolei's would never want to raise a child of mixed race, but that was a chance I would have to take. If the child were Dillon's I would raise it myself, but if it were Connor's I would give it to Adeline, and let Adeline keep my secret.

I was more firmly decided that if the adoption went smoothly, I would not even mention to Mark that I had sex with Dillon. Maybe then, I could pursue the relationship with him that I was already wanting. My secret would be safe, hidden behind all the other secrets I was too troubled to share, and yet Mark had a way of getting me to open up.

I walked down the steps and sat at the table. The hustle and bustle of the morning was humming all around me. Alice was feeding Eva while Dory and Tamar were running through the house chasing each other and screaming at the top of their lungs. My stomach was not feeling so well. I hadn't eaten a bite and was already having terrible heartburn and acid burning up my throat. I ate some Rolaids and waited for the acid to subside, because although my stomach was upset, it was also empty.

"Tamar, Dory stop that running!" Alice screamed, "Oh, it's no use I'll be glad when their father gets home and tans their little hinnies." Alice smiled at me looking rather haggard.

"Have you had breakfast yet?" I asked.

"Are you kidding? I don't have time to eat chasing them around and keeping this one fed."

“Well, how about I make us some flapjacks.”

“Flapjacks? Is that like pancakes?”

I laughed. “Yes, Alice, they happen to be the same thing. My mama always called them flapjacks.” It was funny to me how things are spoken differently in different homes and locations. I have a cousin who says "pop" instead of Coke or soda, and an uncle who used to say fair to middling every time you asked him how he was.

Alice chuckled, and I started pulling out a mixing bowl and skillet and began to get the eggs, flour and milk out of the refrigerator. “Where’s Miss Renée?” I asked, wondering where she could have gone at such an early hour in the rain.

“She's taking care of a sick friend from church. Jane, I think is her name. She’ll be back after a while.”

“I have made a decision, Alice.” I looked up at her with serious conviction on my face.

“Really, Jade, about what.”

“I’m going to give the baby up for adoption.”

“Wow, Jade. Bless your heart. Honey, are you sure?”

“Yes, Alice I’m sure. I’ve found a very nice couple. It's the people who commissioned a portrait of their son. They can’t have any more children, so they want to adopt. They are very well off and can give this baby so much more than I can."

"Yes, Jade, material wise, but what about love?"

I looked into Alice's wise eyes and wished that I could explain, but couldn't find the right words.

"They will be able to give this baby a mother and a father and a great education, and they are good people."

"How do you know that, Jade, you've only met them once?"

"I don't know Alice, I just feel it in my soul, and I am planning on talking with them again this Sunday when I take their painting to them. We will go over all the details. I've made my decision, and now I am not going to dwell on it anymore."

I put the Karo syrup in a small pot and onto the stove's back burner to heat slowly. I watched the batter make bubbles over the top of the pancake and gently flipped it over looking at the golden brown circular rings left by the skillet.

Miss Renée came through the front door and grabbed Dory in mid-run. "You better calm down missy!" she said with good humor and a glint of delight. Her long blonde hair was tucked behind a scarf and her eyes sparkled with love. She took off her raincoat and draped it over the couch. "Good morning everyone. What's that smellin' so good?"

"Jade's making pancakes or flapjacks, as she says." Alice smiled and pulled the baby from her breast and began to pat her back until she let out a much too loud burp for such a tiny person.

"Jade's got some news, too," Alice said quietly.

Miss Renée looked up from admiring the baby and locked her eyes with mine. "Is that so, well don't keep me waiting?"

I looked back at her, swallowed hard and said, "I've decided to put the baby up for adoption."

She sat there quietly, her eyes scanned the room while her brain was turning this over like the flapjacks I had prepared for breakfast. Finally, after a long pause she said, "Well Jade, it's your decision. I can't stop you, and I am sure you've prayed about it." She said it as if it were more of a question than a statement of fact. "Have you told Mark yet?"

"No, you all are the first to know, but I plan on telling him soon."

"Jade, you have to follow your heart, and so I hope that you are not letting others interfere with your plans. Always know that nothing is final and you still have time to change your mind."

Miss Renée walked to the stove, still holding the now sleeping infant. She cupped my chin with one hand and lifted my eyes to meet hers. "Know that I will support you no matter what. You do know that, don't you?" I nodded my head and realized how wonderful God had been leading me here to this house filled with women and laughter and children. There was a spirit of love in this house and it dwelt in these people. I placed a stack of flapjacks on the table in front of Alice and Miss Renée and the pot of warm syrup along with the butter dish. We all sat there together eating this simple but comforting food. I took the first bite of the fluffy cake soaked in syrup and closed my eyes. I prayed silently, "Thank you, Lord God, for new beginnings and for the mustards seeds you've sprinkled along my path!"

Chapter 35

I met with Adeline and Francis on Sunday afternoon. After they admired the portrait of their son. Francis gave me a check and they both thanked me. I felt like they were really pleased with what I had done, and not just putting me on for selfish reasons.

We walked into the dining area of their lovely home. They had prepared finger foods and ice tea, tiny crackers with crab dip and cheese with a black olive slice adorning the top. I was very nervous, my fingers fidgeting with the hem of my maternity top. I was trying very hard to study them both. I was looking for details deep within their soul, details that would unearth the top layer of self in each of them, and get down to what lay beneath. Were they people with morals, integrity, character, and compassion? I didn't know. But I felt like I could learn a lot about people in a short time if I watch them carefully.

Francis was a dark-haired man, tall and well built, with dark eyes. He looked Italian or Greek maybe, and his skin was the color of mellow wood tones. He seemed calm and very casual while Adeline seemed very excited. She wanted a girl, but a little brother for Fredrick would be good, too. She didn't want him to be an only child, and having a playmate would occupy his busy mind.

"Have a seat, Jade," Francis said motioning to the elegant tapestry cloth dining chair he had scooted out for me. His voice was low and strong, a man of great confidence, I thought.

"Jade, we want you to make yourself at home. So if there is anything we can get for you, you just ask, okay?" Adeline said sweetly. She looked stunning. Her hair was done in a French twist. The various shades of soft natural blonde flowed into the roll in the back. It gave her a very sophisticated look and allowed her delicate facial features to show. She had a beautiful, sparkling comb in just the right place, and she was dressed in bright green which complimented her eyes. In a word, she was a looker.

"Thank you," I said. I began to feel like I was on some sort of movie set and everything that was going on was just part of the script.

The handsome Italian spoke, "Jade, we understand you are willing to give this baby up, is that correct?"

Before I could answer, Adeline was pouring me tea and offering me sugar cubes and lemon wedges. "Umm, yes, that is true," I said with a slight frog in my throat.

"Adeline tells me you are a widow?"

A lump was forming in my throat in place of the frog. I was fearful to tell any more lies, especially since I had made that commitment with the Lord a few weeks ago. "Well, yes, and no." I felt a bit trapped now.

Francis frowned and moved on to more interrogation. "How do your parents feel about you giving this baby up for adoption?"

“My mama died last year, and my daddy is not a part of my life anymore.”

“I’m sorry to hear about your mother, Jade. How did she die, if I might ask?”

“She died of lung cancer. She was a lifelong smoker. They had just issued a surgeon general’s warning on the packs being sold. Once my mother was concerned about her favorite habit it was too late.”

“Do you smoke?” he queried.

“No. I never have.” As soon as I answered him I was taken back to that large sycamore tree, and Johnny and me fighting the wind to light our first and our last cigarette.

“Do you have every reason to believe this baby is healthy?”

“Yes, Mr. Kopelia, I know this baby is healthy.” I was certain my baby was healthy. I just didn’t know what color it was.

“Jade, Francis and I want you to know that if you are prepared to hand us your child to raise as our own, we will pay for all your medical bills, and Francis will even pay for you to attend an art school here in Kansas. We want you to know that we will see that this child has everything and more, including all the love you can imagine."

I looked at Adeline's porcelain skin and soft blue eyes speckled with brown. She was seriously searching for any doubt. "Are you a hundred percent positive, Jade, that you are willing to give this child up completely?"

"Yes, I am. I've thought long and hard about this and I am sure it's the best thing for the baby and also for me." I was aware, of course, that direct adoptions like this were always open to problems later down the line when the birth mother felt guilty over what she had done. This could make trouble for the child and his adoptive parents, so I understood why they wanted to be certain.

"I have taken the liberty, Jade, of having some paperwork drawn up by my attorney," Francis spoke in a matter of fact tone, with that take charge confidence of a man of wealth and power. "If you would just look over these and sign on the places marked, we can begin the process immediately. And, of course, we will need a copy of your husband's death certificate."

I gasped, and then tried to cover my shock by taking a nice gulp of tea. What was I going to do now? I really was caught. When I composed myself a bit, I said softly. "What if the birth father is absent and cannot be located?" Then I added even more softly, almost a whisper, "I wasn't completely honest about the father. But I'm sure it will be just a technicality we can get through."

"How are you feeling, Jade?" Adeline asked. Francis said nothing.

"I feel good," I answered, unsure about the decision I was making that would change the course of my life forever. Knowing that a tiny life forming inside of me would be held by another and loved by another. I would have to deal with giving away this life that I had carried for nine months. The word *good* now seemed so shallow for how I felt. I sensed time and space shatter and all the thoughts I had of raising a child and protecting it from evil and the abuse of the world. I felt every emotion of the day when my mama held my hand before she died. I could still hear her faint, weak voice, "Jade promise me you won't marry a man who drinks."

"Do either of you drink?" I blurted out awkwardly.

"Just socially, why do you ask?" Francis was looking at me intently.

"I do not want my child being raised by an alcoholic. It's very important to me." I was returning his intent stare with one of my own, as I studied his eyes for any trace of fear.

He smiled, kind of thin-lipped and said, "Now, don't get me wrong, we drink. It's just rarely and only on holidays or special occasions." I thought he was annoyed that I was interviewing them, instead of it being solely the other way around. I figured I was doing them a favor just as big, if not bigger, than the favor they were doing for me.

I had one more question for them both. "Will you raise this baby to know God and the teachings of the Bible?

Adeline answered first. "Of course, Jade, we will teach this baby along with Fredrick all about Christianity and the faith. Francis is Catholic, but I was raised Methodist. I guess the combined faith will be enough for this little one. Fredrick and I attend church every Sunday and Francis accompanies us when his schedule allows."

I thought about what she had said for a minute. But what I wanted wasn't formed in a religion but a friendship. It was the sixties, and there were radical hippies screaming against politics and fighting for freedom and peace and love. They had their own lingo, words like groovy, hip, and cool. Then there were the partying Jesus group's that made Jesus into a cool guy who was down with everything you did. But the worst, were the stuffy religions that I could not abide with their kneeling and standing and repeating and following an order of routine brought by man. I just wanted my child to know God as the only true and Living God, and Jesus as Savior.

I finished up the meeting, signed the papers, and left wondering if what I had done was truly the right thing. I decided to stop by and see Mark. I wanted to know what he thought about the whole situation. The Kopelia's had sent their car for me, and now I directed the driver to Mark's place.

I waddled slowly up the sidewalk and down two steps to his apartment. I knocked on the door and waited briefly. At this point, my mind was spinning out of control. "What had I just done?" I felt like it wasn't real; none of my life seemed real anymore. I had traveled so far from Braxton and the only life I had ever known was mama, Johnny, Miss Cotton and daddy. I suddenly felt sorely alone, and the future was inconceivable, unbelievable and unavoidable. I was snapped out of my whirlwind by a familiar voice calling my name.

"Well, hello, Jade."

Mark smiled, his dimples caving into his cheeks. He stepped back and held the door open for me with one hand and the copy of a hardbound novel in the other.

"Sorry to just drop by, but I miss you! By the way, I am also going to need a ride home." I raised my eyebrows and gave him a grin, nervously wondering what would spew out of my mouth. "Mark, I need to talk with you. Is this a good time?"

"Shoot, Jade, I'm all yours." He took my hand and led me to the couch. When I turned to sit, he held both my hands and helped me ease down and settle my considerable self into place. Then he sat next to me. He gave me his complete attention, which made me feel like a spotlight was beaming down on me.

"Okay, well, here goes... I have decided to give the baby up for adoption, and I just met with the new family to be. They have great means and are very eager to become parents to this little life." I held my breath and waited for his approval. I looked into his face, but it revealed nothing.

Then he said, "Jade, that's a really big decision. Do you feel good about it? I mean do you have a real peace within?"

I looked at Mark and I wondered if I had peace, but I knew by the layers of guilt that were forming that I didn't. I don't know if it was all my hormones out of control or just my situation, but I couldn't control myself. Suddenly, without warning, I burst into tears.

Mark reached for my hand and said, "Okay, it looks like the peace isn't perfect. So, talk to me Jade, tell me what's going on and making you second guess your decision." He lifted my head and began to push my red curly hair back out of my face and wipe my tears with his fingers. "Come here." He opened his arms and pulled me into his chest. I laid my head there and tried to breathe again.

"I have a secret, Mark, and it's so big and so ugly that if I tell it, no one will ever want me around again, and no one will want my baby."

Mark shook his head as he smoothed my hair again. "Jade, that is just plain not true; I will want your baby. Anything that is a part of you, I will want." He pulled my face up to his and lightly brushed his lips on mine, so softly I almost didn't feel it. I closed my eyes and let him kiss me again, kiss all my pain away. But the whole time he kissed me, I felt guilt that I was keeping this huge secret and his kisses were so soft and loving, like nothing I had ever experienced. I wanted to just let him hold me and never let go.

"Mark, wait," I pushed back. "I'm not a good person. I have done a lot of very wicked things, and I want you to know that you deserve so much better than me and this baby. Well, this baby deserves much better, too."

"Jade, what are you talking about? I already know that you were raped. That is not your fault! Stop being so critical of yourself. You are one of the most loving, giving people I know! And I love you."

I looked at him shocked that those words had come from his lips. "Mark don't say that, you don't know me. I'm not the good person you think I am. I'm not . . ." My voice trailed off. Tears began to fall again and Mark sat back and pondered what to do with such a hormonal woman. "I'm just going to get this over with, but I need to tell you in the car so that if you never want to speak to me again I won't have to walk back to Miss Renée's or ride in shame in the silence of your car."

"Jade, please give me a little credit here. That is not going to happen. There is nothing you could do or say to change the way I feel about you."

"Mark, there is something you should know, that happened after I was raped. I, I, I…" I stuttered. I shook my head, took a deep breath and pulled the plug on the not-so-successfully buried truth that Mark had to hear. "I was terrified and I was being stalked by the man who raped me. He was coming to my high school and he was stopping by my daddy's house and was following me and threatening me. I was so scared and so fearful that I sought out a friendship with a young man I had known since childhood. He is a man of mixed color, and in a desperate attempt to make myself rid of what was done to me, to feel like I was normal, I had sex with him once. At first I felt better because he cared for me and didn't steal "it" from me. He went off to college a few weeks later. When I realized I was pregnant, I also realized I had no idea whose baby this is." I looked at him, my face was contorted and I squeezed my eyes shut tight, but it did no good, the tears got out anyway. I was sobbing now. I was a complete royal mess! Thank God for the box of tissues on the end table.

I couldn't breathe. I was waiting for Mark to say something, anything. Instead, he opened his arms again and laid my head on his chest and he patted my hair. He brushed his hand across my face and he kissed my forehead. I began to calm down. Then he spoke. "Jade, I am going to make you a promise. One that you have my word on. I will never let a man hurt you as long as I have breath in my body! And this baby, I don't care if its purple or green, I will be right beside you through everything. Don't you understand that when I said I love you, I meant it?"

I guess I hadn't believed real love existed, not between men and women anyway. I had never seen what that looked like. I had seen my daddy love my mama and kiss her and tell her she was gorgeous just as Mark had me, and then turn around and knock the hell out of her. I really couldn't fathom that a man could love someone as polluted and ruined as I was.

Mark continued, "Jade, you must realize that none of this is your fault. It's not your fault that this man took your virginity and robbed you of something beautiful and then stalked you and kept you a nervous wreck. It would only be human for you to look for someone to be there for you, to protect you, and that is all you did. You are not wicked; those men were wicked, not you."

I sighed and shuddered and tried to regulate my breathing. What he was saying was wonderful, but so foreign to me that I couldn't really believe that it was true, even though I really wanted to. I sat there for the longest time, resting my head on his chest and listening to his heartbeat and the movement that was pushing and trying to free itself from my belly.

"Lord God, you are so incredible," I prayed to myself. "You've taken the broken and rough pieces of my life, and you are beginning to smooth me in your rock tumbler!"

Chapter 36

I woke up at three in the morning with a dull ache in my lower back. I went into the bathroom to empty my bladder. I had just raised up from the commode, pulled up my pajama pants, and started wobbling toward the bedroom when I felt it. My water broke! There was a warm, moist feeling running down my legs and a low shock in my spine that almost knocked the breath out of me. I then looked down at the huge puddle of water spreading over the tile around my bare feet. I got out of the pajama pants, got my towel to dry myself, soaked the puddle up, and tossed the towel and pants into the bathtub.

"Miss Renée," I said rather softly, tapping on the outside of her door.

"Yes, Jade?"

"It's time."

"It's time? What time is it, Jade?" Her voice was muffled and fuzzy from sleep. I could tell she was deep in sleep mode.

"Miss Renée, my water broke and I am really scared."

"Your water broke?" she was processing this news. Her rather soft, slow voice, mimicked again, "your water broke," then abruptly it turned to a voice that carried to the rafters. "Your water broke! Oh my goodness, I, uh, I'm coming, Jade. Umm, let me get dressed and you call the doctor."

I went back to my bedroom. I slid my bag out from under my bed where I had stashed it weeks before. It had everything I would need for a night or two in a hospital. I had packed nightgowns for the baby with draw strings on the bottom. One was pale yellow with little birds on it and the other one was light green. I had packed a toothbrush, nightgown, some lotion and powder and baby socks, tiny little booties with furry balls on the end. I lifted the case and slipped on my house shoes. I figured there was no need to get dressed, so I threw a housecoat over my pajama top. I made my way into the kitchen and looked for Dr. Johnson's phone number in the index card holder when another full contraction made me lose my breath.

"Miss Renée!" I hollered, "Miss Renée!"

I really didn't know what to expect, but I knew that another life was trying to make its way out of a dark cave and into the light. It had been hibernating for almost nine months and I was not sure I was prepared for this moment, nor could I conceive how it could be possible.

In a panic, Miss Renée came flying into the kitchen, a scarf tied over her morning hair, car keys in her hand. "Let's go, Jade, we need to get you there." She told me to get in the car and she picked up the phone to call the doctor. By this time Eva was screaming and Dory was wide awake. Alice looked rather surprised to see that we were going to the hospital so early.

"Jade, your baby couldn't wait till nine or ten o'clock to make an entrance. He must be in a hurry to make an appearance." She smiled at me, a knowing grin. "Don't you worry you are going to be just fine."

Dory started yelling, "The baby is coming; the baby is comin'!"

In the midst of all this, I worried about what to tell these little ones when I returned with no baby. What would I say? How would I explain?

"Can you call Mark, Alice?"

"Sure, Jade, I will call him as soon as the sun comes up!" She winked and picked up Dory. "You, Miss Dory, are going back to bed. The chickens ain't even up this early!"

I waddled down the steps and made my way to the car. It was pitch black, and I wanted Mark more than anything. I would tell another lie and say he was the father just to have him stroke my hair and hold my hand. But I didn't want him looking at the delivery process, and I had heard the afterbirth and the blood was a bit more than even the most caring of fathers wanted to take in. The fathers came to see the baby after it was washed and clean and wrapped in a soft blanket.

"Jade, I know it's the last minute, but I wanted to talk to you about this baby again. I know you said you want to give it up, but what if you really don't? I mean what if you are just worried about what other people will think?" Miss Renée was relentless about this.

"I don't know, Miss Renée. I can't seem to sort it all out. I wish I knew the answer, but I just don't. Nothing seems right to me. I can't see how anything good could come out of me keeping it. I mean if it's Conner's and it's a boy and it reminds me of him, I just don't think I can be sure I could love the child like I need to."

"Oh, Jade, honey, a mother always loves her children. A mother looks at her children and right away there is a connection that can never be broken. Right away there is a river of love, a river so deep you could swim in it. It's the way of nature. A mother instantly protects and loves her children."

I pondered her words and waited for the next contraction with fear that it would become stronger and harder. I didn't know how I was going to bear it. I was clenching my fists so hard my fingernails were digging into my palms. Renée waited for the pain to subside and then looked at me and said, "I don't know if you are aware, but this baby could be Dillon's, and if it is, you may not know it's a colored baby right away because they are often born with pale olive skin that gets darker as they grow. Africans develop their pigment in a week or two after birth. And they have blue eyes at birth a lot of times. You will have to wait several weeks before you can even give the baby to Adeline and Francis."

I tried to soak in everything she was telling me. "I'm going to keep the baby if it's Dillon's," I said.

"Good, Jade, I think that is good."

We entered the emergency room and the nurse was waiting with a wheelchair. They took me to a room and got me prepped. That's what they called it. I wasn't sure why but I had to drink something that the nurse brought me and take a suppository. She told me to sit on the commode and empty my bowels. I was having contractions and voiding my bowels at the same time. I couldn't understand why this was happening to me. Suddenly, I was feeling so alone and so scared. How was I to be a good mama to this baby? Could I die while having this baby? I wondered secretly and began to pray with all my might. "God please don't let me die, and please don't let my baby be the wrong baby." As soon as I said it my heart grabbed me with regret. How could an innocent baby be wrong? How could a beautiful life inside of me be wrong? This baby could be just like me for all I knew, or just like Mama. This baby could have such a great personality that no one could resist it. I couldn't wait to see my baby. All of a sudden it didn't matter if I had any money or a place of my own or what color the baby was. All that mattered was looking at this little life and loving it.

The nurse came and took me back to the birthing bed. I had a gown on that was open in the back, not covering much. The metal stirrups for my legs made me nervous. How was I going to push this baby out of me? They put an I.V. in my arm and hooked me up to a monitor of some sort. Miss Renée was right there with me the whole time praying and asking God to ease my pain and to give me wisdom and direction. I could feel her prayers literally enter my body and bring a peace even through the intense pain.

Four hours had gone by and my hair was matted from sweating and moving my head around on the pillow. Then the pain became thunderous. I kept passing out and coming to from the jolts of contractions that seemed to catapult through my body. After ten hours of labor the doctor said he was going to give me some medicine to speed up the process and that my pain would get harder and come closer together. But that as soon as I dilated enough he could give me a shot in my spine and numb me from the waist down. I was all for that and yet terrified that the contractions could get any stronger. I was drenched in sweat and terrified that I might die giving birth.

An hour later after pushing and pushing the baby crowned. And then with one swift push it seemed the doctor pulled the baby from my womb and into the world. "It's a boy!"

I heard that first, and then they were holding him before me. He was covered in blood and screaming at the top of his lungs and still he was the most beautiful creature I had ever laid eyes on. They counted his toes and then his fingers. "One two three four five, and ten fingers. Jade, let me count those for you, one two three four five."

I looked at my son and I searched him. He had a head full of dark, softly curled hair that looked like silk, pale skin, and big eyes. They weighed him and measured him: eight pounds and three ounces, twenty-two inches long. "Young lady, that's a big baby for a tiny girl like you!" The doctor smiled at me and seemed just as excited about bringing this new life into the world as I was. I was so relieved. The lumberjack doctor had made me feel so ashamed.

As soon as I saw my baby I wanted to hold him. But they swiftly took him away and bathed him and put a tag on his foot. They said they would bring him back to me shortly. I closed my eyes and cried. How wonderful and how mysterious life was. My son looked just like my brother Johnny, a spitting image of Elvis. I smiled, thinking about all the fear I had held onto for no reason. All the doubt and all the worry, and what good did any of it do?

When I awoke the sun was shining through the window and the nurse was pushing my baby through the room in a little glass cart. "Would you like to feed him?"

"Yes," I said, picking him up and pulling him close to me.

Miss Renée had walked in behind her. Apparently she had been watching him get his bath and get pushed in his little cart in front of the delivery room window. This was the center stage where everyone stood anticipating a look at the newest member of the human race that had come into the universe. "Isn't he beautiful?"

I smiled and looked at his tiny fingers that had grasped onto my finger. "Yes, he is the most beautiful thing I have ever seen!"

"Jade, you have a certain someone who has been waiting a long time to see you." I knew she meant Mark.

"Send him in." I held my breath and wondered what Mark's expression would be at the sight of my baby. His tall lanky body strolled in the room, and his terrible posture pulled him over slightly. He had a smile on his face and a twinkle in his eyes. He held a small box in one hand and the tiniest baseball cap I'd ever seen.

"Congratulations, Mommy!"

"Thank you." I smiled, looking into his kind eyes that made my heart feel things it never had.

"Would you like to hold him?" I asked, and I held him up for Mark to get a better look.

"I would, but first there's something I need to do." Suddenly Mark was kneeling by my hospital bed and holding out the small box and raising its cover. "Miss Jade Gentry, in the short time I've known you, I seemed to have fallen madly in love with you. I have often wondered if you have felt this same sort of insanity." He winked and continued talking. His dimples were adorable and so were his laughing eyes. "This baby is going to need a father, and so I said to myself, "Mark, do you think it's possible that Jade and this baby would like to become Mrs. and little Mr. Richards?'"

I wanted to scream yes from the rooftops, but each time I tried to answer he interrupted me.

"I promise to raise this child as if he were my very own and never treat him differently... even after you bear the other five children I've always dreamed of having. What do you say?" He winked again. His blond curly hair and bright eyes made me feel alive inside, more alive than anything besides the little life I was holding.

At last I could speak: "It would be an honor!" I was crying and tears were dripping on little John's receiving blanket. The wedding ring was made of an imperial Jade stone with two tiny diamonds on the sides. He said he picked it to match my eyes, but that he could find no stone as lovely or as green.

Miss Renée threw her head around the doorway. "Well?"

"She said yes!"

"Praise God! This baby is going home!"

Renée walked over to my bed and picked up my hand. "What a gorgeous ring," she said.

"I know, isn't it splendid?" My facial expression went from pure joy to biting the inside of my jaw and pulling on my lip. "What is it Jade?" Renée knew me too well. "What if I can't get out of this adoption? What if the courts and that expensive attorney they hired come and take my baby away? Plus, I signed my name and promised to keep my word."

"Now, now, Jade don't get all worked up. We both know that the ink probably hasn't dried on the paperwork yet, and surely they realized when you sat down with them that you were young and uncertain." I nodded, hoping she was right. I looked down at my son and couldn't imagine one second without him in my life. Tears started to well up in my eyes, and before I knew it Mark was trying to console me as well. "Jade it will all be just fine. Don't you worry. If I have to, I'll hire an attorney myself."

"Listen here, Jade, I'll call Adeline and tell her the adoption is off. Don't worry or let any guilt come on. They will find another baby; the right baby." I nodded in agreement and let out a sigh of relief.

"So do we have an official name?" Mark and Renée asked in unison.

I looked up at Mark and smiled. Could a baby have four names I wondered? Why not! "My son's name is going to be John Mark Isaac Richards!"

Tears seem to well up in his eyes and he turned his head towards the window. "I love it," he said. "I think it's perfect," and then he kissed the hand he had placed my ring on.

Chapter 37

Miss Renée came by the hospital the next day at feeding time. I was tired but excited when they carted little John Isaac into the room. He was so soft and tiny and I could get lost in his delicate features. I felt so relieved that I had decided to keep him for myself.

"Jade would you like for me to contact your brother, Johnny, and Uncle Ed so they can see the baby?"

I had been pondering that all morning. It was funny how she intuitively seemed to know my thoughts.

"I'm not sure just yet, Renée. After you explained that the baby's eyes may actually change color and that Caucasians eyes are usually blue at birth, I've not calculated what to say to them. I know they will have questions about Mark. If I tell them I was raped and then Isaac starts to get pigmented skin, Johnny might take the matters in his own hands and hurt Dillon or worse. Plus, Braxton's so narrow-minded, a man could get strung in a tree or fed to the alligators without anyone questioning his whereabouts." Suddenly I felt sad again.

"Jade, honey, there is no reason for you to explain anything to them. You don't need to disclose what happened to you at your daddy's house. It's none of their business, and furthermore, for the wellbeing of your child, I would stop trying to figure out who the father is and just love your baby. He is a part of you and soon will have a wonderful father to help raise him."

I nodded, as tears began to well up inside of me. Now, now, Jade, you must not fret. God has seen you through up until this point, and He will continue to guide you."

"You're right. I sniffled and wiped my eyes. I guess now is as good a time as any for Johnny, Julie and Uncle Ed, to see the baby! I smiled at Renee, feeling relieved by the wisdom she was often giving me. She stood up and lightly kissed my forehead, then took her hand and stroked Isaac's soft tufts of dark hair. "Pretty boy," she said. Her expression towards my son was almost as good as if my very own Mama were standing right there with me. Almost. I still had more questions for her that were troubling me.

"How did Francis and Adeline take the news that I've decided to keep my baby, Renée?"

"Well, Jade, that was easy. I just told them that you had not been truthful with them, and I implied that the baby's father was possibly a mystery. It seems they wanted to have a more complete history on the father of the child." She raised her eyebrows and made a face that seemed to say "ignorance."

About the time Miss Renée was headed home to make phone calls and get the bassinet moved up to my small room, Mark waltzed in the door. They exchanged pleasantries and she left us to be alone with the baby.

"Hello, gorgeous!" Mark said as he made his way to the bed. I couldn't understand what I had done that was deserving of such a man. "Hello Mark, do you want to hold the baby?"

"Our son, you mean?" He smiled, his almond eyes dancing with excitement. "Of course. Why do you think I'm here?" I smirked gleefully and instructed him on how to support the baby's head and neck and hold him properly. He scooped little Isaac up like it was the most natural thing he'd ever done. The baby whimpered and then rested his head on his shoulder, letting out a soft sigh. Mark rubbed his back gently and spoke in the cutest baby voice ever. "We're going to get along just fine aren't we little fellow. Tell your mom to relax. Now, now, it's going to be alright, daddy's here."

I couldn't help but take a snapshot of that moment in my brain and file it under "best memories" thus far. "I love you," I mouthed in a whispered tone. He looked down at me and didn't even have to say it back. I knew what he was thinking.

"Jade, you need to get your rest and recuperate because we have a wedding to plan."

"Oh my goodness, I know!" I said in a voice that squeaked with excitement. "I can hardly believe it. My life has been changing drastically, and I keep having to pinch myself to see if I'm awake."

Mark chuckled, "You are awake alright and you're all mine!" He clasped my hand with his free one and looked down at the beautiful ring he had slipped on my finger just hours before. "I love it, Mark! I can't stop looking at it. Between looking at the baby and the ring, I feel like doing somersaults down the corridor of the hospital."

"I'm so pleased," he said. I couldn't decide on whether to get you a diamond or the Jadestone, but now I am happy I chose the Jade."

"Mark, when I became pregnant, I thought my life had ended. I couldn't imagine anyone ever wanting to marry me. I felt so worthless and so dirty, but you, you have helped me by polishing, sanding, and smoothing away all my rough places. This ring is perfect. I don't know how I would have gotten through everything without you."

He shook his head lightly and said, "Jade, you sell yourself short. I think you are one of the strongest bravest women I have ever met, and since you came into my life I have never felt happier. True story. You bring me such joy." He smiled and placed the baby back in my arms. "Now get some rest and I'll be back in the morning to pick you up and get you safely delivered to Miss Renée and Alice's until you are ready to become Mrs. Richardson."

"Okay, boss. Geez, give a girl a ring and you think you can just order her around?" I smiled and he knew I was being sarcastic. The nurse came in and placed the baby back in the cart and wrapped him up tightly in the receiving blanket. Mark dimmed the lights and kissed me goodbye. My eyes were heavy and I was still exhausted from the labor. I snuggled into the pillow and closed my eyes.

"Dear God, It's me, Jade. I stand in awe of you and how you work everything out when we place the reigns in your hands. You have turned my sorrow into dancing! You've really polished this gem and I am beginning to shine. I trust you and I love you!

P.S. Please tell Mama that I'm doing fine and that she has a new grandson."

Author's Notes:

The information on peacock feathers was obtained at:

http://www.jeffreykedwards.com/?p=367

Made in the USA
Columbia, SC
09 October 2020

22269529R00231